For Don, Evan, and Garrett
my love, my life, my meaning

A Kiss for Maggie Moore

Micki R. Pettit

Black Rose Writing | Texas

ISBN: 978-1-68433-838-2
PUBLISHED BY BLACK ROSE WRITING
www.blackrosewriting.com

Printed in the United States of America
Suggested Retail Price (SRP) $19.95

A Kiss for Maggie Moore is printed in Book Antiqua

SECRET LOVE (from *Calamity Jane*)
Words by PAUL FRANCIS WEBSTER Music by SAMMY FAIN
Copyright © 1953 (Renewed) WC MUSIC CORP. All Rights Reserved
Used By Permission of ALFRED MUSIC

LITTLE JOE THE WRANGLER (from *Songs of the Cowboys*, 1908)
Courtesy Nathan Howard "Jack" Thorp (1867 – 1940), an American collector and writer of cowboy songs and cowboy poetry

OH MY DARLING, CLEMENTINE
American western folk ballad credited to Percy Montrose, 1884

Cover design by Cait Jones

*As a planet-friendly publisher, Black Rose Writing does its best to eliminate unnecessary waste to reduce paper usage and energy costs, while never compromising the reading experience. As a result, the final word count vs. page count may not meet common expectations.

A Kiss for
Maggie Moore

THE WEDDING

She is wearing white. Baby's breath plays peekaboo with the folds of her braided hair. Her face, somewhat red from all the bridal attention, glows beneath a veil delicate as fairy wings.

His face is glowing, too. He is a man in love, exuberance in every line of his dimpled, lopsided grin. An expression that never ceases to both astound and annoy me.

I stand beside them, wearing panty hose no less, in a puffy-sleeved froufrou dress she has chosen. I am the maid of honor. Oh, to be the bride.

"Lord, look mercifully upon these two who have come seeking your blessing. Let your Holy Spirit rest upon them so that with steadfast love they may honor the promises they make this day."

The low, droning voice of Reverend Bauer melds with the sound of the Sanctuary's antiquated furnace. It's hard to tell which blows hotter air. Together they lull me into a nostalgic stupor.

"Take her right hand in yours, and with the vows that bind one another repeat after me: I, Buckingham Howard Majors the Third . . ."

● ● ● ● ●

". . . Buckingham Howard Majors the Third!" he shouted with hands on hips, looking like a general who had just taken a hill. My hill.

"A third of what?" I shouted back.

"Not a third. *The* Third."

1

"Well, I'm Margaret Emma Moore—*The* First. That means I'm number one. Get it, Mr. *The* Third?"

"Oh yeah? Well, I was here first."

He had a point, but I wasn't going to back down.

"You lie! You lie like a fly with a booger in its eye!"

"Wait a minute—Margaret?" His voice turned smug. "Why, you're just a girl."

JUST a girl. It wasn't the first time someone had mistaken me for a boy. Nor was it the first time someone had said those words as if being a girl wasn't good enough, but this time the phrase stung. He was a dead man. I took my best as-seen-on-television boxing stance. "You take that back," I demanded.

He crossed his arms and tilted his head as if reconsidering. He obviously outweighed me, but I was meaner. Mr. *The* Third didn't want to tangle with me, so he did the next best thing to winning: he negotiated.

"Well, if you'll share the hill, I'll share this." He pulled a fistful of smashed jelly beans from his pocket.

Never one to turn down anything edible, I accepted.

"My friends call me Bucky," he said, holding out a hand to help me up our jointly claimed pile of construction rubble. That's when I saw his dimple for the first time.

I took his hand, and he took my heart.

•　　•　　•　　•　　•

"...take thee, Melinda Ann Thomas..."

•　　•　　•　　•　　•

The new girl was wearing a school dress fancier than anything I'd ever seen, much less anything I'd ever wear. Her hair was the color of autumn grass, golden with a hint of red. It was tamed by two fancy French braids, each embellished by a bright blue bow that perfectly matched her dress, and her eyes. She was sitting on the rusty rail of

2

the old railroad tracks. No train had ran them for years, so they were ours to travel.

Bucky spotted her first. We had been scouting Indians, certain that any minute a whole war party would appear over the horizon and lead us on an adventure—just one of many imaginary scenarios Bucky and I had acted out since we made peace atop the pile of house-making leftovers.

"Who you s'pose that is?" Bucky whispered

"Don't know. Never saw her," I whispered back. "Maybe it's the Medicine Woman."

"Hmm," he wondered. "Let's get closer."

On hands and knees, we inched our way through the tall grass alongside the tracks, Bucky in blue jeans and a T-shirt, me in hand-me-down overalls.

When we were about six ties away, she moved, plucking a dandelion that had gone to seed.

"Ah, an unsuspecting damsel," I whispered, immediately changing pretends. Bucky didn't respond. Instead, he fixated on the dandelion, as if he were the one examining the bygone flower. She had enchanted him. I didn't like it. Not one bit.

Since Bucky had ceased to be part of the plan, it was up to me to find out exactly who this princess was. Leaping into the air, I gave my best monster-on-the-loose scream. The effect was disappointing. She stiffened, but didn't scream back.

When you attempt to scare someone and it doesn't work, you have to redeem yourself quickly. I tried again, knowing full well I probably looked like an idiot. Although Bucky stood up and glared at me, the girl seemed amused.

"What's your name?" I asked. "And why are you here?"

"Melinda," she said, standing to brush the dirt from the backside of her dainty dress. "Melinda Thomas. I hope you don't mind, but I've been following you. I'm your new neighbor."

Something about her tugged my heart, like the need to nuzzle a sleeping puppy. She extended her arm for a handshake. An offer of friendship, if I would only take it. The formality suited her, and I liked her show of respect. I decided she would fit in just fine.

At least until she smiled at Bucky.

$\bullet \qquad \bullet \qquad \bullet \qquad \bullet$

" . . . The ring? May we have the ring, please?"

Reverend Bauer is addressing me. Suddenly, I'm the focus of all eyes.

"Mags, tell me you've got the ring," Bucky whispers.

"Of course, I've got the ring." I'm wearing it. Unfortunately, the blasted thing won't come off without a fight. I discreetly stick my finger in my mouth and pull one-and-a-half karats over my knuckle with my teeth. Then I hand it to the groom.

Bucky gives me one of those "I don't believe you did that" looks. Melinda smiles.

Taking Melinda's delicate hand, Bucky raises it to his lips before sliding the ring past a manicured nail and over a long, dainty finger. I watch it come to rest where it really belongs.

Still, I wonder...

"Whom therefore God has joined together, let no one put asunder. You may kiss the bride."

$\bullet \qquad \bullet \qquad \bullet \qquad \bullet$

Bucky's eyes were squeezed shut, his puckered lips slowly moving toward their target. Fully alert, Melinda awaited the inevitable encounter with no outward show of fear. When their lips touched, Bucky's eyes sprang open and Melinda's closed.

"Wrong, wrong, wrong, wrong, wrong!" I interrupted, stealing the moment. Bucky stood up from the clubhouse bench, seeming a little too upset by the intrusion.

"I thought it was okay," Melinda assured him.

"Yeah, Mags. What do you know?" Bucky snapped.

I defended my pronouncement. "There was no movement. I mean, come on. Everybody knows you got to at least move your head." Using my fist as an imaginary partner, I closed my eyes, tilted my head

4

upwards and rolled it from side to side with dreamy abandon. Satisfied with my demonstration, I opened my eyes to Bucky's smirk — he knew I was no more practiced in the art of kissing than either of them. Melinda, however, was impressed.

"Should we try again?" she asked me.

"No," I sulked. "This is stupid."

"Well, it was your idea in the first place," Bucky reminded me.

I licked the split in my upper lip that always came with the dry winter air. The hideous thing had kept me from being the one to give Bucky his first kiss. And mine.

"It was an experiment," I said. "And a dumb one at that."

"Well, what should we do now?" Melinda asked with new enthusiasm.

Suddenly I was annoyed; when it came to imagination these two had none. All Bucky did was get us into trouble, and all Melinda did was . . . be perfect.

"I don't know. You're the new president. You figure it out. I'm going home."

After paying due respect to our official clubhouse mascot, Hector, a Clorox bottle made into a pig, I left through the blanket that served as the clubhouse door.

I didn't really want to go home. There was still plenty of daylight left, and supper was still a few hours away. I was about to go back in when I heard Bucky tell Melinda, "Ah, let her go. She's in a snit and won't be much fun anyway."

That made me mad enough to run all the way to the fence. Before separating the barbed wire, I looked back at our ramshackle clubhouse. No one came out.

"Who needs them anyway," I told myself as I pushed down the lower wires and slipped through. Besides, it wasn't like they could come up with something worthwhile to do without me.

I should have never left them alone.

PART ONE
The Summer of 1968

CHAPTER 1

The house where I did most of my growing up was pink, about two shades darker than cotton candy. Not a conventional color for rural Wyoming. Then again, the families who lived along Old Orphanage Road were anything but. We were a colorful bunch who coveted elbow room yet understood the need for neighbors.

The Bales and their Barn had arrived first. Built in 1920, the Barn was a relay station for illegal booze back when our neck of the woods was beyond both city limits and the local sheriff department's jurisdiction. Few people in Wyoming, including the sheriff, paid much attention to laws that forbade them to partake in whatever the hell they wanted, and Mr. Bales took advantage of the situation. He hired some local musicians, added a few outhouses, and made the Barn the most popular speakeasy this side of Thermopolis.

Respectability didn't enter the picture until Mrs. Bales did. Not that she was averse to downing a beer with a whiskey chaser, but Elizabeth Bales was first and foremost a do-gooder. Her pet project was establishing a county orphanage to be built on the twenty acres her first husband had acquired in a poker game. Unfortunately, he lost the property to Mr. Bales in the same fashion then shortly after keeled over from a bad liver. Apparently, Elizabeth's affections came with Mr. Baleses' winning hand. After allotting the appropriate mourning time to hubby number one, they married. Once again, the twenty acres were in her possession. However, her new husband's illicit establishment—within eyeball distance of her proposed orphanage site—was a potential contribution to juvenile delinquency. In the throes of love, Mr. Bales shut down operations. The Barn was converted into an honest-to-goodness home, complete with kitchen and indoor toilet.

As for the county orphanage, it was doomed from the get-go. Construction began shortly after prohibition ended then moved at the pace of a hobbled horse. During a wild spring thunderstorm, its newly erected thirty-foot flagpole took a direct hit from a lightning bolt. Nothing was left on the premises but charcoaled skeletons.

The orphanage never was rebuilt, but names being names, and people being people, the route would forever remain Old Orphanage Road.

Mr. and Mrs. Bales hung on to their undeveloped land until the early sixties when they decided to sell. My father was the first in line to buy. A painter by profession, Dad was giving the Barn the last of its red coats when Mr. and Mrs. Bales took a shine to him. Never having had any kids of their own, the couple relied on townsfolk to look in on them. They were also lonely, so Dad, who could be quite charming, convinced them they needed some company. He had just enough money for a couple of acres. They agreed to whittle down their land.

Dr. Simms was second. He tried to buy the remaining acreage, but Mrs. Bales had come to like the idea of having a neighborhood and wouldn't sell Doc anything more than five.

Our house—a modest three-bedroom with a basement—was the first to be framed and the last to be finished. Every weekend Dad would drive the backhoe, pour some cement, pound a few nails, and do whatever it took to move construction along using whatever money he'd managed to come by that week. Dr. Simms and family was living in their modern showcase long before we had a roof. While they had floor-to-ceiling windows, two fireplaces, and an attached two-car garage with an automatic garage door opener, we were happy to move in as soon as ours had a functioning kitchen and a flushable toilet. It didn't matter that the floors were bare plywood, the bathroom lacked a sink, and the living room walls were unpainted sheet rock.

Dad had been sold on aluminum siding by a smooth-talking fishing buddy turned salesman. A rather off-putting shade of pink, the siding came primed for painting, however that wasn't on my father's list of priorities.

The color offended Dr. Simms. He rang our newly installed bell one evening at suppertime. "When the hell are you going to paint over that damn pink? It cheapens the whole damn area." Showing remarkable restraint, my father reminded the good doctor that if he ever got around to paying his bills and came across one owed for a certain paint job on a certain reception area, some people might have enough money left over to buy a bucket of paint. The doc went away in a huff. Two days later Dad received a check in the mail. He immediately went out and bought pink exterior paint.

About the time of the paint feud, Big Buck Majors, a businessman who owned the biggest car lot in town, started building a home for his family just catty-corner from ours. Construction on the Padilla home began around the same time.

Mr. Padilla had been a successful rodeo clown, growing up in the border city of Juarez and traveling both the Mexican and United States rodeo circuits. Two days after arriving in our city with his long-suffering wife, five *niños* and a *bambino* on the way, he took a bull's horn to the gut and landed in the hospital. Surgery was touch and go, but the afterlife didn't stand a chance, not with Mrs. Padilla lighting candles and reciting rosaries to keep her husband in the here and now. When Mr. Padilla woke, he claimed the Virgin came to him in a vision, delivering a bedpan along with a message that further instructions were forthcoming.

When his bandages were removed for the final dressing, Mrs. Padilla took one gander at her husband's gut and fell to her knees. There on his abdomen, etched in scar tissue, was the Virgin Mary standing in front of a big red house.

Not sure of his vision nor his emerging scar, Mr. Padilla loaded up the family in their rickety pickup and set out for a drive, hoping to sort things out. As fate would have it, they blew a tire on Old Orphanage Road, not thirty yards from the Barn—the big red house.

Mrs. Bales happened to be on the front porch in her nightgown taking in the morning sunshine and combing her long white hair. Apparently, she was the spitting image of the Virgin on his belly, because when she looked towards the road, Mr. Padilla was running towards her followed by five hollering kids and a very pregnant woman. *"Nuestra Señora, Nuestra Señora!"* They chased Mrs. Bales clear past the frog pond before she finally tuckered out, at which point Mrs. Padilla went into labor.

Although a harrowing experience for all, it worked out for the best. Mrs. Padilla gave birth to a healthy seven-pound girl who she named Elizabeth, after Mrs. Bales. And Mrs. Bales sold them two acres at a price they could afford.

Doc Simms kept his eye on the Padillas' house as it sprang to life, pleased until the landscaping began, as Mrs. Padilla was enamored with statues, in particular Madonnas. No less than thirty Ladies graced the outside of her home, along with a variety of saints, weather vanes, and tropical birds. To add insult to Doc's injury, my father helped Mr. Padilla paint the outside of his home a lovely shade of green. The color complemented the arrival of Mrs. Padilla's mother's turquoise trailer.

During the Padilla fiasco, the five acres sandwiched between the Simmses' and the Majorses' were purchased by Walter Esmond Thomas. The Colonel, as he came to be known, was a widower, and Melinda his only child. Their quarters went up without a hitch, meticulously built then meticulously run by Mrs. Mavrakis, the Thomases' housekeeper and Melinda's confidante. Bucky and I welcomed Melinda into the fold.

The last to arrive were the mysterious Fricks. The Fricks didn't build a new house, they brought one of their own. Hailing from a time when it was fashionable to live in the middle of town, the house had been abandoned after the war and eventually sold, becoming Clemens Funeral Parlor until they decided to tear it down and build a modern air-conditioned facility. Enter Mrs. Bales and the Historical Society, who were appalled at the dismantling of the grand old home on Main Street and found a buyer.

The workers spent two months maneuvering the defunct dwelling onto its new foundation. And then nary a Frick showed up. Eventually, Dad doubted such a thing as a Frick existed, although Mrs. Bales assured him that a Frick lawyer certainly did. Doc withheld his opinion.

So, on one side of Old Orphanage Road we had the well-to-do dads — the Doc, the Colonel, and Big Buck. On the other side lived the working class, the Padillas and my family, along with the yet-to-be-seen Fricks. The Barn was in a class by itself.

Mrs. Bales had handpicked us all, bringing us together on the outskirts of our expanding town. Our neighborhood — the backbone of who I, Maggie Moore, was and what I would become — shaped the indelible friendship between me, Bucky Majors and Melinda Thomas.

1968 was a tempestuous year for our country. Although slow to come to the rodeo, even Wyoming was beginning to feel the effects of change. But at just twelve years old, my best friends and I had yet to open our eyes to anything happening outside of our own environs. We had more important things to do. Life was still about playing outside and staying out of trouble.

CHAPTER 2

A prisoner of the annual spring piano recital, I squirmed in my front-row seat in the First Presbyterian Church's fellowship hall, chewing my left thumbnail while inadvertently flicking the nails of my right until Mom coaxed both hands to her lap and held them captive.

"Sit still, Margaret," she whispered in my ear.

I transferred my anxiety to my feet. Toes together, toes apart, toes together, toes apart. I was wearing black patent-leather shoes, my good shoes, now scuffed from stepping on my own feet. Toes together, toes apart. With stealth-like swiftness, my mother's other hand clutched my knee. When my stomach responded with an angry growl, Mom rolled her eyes.

As Tommy Majors struggled through his performance of John Thompson's "Swans on the Lake," my stretchy headband crawled down my forehead, its bow eventually reaching the bridge of my nose. When I raised my chin to peer out, Mom let go of all appendages and repositioned the headband. She had fussed over my unruly brown hair for an hour, ratting, arranging, spraying, rearranging, and eventually making me three inches taller. Given what she had to work with, Mom was pleased.

I hated it.

I also hated my hand-me-down dress, courtesy of Patricia Simms. Mom did ironing for Mrs. Simms, which meant I knew more about the Simms' wardrobes than I cared to. This particular dress sprouted pink flower petals from oversized white polka dots. It also had an annoying lace collar and an even more bothersome full skirt that was unfashionably two inches below my knees. Definitely more Patricia Simms than me. Too bad she and her beehive weren't the ones wearing it while waiting to make a fool of herself.

Piano penance was at last over for Tommy. As polite applause followed him back to his seat among the first-year students, Mrs. Majors smiled proudly in the audience while cradling a snoring four-year-old Bart. Big Buck Majors, more at home during a baseball game, whistled and shouted his customary "Atta boy!" but Tommy was more interested in the opinion of Miss Lamoreux. He waited until she expelled the "high-pitched sigh" indicating approval—as opposed to the "low-pitched sigh" indicating abject failure—before sitting down. Then she signaled for Melinda to take her turn.

Half the kids on our side of town took piano lessons from Miss Lamoreux, the school system's music teacher. I wasn't one of them. Yet here I was, awaiting my turn in the spotlight. It wouldn't be long now.

As Melinda began to play "Moonlight Sonata," all coughing and scratching stopped. Miss Lamoreux didn't believe in saving the best for last—it was counter-productive to the self-esteem of the other kids—and Melinda was most definitely the best. Watching her work the piano was like watching a fine roping horse with a cowboy's catch. She teased it, coaxed it, soothed it, her fingers always in control, diving then dancing across the keys, never separate from the music they made.

Melinda had been taking piano lessons for years, starting before she could read. Certain she was a musical genius, I never tired listening to her play. My favorite place to do so was on her living room floor looking up the soundboard of her baby grand.

We had a piano once. Dad found it abandoned on the edge of Burton's alfalfa field, home to a family of skunks. Thinking it might make a nice birthday present for my brother Brian, Dad asked Mr. Burton for permission to haul it away. This bit of family lore happened when I was still in diapers and my brother Brian was aspiring to be Elvis. He had his heart set on a guitar and wasn't impressed with Dad's gift. Neither was Mom, with its sound or its smell. Dad knew when to say "uncle" and suggested they put the poor thing out of its misery, one of the rare times he and my brother agreed. The next morning, they took the piano to the dump and shot it, key by key.

After the final drone of the bass clef Melinda stood then searched parental heads for her father, finding the Colonel at the back near the rectory door. He nodded his approval then bowed out. Despite receiving a "high-pitched sigh," Melinda was noticeably disappointed as she returned to her seat.

As Miss Lamoreux summoned her next student, Bucky leaned forward and shot me a smile past five pairs of crossed knees. "We're on deck, Mags," he whispered. How could he be so confident?

Bucky and his brothers took piano lessons because their mother never had the chance and "by God, my kids are going to learn." Bucky caught on well, completing three books his first year. He'd chosen "The Spinning Song," a tricky piece, for his first piano recital, and performed it with aplomb. But while others advanced, Bucky maintained. A captive of his previous accomplishments, he gave an encore performance of "The Spinning Song" at his second recital, and his third. Miss Lamoreux had demanded that his fourth—and most likely final—feature a different song.

That's where I came in. Although we didn't have a piano in the house, we did have a well-loved phonograph. My family was eclectic in its musical tastes. Dad favored jazz, Mom preferred western, Brian took to rock-and-roll, and I was smitten by musicals. Well known for my big mouth and my ability to carry a tune—if I wasn't smarting off, I was singing—I lead songs on the school bus and always got the solo at the school Christmas pageant.

Melinda was the one who had bamboozled me into teaming with Bucky for the spring recital. "He's pretty nervous about performing," she told me in private. "Of course he'd never admit it, especially to you."

"Too bad I'm not in it," I said. "He'd do just about anything to show me up."

"You singing while he plays? What a terrific idea," Melinda said, proving she knew exactly how to play me. Of course, I only agreed because it would be something to hold over his head.

When Melinda presented her big idea to the parties concerned, Miss Lamoreux was delighted. Bucky was dubious.

Coming up with a song wasn't easy. It was either too hard or too high, too long or too stupid. We finally settled on "Secret Love," which Doris Day sang in the movie *Calamity Jane*. It was a sappy song, but I could identify with Calamity, and it was simple enough for Bucky.

But two weeks out from reckoning, Bucky still wasn't able to make it through without a mistake, much less have it memorized, and Melinda had called an emergency clubhouse meeting.

"Sorry I got you guys into this," she lamented from her presidential stool.

"Save your apologies," Bucky moaned, face down on the community bench. "Just figure out how we're going to get out of this."

"You could pretend you're sick," I offered.

"Tried that last year, and the year before. Mom said unless I had blood coming out of both ears, I better have my sweet hiney on the piano bench. Let's face it. We're going to stink."

I was in no mood to stink. "Okay. Here's what we're going to do. Bucky, you'll play the first chord all dramatic, then back off and play as softly as you can. Better yet, don't play at all and just pretend you're hitting the keys."

Melinda caught on. "Sort of pantomime it?"

"Yeah, and I'll sing real loud."

"Oh, right," snarled Bucky. "You'll shine while I look like an idiot? Nope, no dice."

I gave the bench a swift kick. Bucky picked up Hector the Clorox Pig and uncurled his pipe cleaner piggy tail.

"I can play the gall darn song. Can't I, Melinda? If only I didn't have to memorize it."

"Maybe this time Miss Lamoreux will let you use the sheet music," offered Melinda.

"Not a chance. You know her saying: 'Take the piece off the page. . .'"

" . . .put it in your heart," Melinda continued, "and make it a performance!'" They ended, both sweeping a right arm to the heavens.

Suddenly the solution was obvious. The sheet music.

"Use it anyway!" I insisted.

"What? Are you nuts? Miss Lamoreux will kill me."

"Better her than me! Anyway, this is your last recital, right? Wouldn't you rather go out with a bang than a bust?"

A deal was struck. I would surreptitiously put the sheet music on the piano when I took my place to sing, taking the heat off Bucky.

"Maggie," my mother patted my knee after applauding Bobby Harper. "You're on, sweetie." I reached under my chair for my handbag. It wasn't there. "Do you have my purse?" I asked.

"*You* brought a purse?"

Yes. Grandma's handbag. The one I used for storage. I had taken it out of my drawer, exchanging Barbie's clothes for peppermint Lifesavers and the sheet music. Then I put the handbag on the coffee table beside the front door so I wouldn't forget it. *Crap. I forgot it.*

My mother repositioned my headband again. "Good luck."

"We have a special treat this afternoon," Miss Lamoreux announced in her syrupy, fixed-jaw manner as I rose from my seat. "A veritable songbird is in our midst. I am sure you all know the vocal talents of Miss Maggie Moore, and we are simply delighted to have her as a part of our spring recital. She will sing the popular Fain and Webster song 'Secret Love,' accompanied by fourth-year student Bucky Majors."

"Atta boy," came Big Buck's voice.

Bucky, a consummate showman, approached the piano and bowed, then grandly brushed off the piano stool as if wiping off the mediocre cooties of its previous occupants. After pompously sitting his sweet hiney down, Bucky cracked his knuckles. I took my place just as we had rehearsed, minus one slight detail, and indicated for him to begin.

Bucky was confused. His eyes queried, *Where's the sheet music?* Mine answered, *Oops.*

It was amazing what panic can do to a fella.

As Fourth-Year Student began to play, excruciatingly slowly, Songbird sang.

Once I had a secret love,
That lived within the heart of me.

A couple of wrong notes from Fourth-Year Student. Songbird still on key, voice clear and amazingly strong.

All too soon my secret love
Became impatient to be free.

Fourth-Year Student, feeling more confident, played faster. Songbird intrepidly followed.

So, I told a friendly star,
The way that dreamers often do.

Now overconfident and carried away, Fourth-Year Student forgot Songbird was present. Songbird reminded Fourth-Year Student with a less than gentle thump on the piano lid.

Just how wonderful you are,
And why I'm so in love with you.

Filling her chest with air, Songbird soared toward her highest note while Fourth-Year Student drew a blank and stopped playing.

I tilted my head, giving my missing accompanist a glare, but his eyes were vacant. He sat frozen with his hands hovering above the piano keys.

"Bucky!" I hissed through the corner of my mouth. Jolted back from God knows where, Bucky's fingers started moving again. But the music I heard wasn't "Secret Love."

Oh, God, not 'The Spinning Song!'
There was nothing to do but try to out-sing him.

Now I shout it from the highest hills,

Songbird flapped wildly. Fourth-Year Student spun out of control.

16

Even told the golden daffodils.

Songbird sang louder, but Fourth-Year Student pounded even harder.

At last my heart's an open door,
And my secret love's no secret anymore.

Songbird prepared for a crash landing, giving it all she had. Meanwhile, Fourth-Year Student goes for a big finish, ending his musical career.

"Atta boy!" roared Big Buck.

The last thing I heard before I fainted was an anguished low-pitched sigh.

•　　•　　•　　•　　•

Passing out was not an unpleasant experience. Rather, it was like stepping into another dimension, one where I could live an entire life in a single swoon. Different people, different experiences, all feeling so real. But when I started to come to, the two worlds began to play tug-of-war. Then the other was gone—like a popped soap bubble.

I didn't mind fainting. What I minded was fainting in front of somebody, and a lot of somebodies at that.

I woke up on a cot in the Reverend Bauer's office, still a little confused. After poking and prodding me and assuring my mother that I was going to live, Doctor Simms left. My mother, convinced this was all because I hadn't eaten, scurried away on a mission to find me something to chew.

I sat up. Everything seemed all right. No broken bones, no headache. The room was semi-dark, lit only by a sliver of light seeping through a broken blind. It homed in on a painting of Jesus surrounded by sheep, illuminating the lone black lamb of his flock.

Slowly the door opened and two faces peeked through.

Melinda entered first. "Maggie? Are you ill?"

Melinda always gave me a way to save face. I quickly fell back into the cot and gave an agonizing moan.

"I think I'm really sick," I said. "The doctor said it doesn't look good."

"That's funny," Bucky chided. "I heard him tell your mom you just got overheated. What's the matter, Mags, couldn't take the pressure? Had to go girly?"

I was on top of him faster than a cat on a grasshopper.

"Take it back, creep! Take it back!"

Melinda sat down on the cot—she had witnessed our brawls many times and there wasn't much she could do—just as Bucky started to laugh.

"I couldn't help it. Honest, Mags, my fingers went into automatic."

"I'll automatic my fingers on you!" Showing no mercy, I tickled him. It was sublime torture, and his pleading only egged me on.

"Stop! Stop! It wasn't my fault."

"You're right!" I took my hands from his armpits. "It was Melinda's. Let's get her."

That was how the cot got broken, the Reverend's pipe and tobacco ended up on the floor and Jesus fell off the wall. That was also how the three of us came to be grounded for the remaining week of school.

Thankfully, summer vacation was just around corner.

CHAPTER 3

"The Friday meeting of the No Name No Purpose Club will come to order."

Melinda rapped on the rusty cowbell donated by my Uncle Willis, bringing an end to Bucky's and my pointless argument.

"First we'll call the roll." Melinda took her presidential duties seriously. "Bucky Majors."

"Why, I'm right here, little missy," spouted Bucky, doing a rather bad impersonation of John Wayne.

I groaned, but Melinda giggled.

"Maggie Moore," she continued.

"Yeah, yeah."

Not stymied by my lack of enthusiasm, she proceeded. "Hector the Pig."

We perused the confines of our haunt. There was no Hector.

"Where'd he go?" I asked out loud.

"I bet that gall darn Bales mutt got in here again," snarled Bucky as he checked the towel-covered dirt floor to see if the dog in question had left his calling card.

I opted for the more dramatic: "I bet he's been kidnapped."

Lacking poop evidence, Bucky nodded in agreement. Melinda, who was also the club secretary, removed the red pencil from behind her ear and made a sweeping check on her Big Chief notebook. "We'll mark on the roll that Hector is absent. Maggie, will you look into this?"

"You bet." I was already making a mental list of possible culprits.

19

Melinda continued. "Because nothing important came from our last meeting, we'll dispense with the minutes. Is there any old business to discuss?"

We talked about the spring piano recital and how it hadn't turned out as bad as we'd thought. Bucky actually overheard Dickie Lagourainis tell Joel Macrae that our act would have won first place in the 4-H Talent Show because the part where I passed out was pure genius.

"Can you believe it?" Bucky shook his head in disbelief. "They thought we planned the whole thing!" I joined him in a good chuckle until Melinda bludgeoned the cowbell.

"Let's move on to new business."

"Okay, okay. I've got something," reported Bucky. "Joe-Joe Padilla asked me if he could join the club."

I was dumbfounded. It had never occurred to me that we might expand our membership. This required some serious thinking.

"What can he contribute?" Melinda asked.

"A flashlight, a really neat gumball machine, and he says he can rip off his brother's transistor radio."

"Hmm," I said pointedly.

"He's a good wheeler-dealer, Mags," Bucky continued. "That'll come in handy when it's fundraising time."

"I like Joe-Joe," added Melinda. "He fixed my flat tire last week. Took the chain off and everything."

But I crossed my arms and assumed a contemplative pose.

"What have you got against Joe-Joe anyway?" Bucky said.

"Nothing! Why are you ganging up on me?"

"Because you're doing that lip thing."

I had a tendency to bite my lower lip when my brain was engaged. "I just think we need to take some time before making any major decision that'll effect our entire operation. I mean, where's he gonna sit?"

That had them stumped. The clubhouse wasn't very big. We had built it the previous fall on the vacant lot between my family's and the Padillas' property using whatever we could scrape up: plywood, chicken wire, a couple of two-by-fours, a refrigerator box, corrugated steel, here a crate, there a shingle, and lots of nails. It came together in a cool, rustic kind of way, even though it did sort of lean. Dad thought a good wind would tear the thing apart, but it had survived the winter.

Our furnishings were meager but sufficient. Aunt Sylvia's three-legged chair, Uncle Willis's cowbell, a Wyoming state flag, and a beat-up mailbox were my contributions, while Bucky brought in the bench, stool and coffee table, all courtesy of the nearby dump. He also kept us stocked with comic books. Melinda provided the intelligent literature, including a dictionary, as well as blankets for the windows, rugs for the floor, and whatever administrative supplies we needed. All this, and Hector too, fit into an eight-by-ten hangout. There wasn't much room to spare. Still, a gumball machine might look neat in the corner. And music would be a nice touch.

"Any more discussion?"

Obviously, Melinda meant any more discussion from me. I said nothing and shot her a toothy smile.

"Fine. All in favor of letting Joe-Joe Padilla join the No Name No Purpose Club raise your hand."

It was unanimous.

"Of course he'll have to pass the initiation test," Bucky announced.

"What test?"

"I don't know. But I'll think of something."

"Now I have some new business," Melinda announced. "My father left this morning for Washington. He's going to be gone most of the summer." There was a catch in Melinda's throat. Even though he was a strict old fuddy-duddy, she worshipped her father. "Anyway, Mrs. Mavrakis will officially be in charge, so . . ."

" . . . SO WE'RE ON FOR *WEIRD THEATER!*" Bucky and I broke out in unison.

Every Friday night Channel 8 presented *Weird Theater*, and tonight's movie was advertised as deliciously scary. *Weird Theater* came on at midnight, well past Melinda's bedtime. I was meant to be in bed no later than eleven o'clock, although Friday was an exception. Bucky claimed his parents didn't mind if he stayed up all night any day of the week.

We had been planning a *Weird Theater* party, complete with popcorn and bedrolls, since school let out, but had only just sprung the idea on our mothers. While Mom and Mrs. Majors couldn't see any harm, the Colonel was predicted to be a problem. Yet now that he was out of the picture, all we had to do was sway Mrs. Mavrakis.

When it came to Bucky and me, Mrs. Mavrakis was a pushover. He tickled her funny bone, and I was forever praising her baking, because no one could hold a candle to Mrs. Mavrakis in the kitchen. Every Tuesday was bread day — Mrs. Mavrakis didn't believe in store-bought — and the three of us would hit her up for dough. She always wore an apron and smelled of flour.

Mrs. Mavrakis had immigrated from Greece after her husband was killed in the Big War. Having met up with the Colonel via a placement agency shortly after Melinda's mother died, she came with them when the Colonel headed west. At five-foot nine with a 54-inch bosom, she could be quite intimidating, but she adored Melinda. With a little persuasion and a tactical appeal for necessary late-night nourishment, our *Weird Theater* party was a shoo-in.

"After we clear it with Mrs. Mavrakis, I suggest we take a nap," Melinda dictated from her presidential high-horse. "It's a long way until midnight."

"A nap?" I protested. "What are we? Two?"

"Not a chance," came Bucky's response.

Melinda tossed her braids. "Have it your way, but this is my first *Weird Theater* and I'm not going to fall asleep in the middle. Bucky, are you sure your mom doesn't have a problem with this?"

"A.O.K. with her."

Of course, the party would be in the Majorses' rec room. It had a ping-pong table and the only color television set in the neighborhood apart from the Simms'. Plus, a wall of cupboards housed an assortment of trucks, trains, racing cars, and green army men, not to mention every Milton Bradley board game and Mattel Creepy Crawler ever made. I never had many toys other than a Barbie and a headless Ken whom I considered more my subjects than dolls, but while I much preferred playing outside, shooting marbles or hanging on the clothesline pole, I still sometimes dreamed of having my own full cupboard of playthings.

After Melinda adjourned our meeting, we headed to her house, where Mrs. Mavrakis was already in place for her afternoon story. Every weekday at two thirty, Mrs. Mavrakis sat down with a cup of coffee and lost her soul to *The Edge of Night*. Afterwards, she'd ring up Mrs. Bales, another devoted watcher, to discuss what they had just seen, reproach the shoddy handling of circumstances, and make a few predictions. Mostly they just gossiped about the characters.

Sometimes we'd watch with her, but Mrs. Mavrakis didn't always welcome our company. For one thing, Bucky asked too many questions, like "Who's that?" and "Why's she so upset?" or "Why doesn't he just tell her the truth?" Bucky didn't always understand the finer points of a soap opera.

As something juicy always happened on Friday—a clever ploy to keep all *Edge of Nighter*s on pins and needles until Monday—Mrs. Mavrakis was wide-eyed and not at all pleased to see us.

"The kitchen jar holds sugar cookies. Help yourselves, and no forget to shut the screen door on your way out."

Cookies were a classic Mavrakis bribe and one that worked on me every time. I started for the kitchen, but Melinda caught my arm.

"What's the scoop for today, Mrs. Mavrakis?" Bucky asked, plopping down on the sofa. "Did that guy ever tell his girlfriend he had a wife?"

The pre-show commercials were almost over and Mrs. Mavrakis was getting noticeably perturbed. She waved her hand at Bucky as if swatting a fly.

"You kids should be outside, in the sun. It's no good to be inside."

"Why, Mrs. Mavrakis! Are you trying to get rid of us?" Bucky gave her a grin that showed off his dimple, Melinda's cue to get the ball rolling.

"We have plans in the making and want to run them by you," Melinda said. I took it from there. "You see, we've been wanting to have a slumber party at the Majorses'. You know, to kick off the summer. And we were thinking that tonight would be a good night because . . ." I decided not to tell her about *Weird Theater*. Grownups seldom understood the benefits of staying up late.

". . . because my Mom said it was all right," Bucky finished. Quick and to the point.

Melinda jumped in with sincerity. "I really would like to do this. I've never been to a slumber party."

"And what does it mean, this slumber party?"

It was almost showtime so we had to wrap it up. "You play games," I rattled off, "you tell stories, and you go to sleep. Oh, and you eat. Can we take some of your sugar cookies?" My father taught me it's best to assume the answer is yes.

"And this is no problem to your mother, Margaret?"

I nodded yes just as the gloomy voice of the TV announcer intoned, *"The Edge . . . of Night."*

"Then this is no problem to me. Now skedaddle before my mind changes."

And skedaddle we did, right to the cookie jar then out the door, leaving Melinda to her nap.

$\bullet \quad \bullet \quad \bullet \quad \bullet \quad \bullet \quad \bullet$

Melinda and I arrived at Bucky's around seven thirty, leaving us just enough time to play a game of Starlight, Moonlight before we'd have to go inside. Joe-Joe Padilla joined us, along with his older brother, Johnno, and younger sister, Maria. Patricia Simms came out, too. Even Bucky's little brothers Tommy and Billy were in on the game, much to his chagrin.

Starlight, Moonlight was our neighborhood version of hide-and-seek only the "it" was a witch and the witch hid instead of everyone else. Whoever the witch caught joined the coven. The last one to *not* get caught was the winner. Master of the Universe. As its name indicated, the game was much better when played after dark.

The moon was on the rise—full and ominous. Johnno, Billy, and I were the only non-witches left. With hands marginally placed over eyes, we waited on the stoop for the others to hide. Johnno was getting impatient and hurried up the conventional count.

"... 85, 90, 95, 100. Ready or not, here we come."

Billy, who was just shy of six years, grabbed my hand. "I'm not ascared," he gulped.

I gave his hand a squeeze and we began our chant.

"'Starlight, moonlight, hope to see the witch tonight. Starlight, moonlight, hope to see the witch tonight.'"

Johnno took off first. His strategy was to run as fast as he could as close to the house as possible, hoping to catch the witches off guard then beat them back to "home free." I chose to let him flush them out. Billy's plan was to stick to me.

Johnno breezed around the front corner of the house. There was too much light for anyone to effectively hide, so naturally that's where Patricia was, lurking next to the front bumper of Big Buck's Impala. Her attempt to snare Johnno was a bust. He sailed past her before she could let out a cackle. Billy and I successfully evaded her by going around the back of the car and keeping our distance. Eventually spying us, Patricia tried to run us down, but was too slow.

Maneuvering along the house's south side was a little trickier. That's where Mrs. Majors had planted her rose garden, and she didn't take kindly to trampled flowers. It was best to stay clear of the bushes and head toward the open field. Johnno seldom took the easy route, braving the thorns along with Mrs. Majors's wrath. Maria and Melinda, hiding together behind a wheelbarrow, let him pass and came after me and Billy instead, chasing us away from the house. But when the winded witches stopped to catch their breath, they made the mistake of taking their eyes off us.

"Time to split up, Billy," I said when we hit the open field.

Billy didn't argue. He just listened. Add dimples and part his hair on the opposite side, and Billy looked like a miniature Bucky.

"Start crawling on your belly toward the fence post. When you get about ten yards, turn towards the house and wait for me to give the word."

"Okay." Billy squealed in adorable little-boy fashion.

"I'll distract them, then loop back and follow you. Okay?"

"Okay." Billy was all-trusting.

I raised my head slightly to look over the grass. Melinda and Maria were combing the area but hadn't spotted us. Billy began to crawl as instructed while I moved toward the girls. This was a golden opportunity to scare the bejeebers out of them. I might get caught, but it would be worth it to hear Melinda scream and make Maria pee her pants. She often did when startled.

I got close enough to see the sparkle of Melinda's golden ribbons. Then I reared back and sprung up from the ground in one glorious swoop to land directly behind them, shouting, "Run, Billy, run!"

Melinda screamed, Maria peed, and Billy ran smack-dab into Tommy, who had come out of hiding to check on the commotion. The two of them landed in the sand pile at the back of the house, both bursting into tears.

"You did that on purpose!" Tommy accused as he cradled his wounded head.

"It's not fair!" Billy whined. "You didn't really catch me. I won't be a witch."

Fighting ensued. By this time Melinda and Maria had recovered and were making their way to the sand pile to try to calm the boys down. I took advantage of Billy's misfortune and continued the trek, rounding the bend to the house's north side. Johnno was there, waiting by Big Buck's boat, taking a breather.

The north side had lilac bushes and a willow tree just off the front corner. It was an ideal locale for ambush, but if you went too far from the house the witches would converge on "home free" and make it nearly impossible to get through. Most of the witches were still at the sand pile. But Joe-Joe and Bucky were out there somewhere.

"Where are they?" I whispered.

Johnno pursed his lips at the tree, where Joe-Joe wasn't doing such a good job at hiding. It was unmistakably his skinny butt sticking out from behind the trunk. Bucky had to be somewhere in the lilac bushes or just around the corner.

"You're on your own, *muchacha*," Johnno informed me as he spat on his palms and rubbed his hands together. We took off at the same time, Johnno dashing between the tree and the bushes, me running to the right of the willow. Joe-Joe flanked his brother just as Bucky jumped off the roof and met him head-on. Johnno was caught.

While the three boys started to wrestle, I took off for the front of the house. But about twenty-five yards from "home free," Bucky spotted me. Even in the twilight I could see his dimple flash.

Suddenly I got butterflies in my stomach. It was our turn. Bucky and me, about to engage.

Ready... Set...

Whooooh-weet! Whooooh-weet!

The porch light at "home free" came on. Big Buck was standing at the front door, his thumb and forefinger in whistle position. Big Buck's whistle was our neighborhood siren—a signal that playtime was over and it was time to go home, no dilly-dallying, no questions asked.

So much for "Master of the Universe." So much for the chase. And being caught.

Johnno and Joe-Joe collected Maria and offered to walk Patricia home. Billy and Tommy called a time-out on their brawl, to be continued inside. Meanwhile, I joined Melinda by the bedrolls we'd left on the porch swing and followed Bucky into his house.

As we descended the stairs to the Majorses' rec room, we realized our party of three was now a party of five. Tommy and Billy had tagged along thinking they were invited to the sleepover. Bucky had to set them straight. When reasoning then threats of bodily harm didn't budge them, Bucky called in the heavy artillery.

"Mom!"

Mrs. Majors appeared at the top of stairs and announced bath time for the two boys. You'd have thought she was sentencing them to hard labor, but their fussing ended abruptly when Big Buck laid down the law.

"Go wash up! Go! And quit your crying, or I'll give you something to cry about."

All whimpering came to an end, and they hurried to the bathroom.

At last we had the place to ourselves. Bucky closed the door, then pounded his head against it. "You see! This is what I have to put up with every day of my life."

Melinda and I sympathized. My brother Brian was ten years older than me and lived on his own. There were certain advantages to being the only kid at home.

We proceeded to stake out our *Weird Theater* viewing site. Bucky won the couch in a Rock Paper Scissors game, so Melinda and I took the floor, spreading our bedrolls side by side, heads against the couch, feet towards the television.

Now how to pass the time until midnight?

After five rounds of Chinese checkers, six games of ping-pong, and a hand of fifty-two card pickup, it was still only ten thirty. Fortunately, Mrs. Majors eased our impatience by showing up with a big bowl of popcorn. She handed it to Bucky.

"Keep it down if you don't want a visit from your father."

After kissing each of us on the forehead, she pointed to the clock on the wall. "And don't stay up too late."

We said our good nights then Melinda suggested we get into our pajamas and save the popcorn for later. That didn't go over well because Bucky and I already had our hands in the bowl. (Mrs. Mavrakis's cookies didn't make it to the party.)

Our eventual pajama donning turned into a fashion show. Bucky modeled the latest in summer sleepwear for boys: a short-sleeved, buttoned-down top and string-drawn bottoms with branding iron designs. Melinda was ready for nighty-night in her white-eyelet Baby Doll ensemble with puffed sleeves, yellow laces, and bloomer bottoms. I had a more relaxed look: Dad's oversized Elks Club T-shirt, complete with mustard stain and a hole in the neck. We agreed my sleepwear was the coziest.

After a bathroom break, Melinda turned out the lights and Bucky turned on the set, keeping the sound down while I gave a haunting rendition of "The Golden Arm." That took us to the witching hour.

As Melinda and I made ready by hugging our knees, Bucky joined us on the floor, claiming the movie would have a better effect if we sat close together. A horrifying scream rang through the room from the television announcer. "It's time for *Weirrrrrrrrrrrrrrrd Theater*."

We responded in chorus. "*Weirrrrrrrrrrrrrrrd Theater!*"

"Tonight, the shocking tale of a man who would not die! *Mr. Sardonicus.*"

I'm sure *Mr. Sardonicus* lived up to its ghastly expectations, but I wouldn't know. Within the first ten minutes, I was sound asleep.

"Maggie. Maggie!" Melinda was shaking me.

I grumbled a bit, and then rolled over.

"Maggie. Wake up! You have to see this."

I opened my eyes. Bucky's rear end was in my face.

"What time is it?" I murmured as I sat up, a bit discombobulated.

"About two, I guess."

"What happened to the movie?"

"It's over."

"What do you mean it's over? What happened?" All I remembered of it was the scratching of fingernails, although that could have been Bucky's snoring.

Melinda went to work on Bucky. "It was soooo scary. I can't believe you slept through the whole thing."

Bucky was coming to. "What's going on?"

"We slept through the whole thing, you big dummy." I punched him in the arm then turned on Melinda. "Why didn't you wake us up?"

"I tried, but I guess some people didn't take their nap."

Bucky stumbled to the couch. "Let's go to sleep."

"No!" Melinda insisted. "You have to come see this."

The rec room had a ground-level window that faced the south side's open field. Melinda took my hand and led me to the desk beneath it. Light was streaming in from outside.

"Since when do we have a streetlamp?" I asked.

"We don't," answered Bucky who was suddenly by my side.

"It's the moon." Melinda whispered excitedly. "Get on the desk and look out."

I hoisted my body and did as she told. The moonlight's effect on the landscape was astounding. Basked in beams, the rocks lining Mrs. Majorses' rose garden glistened with authority.

"Wow," Bucky exclaimed as he jumped up and pressed his nose to the window pane. "You can see all the way to Sand Hill."

Melinda reached up, unlatched the window then rolled it open. "Let's go outside."

Bucky and I were shocked. It was unlike Melinda to suggest anything so daring. But a great idea is a great idea.

"Shouldn't we put on our clothes?" Bucky asked.

"I don't see why," I told him. "If we get caught, would it change anything?"

"Guess not." Bucky heaved himself out the window. After giving Melinda a boost through, I climbed out.

It was like stepping into a black-and-white film. Everything had taken on a silver tone: the bicycles strewn over the Majorses' front yard, the briars lining Old Orphanage Road, the dilapidated snow fence just over the western horizon.

The moon made Melinda bold. "Why don't we take a walk?"

Without waiting for an answer, she headed toward the road then made a surveillance stop at Bucky's mailbox. We scrambled to catch up. Except for a chorus of crickets and ol' Hooty the owl, there was only silence. No sign of any Majors stirring. I did a sweep left towards my house, its pinkness masked by the night's glow. Quiet there. At Melinda's and the Simmses' as well. All the neighborhood lights were off . . . except for one.

"Look!" Bucky croaked as he pointed to the Frick's.

For nearly a year the Frick house had stood vacant, its Victorian splendor diminished by an occasional tumbleweed. Now there was an unmistakable glow coming from inside the smaller of the two turrets.

"Do you suppose the light's been there all along?" I whispered, groping for an explanation.

"I've never seen it before," Melinda answered.

Bucky's nostrils flared. He smelled adventure. "Maybe it's a prowler."

Melinda took a step backwards. "Maybe we should go back inside."

Bucky shook his head. "No sirree. Not when there's a chance to be an honest-to-goodness hero. We gotta check this out."

I'd been intending to agree with Melinda, but Bucky had a way of roping me into his escapades, and vice versa. Not wanting to go back to the house alone, Melinda fell in line.

With pounding hearts, we quietly made our way up the Frick front walk, taking cover behind a stack of cinder blocks left by the workers. Sure enough, someone was there, moving about behind the lace curtains illuminated by a candle. We saw a robed figure pause by the bay window, light a cigarette, then stagger past.

"It's a ghost," I gasped.

Melinda wasn't so sure. "I don't think ghosts smoke."

"We gotta get closer," Bucky said.

Leaving the protection of the blocks, Bucky snuck up the porch stairs, Melinda and me close behind. The bottom of the bay window was about three feet above the porch floorboards. We scurried underneath it and squatted down with backs to the wall.

"Okay," I mouthed to Bucky. "What do we do now?"

"Peek in the window," he mouthed back.

In synchronized silence, we positioned ourselves for a look, heads rising to the window like balloons being filled with helium. The room was empty. Only a candle on a shelf in the far corner remained. Then we heard it.

"Momma, Momma. Let me out."

Burst by the shrill plea, we dropped to the porch. It took a moment for me to gather my wits. "Did you hear that?"

One look at their terrorized faces I knew they had.

"Maybe the Fricks are like those people who steal children and sell them overseas," Bucky whispered.

"Or maybe there's a witch inside who traps little kids and eats them," I said.

We heard it again.

"Momma, Momma. Let me out."

Melinda was ready to act. "We have to get help."

I held her back. "Wait a minute! Let's think this through. We're gonna get in big trouble."

"Yeah, but afterwards we'll be heroes," Bucky said.

Squawk, squawk.

As soon as I heard the bloodcurdling screech, I cleared the front porch steps in one leap and was on my way to the road when I realized my friends weren't with me. Looking back, I spotted Bucky head-first in an empty planter box, while Melinda was plastered against the house, paralyzed by fright.

The front door was open and on the porch stood either a Frick or a witch.

Knowing I had to save them, I defiantly walked back to get a better look at what I was up against. "If you do so much as pluck out one eyelash," I hollered, "I'll sic my father on you!"

"Who's there? Who's come to call?" The Frick witch, who wasn't much taller than me or Melinda, was wearing a long lacy robe that offered only a hint of coverage for the sheer negligee beneath it. She had a drink in one hand and a cigarette in the other. Perched on her shoulder was a bird straight out of a *National Geographic* magazine.

"Momma, Momma. Let me out. *Squawk.*"

Melinda let out a *squawk* of her own, and Bucky, who had righted himself, clung to the planter's side.

"Look, Francine, we have visitors." She leaned against the doorjamb and took a slow drag. Using her cigarette as if it were a magic wand, she pointed it toward Melinda. "One," she counted with a jab, "two," to Bucky, then swirled and swirled it until she found me. "Three. Perfect. Please, do come in." No one budged. "Come on," she coaxed with her hand. Slowly turning toward the open door, first her body, then her head, she glided into the house.

"Come to Mamma. Come to Mamma. *Squawk.*"

As if hypnotized, the three of us obeyed.

A churning mixture of cigarette smoke, candle wax, and mildew filled the house, each competing for dominance in the stagnant air. There wasn't a stick of furniture, just a couple of boxes stacked here and there and a birdcage draped in black.

We followed the woman into the front room.

"Scotch?" she asked in a husky voice that hinted a twang. Bucky was first to break from her spell.

"Huh?"

"Would ya'll care for a scotch?" she asked him directly.

He blinked back.

"Oh, what am I thinking? I can't offer y'all a scotch. I haven't anymore glasses." She expelled a throaty laugh followed by a series of snorts followed by a coughing fit followed by a perfect imitation from Francine.

Drawing on my courage, I asked, "Are you a witch?"

"Hmm. A witch. Hmm. I've had a couple of husbands call me that. Come to think of it, they've called me a lot worse." Once again she went through her tittering routine.

She sure sounded like a witch, but I was beginning to have my doubts. "Are you a Frick?"

The women drew in an exasperated sigh before reaching for a near-empty Cutty Sark bottle that sat precariously on a cardboard box. After emptying its contents into her highball, she handed it to me. Inhaling what remained of her cigarette, she thumped the butt through the bottle's neck then reached into her pocket for another. All the while, the bird bobbed on her shoulder, concerned about the unlit Winston dangling from the lip of its perch.

"Where's that friggin' Zippo?" the woman muttered, the cigarette dancing with each word.

"Where's that friggin' Zippo? Where's that friggin' Zippo? *Squawk.*"

Obviously this wasn't the first time the woman had misplaced her lighter. After a frantic search, she finally located it beside one of the candles on the fireplace mantle. Once she'd lit up, she absentmindedly set the Zippo down again. I handed the glass back to her and repeated my question.

"So are you?"

"Am I what?"

"A Frick."

She took a contemplative drag and let the smoke seep from her nose. "Yes, ma'am, I am. Rebecca Frick. Once upon a time, and now once again, but I'm not one to dwell." Her focus switched to me. "And you must be . . ." She peered into my eyes. "When's your birthday, honey?"

"August 14th," I replied, completely confused.

"I knew it. A Leo. Sure of yourself, and you don't take criticism very well, do you?" She turned her attention to Bucky who still didn't seem convinced she wasn't a witch. "And you? You are a . . . You were born . . ."

"Huh?"

"His birthday's September 17th," Melinda supplied.

"Didn't I tell you, Francine? A Virgo." By the way she blew the smoke out of the side of her mouth, a Virgo was not a good thing to be.

Melinda, clearly wanting to be included, raised her hand. "What am I, Mrs. Frick?"

"Oh, no. No. Not *Mrs. Frick*. Frick was my daddy's name. Just call me Rebecca."

"My father would never allow that."

Rebecca Frick gently fingered a strand of Melinda's hair. "Well, then you can call me Miss Rebecca."

"What am I, Miss Rebecca?" Melinda asked again. "January 29th."

"An Aquarian. And you, lovely one, are stronger than you think. Never forget that."

I wasn't so sure about her astrological assessments, but Rebecca seemed wise beyond years. Her age wasn't easy to decipher. One moment the candlelight would be kind, bringing a girlish glow to her cheeks and a fiery passion to her eyes, then the next it would capture the terse pucker of her lips and the grayish hollows below eyes ringed by faded makeup. Her black shoulder-length hair, abused by too many trips to the beauty parlor, held no shine. Her long fingernails, suffering from chipped, frosted polish, were overdue a manicure. And there was that smoker's hack.

Still, Rebecca Frick was bold and sincere, and I admired that.

Bucky got his voice back, and we made our introductions. Not for a second did Rebecca seem to think that three kids in pajamas paying her a visit in the wee hours was odd. She chatted away as if we had come for afternoon tea. Apparently, Rebecca had just arrived from San Francisco. Her belongings would soon follow, and she had quite a few belongings, most of them paid for by her father, J.P. Frick, who had made a fortune in oil.

"It's a dirty, ugly business, not unlike my daddy," she told us.

Rebecca was divorced. Three times. A rarity in our area. Her first husband was the passing fancy of a child. Number two was in the import-export business, which was how she'd acquired her fondness for birds like Francine, who was an African Gray and had quite a vocabulary, most of which was unsuitable for mixed company. Rebecca's third husband was a horse breeder from Kentucky. She'd fallen in love with Wyoming on a buying trip. "It's gutsy here, and people don't give a damn if you drink or smoke or flaunt your carefree nature." It wasn't exactly hip though, something she planned to remedy.

I could have listened to Rebecca's stories for hours, but Bucky was nodding off, and we were out illegally. After settling Francine in her cage, she walked us to the door.

"Now, don't be strangers, y'all hear? Feel free to drop by anytime. No need to call ahead."

We left her on the front porch blowing smoke rings at the moon. An honest-to-goodness Frick.

"Such a sad lady," Melinda reflected.

Bucky yawned. "I think she's weird."

"True and true," I said. "But I like her."

CHAPTER 4

Rebecca's arrival caused quite a stir in the neighborhood. Mrs. Bales headed the Welcome Wagon, and afterwards phoned Mrs. Mavrakis with her assessment. "I'm not one to judge, but I'd go so far to say that she's got a screw loose."

Dad sized her up as a "fruit cake." He and Big Buck headed over to give her a friendly "how d'you" and caught her sitting crossed-legged on the porch, chanting what Dad could only describe as "some foreign mumbo-jumbo." Rebecca, who was wearing a shocking-pink and lime-green bikini and knee-high boots, invited them to sit with her and "feel the love." They both politely declined.

The Padillas paid their respects to our newcomer, bearing tamales. Rebecca was delighted. She spoke a fair amount of Spanish, the result of employing numerous south-of-the-border cooks, maids and grounds keepers. Even Francine could turn a few Spanish phrases, most of which made Mrs. Padilla and *Abuela* blush.

The three of us had a hard time not letting it leak that we were the first to make Rebecca's acquaintance. I looked forward to having another run-in, but she took off for some kind of retreat somewhere in California. In the meantime, there were more important things to think about. Like who would take a Clorox pig and for what reason?

I was pondering this one morning during my sprawl time. The summer sun had already pierced my bedroom window, and I was on my back, hips raised and legs extended over my head so my toes could explore the outline of my headboard. That was how I got my best thinking done.

The clubhouse wasn't exactly theft proof. Then again, neither were any of the houses on Old Orphanage Road. Nobody locked their doors, with the exception of Dr. Simms. Patricia Simms actually had to carry a key.

I dropped my legs and flipped onto my belly, this time tracing the cold metal headboard with my fingers. Its shiny brass had been painted brown. My bed now, but it used to be Grandma's. God, I missed her. The fourth child of nine, Grandma'd had carrot-red hair and a temper to match. She lived a hard life, denied her dream of becoming a teacher by a coal-mining father who saw little value in educating women beyond anything other than doing chores. So she'd done the only thing she knew to get out from under his control: she ran off with my Grandfather, another coal miner. After he died of Black Lung, Grandma became adamant that her two boys would never set foot in the mines.

Grandma died in the summer of '66, one month before her sixty-fourth birthday. Way too young. I still remembered her hands, callused from years of milking cows, churning butter, shucking corn, kneading bread, beating rugs, and ironing sheets.

"Maggie, your mom's got breakfast on the table."

Dad poked his head through my bedroom door and blew me a morning kiss. I caught it in my fist and slowly unfurled each finger one a time, then gobbled it down before it could escape. After he left, I stood on the bed and parted the window curtains. No clouds, no wind. Just the clear blue sky and the dandelion-dotted ground. It was a June day custom-made for an outing. I put thoughts of Hector and Grandma aside and made ready for a horseback ride with Bucky and Melinda.

Being born in Wyoming, you'd think that I would've had a natural thing for horses. I didn't. In my estimation, horses' behinds were right up there with bees and electricity—potentially dangerous and something to be avoided at all costs. As a five-year-old I had witnessed firsthand the damage a swift kick from a 1200-pound horse could inflict on the trunk of a black '58 Hillman. I'd had a healthy respect for the equine backend ever since. But in spite of my fears, I loved to ride.

My mother was a genuine cowgirl, riding before she could walk. Seriously. As the story went, one day Granny Lane had gone into town and left her thumb-sucking baby, my mom, in the care of her whiskey-swigging brother, Foshen. When she returned, it was to find my mother with her squatty legs straddled atop Foshen's black Shetland pony, Prince, clutching the little horse's mane as it lowered his head to chomp grass. Mom was content. Foshen was passed out in the bunkhouse.

Great Uncle Foshen eventually gave Prince to my mom, who rode him to school and learned to put up with the pony's penchant for dumping whatever and whoever was on his back. Horsemanship was a way of life for Mom—raising them, riding them, depending on them—until she married Dad and traded the wide-open country for a small apartment downtown. A necessary adaptation for their newlywed budget.

Mom cursed as we rattled down the washboard in our dust-coated station wagon. "When the heck are they gonna do something about this darn road?" she said, her words vibrating with each bump.

We were heading out to Uncle Willis and Aunt Mina's place in Bighorn. My cousins were grown and working on ranches of their own, so my uncle and aunt welcomed every chance for company and riders for their horses. They pastured six.

Bucky and Melinda were bouncing in the back seat. Bucky was wearing the straw cowboy hat, which he only wore when we went riding. Otherwise, he had on the season's baseball cap. Like his father, Bucky preferred wheels to horses, and he couldn't ride much better than me. Still, when you lived in Wyoming, wearing a cowboy hat was your birth right. I also had one on. So did Melinda.

"Are you going to saddle up with us, Mrs. Moore?" Melinda asked as the station wagon came to a halt at Bighorn's only stop sign.

"Not this time, honey. Why don't you take Lightnin' today?"

Melinda was all smiles. Lightnin' was a handful who had belonged to my cousin Johnny until Johnny wrapped Uncle Willis's new Ford around a wandering telephone pole. "It just came out of nowhere,"

Johnny explained. Uncle Willis figured the empty bottle of Jack Daniels lying on floorboard was a more likely accounting and took Lightnin' as temporary payment.

Lightnin' was a cutting horse, and a fine one at that: a seven-year-old gelding, big and sleek and black as coal with a silver blaze down his forehead. It took dauntless nerve to ride Lightnin'. The horse had huge, flaring nostrils and could smell fear in your sweat; if he didn't respect you from the get-go, Lightnin' was in control.

Lightnin' never troubled Melinda. Like my mother, she had a way with horses. One well-chosen word or well-directed motion made any self-respecting horse gladly do her bidding. Melinda had horse confidence, and she had more horse sense than Bucky and me put together. She also took riding lessons, while Bucky and I learned by trial and error. Mostly by error.

"If she wants him, she can have him," Bucky whispered in my ear. As we turned onto Main Street, I nodded in agreement.

Bighorn wasn't much of a town; with a population of 100, it had one general store, two gas pumps and three bars. You could see from one end of Main Street to the other, and at that other end stood Uncle Willis's and Aunt Mina's modest home.

Aunt Mina knew we were coming and had left the front gate open. As we pulled into the drive, Ben, Uncle Willis's cattle dog, greeted our station wagon. He immediately marked the two front tires then circled the station wagon. Bucky knew the drill but opened his door anyway, ready for Ben snapping at his heels and warning him to get back in the car.

"Ben! Let up!" Uncle Willis hollered from the chokecherry-covered porch.

Ben whimpered then retreated to his doghouse. Safe from molestation, we got out of the car as Uncle Willis hobbled over to greet us.

A cowboy through and through, Uncle Willis liked dogs, whiskey and women, in that order, and when kicked by a horse was known to return the favor. He didn't like to air his dirty laundry and had no respect for those who did. His legs were bowed from having one too many horse between them, and he walked with a broke-one-too-many-horse limp. Stubbly white whiskers camouflaged the creases of his leathered face, and a piece of chew protruded from inside his lower lip.

"Come out, Mother. Sister's here with the young'uns." Uncle Willis wasn't big on names. "I see yas kids made it outta bed." Before I could respond he spotted a passing bug and spit out a wad of tobacco, skillfully hitting his target.

"Mind your manners!" Aunt Mina's voice rang out from the kitchen.

Uncle Willis mumbled, "Woman's got eyes in a back of her head." I didn't know if he was talking to us or the freshly tarred beetle.

"Well, invite them in, Willis." Aunt Mina joined us in the driveway drying her hands on the dishtowel that she'd tucked in her blue jeans. Aunt Mina didn't take any flak from Uncle Willis. Like most ranchers' wives, she worked like a son-of-a-gun. Although Uncle Willis' cattle running days were over, Aunt Mina maintained her pre-retirement status running the house. She could out-chore her husband, out-smart him, out-yell him and out-drink him. What Uncle Willis lacked in affability Aunt Mina more than made up.

"Pay no never-mind to that grumpy ol' coot," she gently chided while doling out hugs and kisses. "His lumbago is acting up again. But it's not a wonder, the way he's been carousing lately." Aunt Mina gave Mom one of those *you know what I mean* looks.

"Gonna be a hot'un t'day," Uncle Willis interjected. "S'pose ta get up ta ninety-five. Did yas bring a hat?"

Uncle Willis sometimes ignored the obvious. The three of us nodded our hat-covered heads.

"Wouldn't wanna have to rescue a body sufferin' from heat stroke just 'cause they forgot their hat."

Aunt Mina took it from there. "Last week Old Man Strickerhouse passed out while working in the garden. His daughter, Gladys — You know her. Big ol' thing with bad teeth? Married Charlie Burton, Big

Sam's son? You know her. Anyway, Gladys found him spread-eagle in the iceberg lettuce with nothing on but his boots and boxer shorts."

"No hat!" Uncle Willis shook his head in dismay.

Aunt Mina herded us toward the house. "Had your breakfast yet?" She didn't wait for an answer. "Willis, while they're having their breakfast, saddle up them horses."

"Maybe they had breakfast. Did ya ever think?" he yelled after her. "Well, have yas?" he barked our way. Again we nodded, but it didn't seem to convince him. "Did ya feed 'em, Sister?" But seeing Mom had already made it to the house, he spit again. "Go in and get yarselves somethin' to eat, and I'll get them horses ready." Uncle Willis shuffled off to the barn with Ben right behind him.

We went inside to eat breakfast. Again. Then Aunt Mina supplied us with sack lunches. By the time we ran to the barn, eager to hit the trail, Uncle Willis was already cinching the last of the horses.

Normally we would have saddled up ourselves, but Uncle Willis was dubious of our abilities, Bucky's particularly because the last time we went riding Bucky made the mistake of selecting Uncle Willis's prized Rudy Mudra saddle and they both fell off within fifty yards of the barn. I didn't fare much better, having had a hard time adjusting the stirrups and ending up with no support for my feet.

Uncle Willis handed me the bridle to Beulah, a fifteen-year-old strawberry roan, spry for her years if a little on the plump side. I had been on Beulah many times and was comfortable with most of her mannerisms. However, she had a tendency to lag behind, and it was a constant battle to keep her from grazing. After I awkwardly mounted her, she immediately headed for something to eat.

"Don't let her get away with that nonsense," Uncle Willis demanded.

"Ah, she's always hungry," Bucky said as he rode up beside me on Speckles, an appaloosa mare. Uncle Willis clinched his teeth and narrowed his eyes.

"Why, the horse is jest actin' up!" he clamored, setting Bucky straight, who was sorry he'd said anything. "Gettin' the better of ya.

That's all there is to it, don'cha see?" He let go a spit, then came alongside the misbehaving animal and me. "Take the reins and give her a good crack on the butt."

When Uncle Willis did just that, both Beulah and I came to full attention.

"That oughta give her something else to think about."

I thanked him for his help, and he shrugged it off. Although I'd never let him know it, I secretly got a kick out of Uncle Willis and his surliness. Like Ben, he had a nasty bark and a potentially nasty bite, but he knew his way around a horse.

Melinda, who had actually inspected her saddle to make sure everything was to her liking, mounted Lightnin' and joined us. Uncle Willis jutted out his chin in approval.

"Where yas headed?"

"Up to the foothills by Little Goose Creek," I told him.

"Well, be home 'fore supper time."

Uncle Willis and Ben kept their eyes on us as we crossed the alfalfa field to the far corner of the pasture. After a few barks and one last hat reminder, they went about their business and let us be.

After crossing onto what was once the Bozeman Trail, we stayed with the road. Melinda and Lightnin' took the lead followed by Bucky and Speckles. I brought up the rear, my unimposing slaps having only a modest effect on Beulah's munching. None of us spoke, each lost in our own thoughts.

I swung a leg over the saddle, hooking it around the horn as I fell into the rhythm of Beulah's smooth gait. What a day! Just my friends and me, with no one telling us what to do or which way to go. Passersby nodded and waved from their trucks as if asking permission to use our road. We owned it all: the wind and its captured crows, the sloping plains, the beckoning mountains, and the horizon that stretched well beyond our eyes.

I rested the reins on the horn, allowing Beulah to plot our course, then placed my hands on her rump and leaned back. Like two powerful pistons, her haunches carried us forward. I closed my eyes, letting motion mingle with sound: the creaking saddles and clip-clopping hooves, the snorts and farts followed by a "pardon me" from Bucky and a giggle from Melinda. A warm breeze rushed by bringing the scent of the ditch's pungent weeds.

Swish, swat. Beulah's tail, on fly duty, sweetly stung my cheek. I leaned forward and stroked her neck just to remind her I was there. Beulah's belly heaved with a sigh.

We had hit a long stretch, and my friends had gotten an uncomfortable distance ahead of me. More often than not they rode together, leaving me in the rear. I needed to fix that. When I repositioned myself on the saddle, Beulah sensed my sudden alertness and perked her ears forward, ready to run.

"Come on, girl. Let's get 'em." A couple of kicks and we were off. I passed Bucky and Speckles with a deceitfully slow lope, and after catching up to Melinda slapped Beulah into high and shouted, "See you later, slow pokes!"

Lightnin' could smell a race before it began, and Melinda was no different. In no time, they were breathing down my neck. Bucky thundered past on Speckles, his elbows high and his butt pounding the saddle. Melinda held back until the time was right, then she let Lightnin' show his stuff. With his tail raised high and Melinda crouched like a seasoned racer, Lightnin' passed me, passed Bucky and would have passed anything else that dared to run.

Something about galloping always made me laugh. Perhaps it was the rush of unchained power, or the tickle of pure joy. Maybe it was the big bite of freedom. The ultimate "Wheeeeee!"

I couldn't catch the others. Melinda started slowing Lightnin' down and when Bucky came alongside her, he made Speckles do the same. I finally caught up and we trotted three abreast.

"Now that's what I call riding!" Bucky declared, out of breath. I was still laughing.

Melinda and Lightnin' looked as if neither had put out any effort. She went for her canteen, and we shared a drink. Bucky reached down and grabbed a tall blade of wheat grass for a chew. I did the same then returned to my thinking.

"I bet they ate him," I surmised out loud, assuming my friends would know where my internal conversation had been. Bucky passed Melinda a quizzical look. She simply shrugged.

"Who ate what?" she asked.

"The thieves," I said to their clueless expressions. "Hector! Our pig!"

"You can't eat plastic," Bucky protested.

"You can if you're a creature from outer space."

Melinda blew out her cheeks then and smiled. No matter how far-fetched my conjectures, she always gave them the benefit of the doubt, but Bucky would have none of it. He took off his hat and grandly swept his brow in a gesture of indignation.

"There ain't no such thing."

"Oh really?" I said, leaving it at that. After a respectful amount of time Bucky broke the silence.

"Besides, what would they want with a pig when there's a whole dang flock of flamingos in the Padillas' yard just waiting to be fried."

"Maybe Hector's not the only object of importance that's missing from the neighborhood," Melinda added. "Maybe we should ask around."

"Okay. I'll ask Joe-Joe if he knows anything next time I see him," Bucky conceded.

At last, my team of detectives were thinking.

"Where's Joe-Joe been lately anyway?" Melinda asked Bucky.

"His dad's got him working out to the Rawlings Ranch mucking stalls."

"Are we set for his initiation ceremony?" I asked.

"Mags!" Bucky pulled back on Speckles's reins, bringing his horse to a halt. "You know we can't talk about official clubhouse business outside the clubhouse."

"Well, Hector is official clubhouse business."

45

"That's different." The difference being that Bucky hadn't come up with an initiation idea regardless of where it was discussed. At least I had given the pig-napping some thought.

We had reached the old one-lane wooden bridge that crossed the Little Goose. Here the road forked, its main route leading to the mountain's top. We temporarily parted company with the creek and trotted down the less traveled pine-lined road. The horses' hooves disturbed a coating of brittle pine needles creating a knee-high layer of dust, the result of a dry summer. Even with the trees' shelter, the sun was blistering. I was glad for my hat.

Two miles in and we came to the Shriners' collapsed pavilion. Although clubs and companies once used it for their annual picnics, they had since moved on to a more refined recreational area run by the forest service. All that was left of the once teeming campground were a few rickety picnic tables with their crumbled fire pits and a scary-looking outhouse. From here, various deer trails lead to various deer places, one being our absolute favorite spot, the Watermelon Meadow.

Bucky guided Speckles to the head of our intended trail, but this time Beulah and I took the lead. We were in for a fairly steep ascent over a rocky ridge, and Beulah loved to climb. Before long the trees grew thicker and the path narrower. The smell of tree sap and decaying leaves folded into the dry mountain air. After Beulah raised her nostrils for a whiff, I gave the horse her head and up we went. After a few zigs and zags she bounded to the top. As we waited for the other horses, who were less confident of their footing, I jumped off to peruse the area. It was as undisturbed as the first time we found it.

The Watermelon Meadow, so dubbed because of the wayward watermelon patch created by an unknown picnicker, wasn't very big, but it was magical. Sunshine trickled through a canopy of quivering aspen to dance over a carpet of mountain grass surrounded by fiery orange spears of Indian paintbrush. Off to one side, hardly a stone's throw away, rolled the Little Goose.

Beulah was in full graze by the time my companions found their way up and dismounted. Lightnin' and Speckles gave Beulah a respectful sniff then all three retreated to a shady spot by the water. Melinda tied their reins to a sturdy branch while I unloaded our lunches. Bucky was already hiking the creek, on the lookout for a flat rock where we could dangle our feet and eat our sandwiches.

"Here's a good one!" he shouted. "No. Wait. I think there's a better one farther up."

"Don't get too far from the horses," Melinda warned. Bucky could get carried away with his search for the perfect spot. Melinda and I stuffed our socks into our boots, which we put beside Bucky's. After rolling up our pant legs, we walked the water-worn rocks of the Little Goose.

This particular section of the creek wasn't wide, nor deep, but it was fast and cold. The winter snowfall had been heavy, and the water felt newly melted. Knowing my propensity to fall in, I took my time seeking out dry boulders to place my tender feet. I liked to deal with freezing water on my own terms, little by little, with no surprises.

I tiptoed and wobbled, balanced and backtracked, baby-stepped and giant-stepped. Melinda was right behind me doing her own delicate dance. From up ahead, Bucky came careening through the water. "Got the food?" he asked before sitting on the flattened boulder he had chosen to be our picnic table.

Melinda showed him the sack.

"Toss it over."

"No, I'm coming," she told him, then braved the creek's cold.

As soon as Melinda made it to the boulder, Bucky held up her arm and dangled our lunches. "Come and get it!" he baited with a grin.

Not wanting to give Bucky the satisfaction of seeing me miserably wade through the water, I sat back on my haunches and in one powerful jump made it over the water and to the boulder with room to spare, surprising all three of us.

"Let's eat." I smiled. Bucky's grin was gone.

It didn't take long to devour Aunt Mina's ham salad sandwiches and chocolate chip cookies. With bellies satisfied, Melinda and I sprawled out on the boulder for a little sunbathing while Bucky crumpled the paper lunch sack, put it under his hat then got to his feet for a stretch. He had another kind of bathing in mind, having spied a swimming hole just off our rock's high end.

He pulled his T-shirt over his head and purposely dropped it on mine.

"Jeez, Bucky, you're blinding me," I teased as I shielded myself from the glare of his white chest.

Bucky ignored my remark. "Anyone for a dip?" he asked as he stripped down to his skivvies. I thought Bucky's chest lacked color but his upper legs looked as if they'd never seen the sun. Melinda giggled, but before I could make a witty comparison to a parsnip, Bucky dove in. When he emerged, he immediately scrambled back to the boulder.

"Is it cold?" I asked sweetly.

"Nnnot a bbbit," he stuttered. "Only if you're a ssssssisssssssy."

Silence. We stared at each other. More silence. Melinda tried to give Bucky his shirt but he wouldn't take it. He stood there righteously shivering.

Slowly, I took off my pants, folded them and handed them to Melinda. I stood. The crystal clear water made the swimming hole visible down to its sandy bottom. Perhaps five feet deep, it was aching to be disturbed yet again. But this time, my way.

I walked down the boulder to the water's edge and tested it with my toe, quickly pulling it out. If my toe didn't like it, I knew the rest of me wouldn't either. But I was not a sissy. I inched myself into the swimming hole, the plan being a slow introduction of each body part. The plan backfired when Bucky gave me a shove and I went in headfirst.

I couldn't breathe for the cold. My feet found bottom and instinctively shot me to the surface. My lungs gasped for warm air. My shocked ears could faintly hear Bucky laughing as he mimicked, "Is it cold?"

Wanting to make my friends suffer as well, I started splashing.

"You're getting the clothes wet!" Melinda screamed as Bucky dove back in. When his head came out of the water, I gave it a dunk. "Take it back," I said as he came up for air.

"Alright, alright. You're not a sissy."

Poised to dunk him again, I ordered, "Tell me I'm a superior human being."

"You're a superior human being," he laughed, raising his hands in surrender. "Let's get out."

"Not so fast." Melinda was wading toward us, showing no discomfort from the icy water. "A superior human being has stamina. Bet I can stay in the longest."

I lowered my chin and crossed my arms, putting my hands in my armpits. "You're on."

Bucky accepted the challenge as well, duplicating my stance. "I can handle it."

Silence.

Melinda's shoulders rose to her ears, and she hugged herself tightly. Still, she remained defiant. "You call this cold?"

"This is like bath water," I said.

"A regular hot spring." Bucky shivered.

Silence.

The painful contest went on until I came up with a better game and sprung it on them.

"Last One Out Is a Rotten Egg!"

By then we all wanted out. I was the first to attempt retreat, but Bucky grabbed my tank top and pushed me down, then leap-frogged over my shoulders onto the shallow rocks. I grabbed his skivvies, bringing him crashing back into the water.

In the meantime, Melinda had made it onto the boulder. "I'm out! I'm out!"

Bucky yanked her hand, pulling her back in. Melinda was laughing so hard she took a big gulp of water and nearly drowned. Bucky grabbed one of her arms and I grabbed the other and we walked out together.

Three superior human beings, cold but happy.

Back on the boulder we found our sopping pants and hung them over a fallen tree that bridged the creek. Settling back on one of the few remaining dry spots on the rock, I clung to the warm boulder and closed my eyes. I could barely distinguish the chattering of my teeth from the roar of the water and my friends' shallow breathing.

Before long I started to drift off.

Down the creek, down the mountain, bareback on my horse, riding double with Bucky, him in back and me in front, his arms around me holding the reins. I tingle. Then he's ahead of me, on another horse with Melinda. They get farther and farther away. I can't catch up. Up the road, up the mountain, up the creek. The water sings. Its song is deafening.

I opened my eyes.

Melinda, still beside me on the rock, had been humming.

"My mother liked the water," she said out of the blue. Bucky rolled onto his elbows and glanced my way to share his surprise. Melinda seldom spoke of her mother.

"She was wild—sort of like Lightnin'—and not afraid of anything much less water. I'm certain she would have loved it here."

There weren't a lot of things that made me quail, but I could never bring myself to ask Melinda what had happened to her mom. So, I asked mine. She told me Mrs. Thomas had died in a car crash when Melinda was only five. When I passed on the story to Bucky I found out he already knew. Melinda had told him. Yet, she hadn't told me.

She did show me a framed picture she kept on her bedroom nightstand. Wearing a full skirted garden dress, her newly-wed mother sat on a swing beneath a willow tree, her hands grasping its ropes and her legs outstretched. Her smile was so real, so alive, you could almost see her kick out her heels and swing upward to the sky, laughing all the while. It was hard to believe the young bride in the photo was gone.

"I used to ask my father questions about my mother," Melinda continued. "What her favorite books were or if she liked Chopin, but he doesn't really like to talk about her. I guess he thinks it's counterproductive to bring up the past."

Melinda shifted her body, letting go of a knee and reaching for her outstretched toes.

"But one night—it was during a snowstorm—I heard him talking to Mrs. Mavrakis in the kitchen. They were drinking sherry. He said he missed my mother most of all in winter, because winter was when he asked my mother to marry him. It was cold and snowing and the wind was blowing, and mother took off all her clothes and ran into the ocean for a swim."

Not missing a beat, Melinda straightened her spine, giving a spot-on Colonel imitation. "'Are you out of your mind?' he asked. 'Get out before I have to come in and get you.'

"'No sir, Walter Esmond Thomas,' she told him. 'Not you and all your fancy brass can keep me out of the water.' He decided right then and there that he was going to propose."

Melinda extended her left hand, as if admiring a wedding ring.

"Do you remember her?" Bucky asked, spellbound by Melinda's story.

"I remember her hands," she said examining her own. "And a scar, right here, just over her brow. I remember her brushing my hair. And if I really think hard, I remember the way she smelled. Sweet, like honeysuckle, but fresh, too, like cotton sheets on a clothesline. She wore red, red lipstick and used to kiss me on the lips so I could wear some as well."

She outlined her lips with her fingertips, then let out a sad, longing sigh.

I knew I should console Melinda, but I was afraid to touch her. Afraid of somehow catching her misfortune as if it were a cold. But Bucky scooted beside her, and laid his cheek on her shoulder. I was suddenly envious of her sorrow.

"Mags?" she said. "You know what I'd like? A song. Sing one, would you?"

I sang our favorite riding song, "Don't Fence Me In." They joined in the chorus, Melinda harmonizing and Bucky wailing off-key.

Her sadness had passed, as had my jealousy, and once again we were three carefree friends with nothing more important to do than mount up and get home before supper. We rode back to Aunt Mina's and Uncle Willis's stable in damp britches, wearing our hats.

CHAPTER 5

Parades were popular in our town, and while the rodeo parade was the biggest, the Fourth of July one was my favorite, mostly because of the picnic and fireworks that followed. Everybody showed up for a parade. If you weren't in it you were watching it. Grandpas in overalls and grandmas in bonnets lined Main Street and Jerome and waited for family, friend or foe to ceremoniously pass in front of them. Kids peeked through their mothers' legs and squirmed atop their fathers' shoulders. Shopkeepers closed their doors and joined their employees on the sidewalk—except for Mr. Archer, the Main Street barber, who set up outside chairs and kept clipping through the festivities.

It was a quarter past nine and already the women were fanning themselves with paper cutouts provided by the American Legion while clutching their Sunday-best pocketbooks. Dressed in the appropriate patriotic colors, Mom and Mrs. Majors were quibbling over who might bring the best potato salad to the afternoon picnic. I hurried ahead, worming my way through the crowd to my favorite viewing spot: the curb in front of Rexall Drug. Located midway along the parade route, it was the absolute best place to catch candy. Too close to the start and candy-tossers were stingy, but halfway through their generosity kicked in and the goodies would fly in fistfuls until they ran out at the parade's end.

Today Bucky would be among them. Big Buck always provided a new convertible to showcase a beauty queen or dignitary, and at least one of his boys rode with them. Bucky had asked Melinda and me to sit beside him and help hold the "Big Buck's Cars and Trucks" banner. Melinda was game, but I wasn't keen on a bunch of idiots staring at us. When he pointed out that put me in the idiot category, we had parted ways. Later, after it occurred to me that acting as advertising assistant meant I would have control over a significant amount of candy, I approached Bucky with an apology, but it was too late. He had already found a replacement, although not Melinda who had refused to ride without me.

As I scooched my fanny between two plump women, I kept an eye out for my loyal friend. Across the street in front of the Western Union station, Mrs. Bales sat under an oversized umbrella, sipping lemonade and acknowledging the well-wishers and hat-tippers from her garden chair. No doubt Mr. Bales would watch the parade at the Bronco Saloon along with a number of other men, including my dad.

To the right of the Western Union, Patricia Simms and her little brother Randy dangled their feet off the balcony of their father's two-story office. I once watched a parade from up there. It wasn't much fun. Doc Simms took offense every time a horse left a load near his reception entrance and yelled at Mrs. Simms as if it were her fault. "Dammit! There goes another one, Martha." Mrs. Simms kept repeating, "Yes, dear. I'm sorry, dear." If it had been my Aunt Mina, she would have clobbered him. Then again, my Uncle Willis would never get upset over a little thing like horse manure.

Patricia saw me looking her way and gave me a perfect "windshield wiper" wave. Last year Patricia rode the Busy Bees 4-H float, and Bucky and I instructed her in waving techniques including the "stiff-wristed rotation" and the "rotating torso," a skill we had mastered by watching the Rose Bowl Parade (required viewing in the Majorses' household). Patricia was a good sport, even if she was too frilly for my taste. I returned her greeting.

Below the balcony the Padilla regiment was marching in search of a shady spot. Mr. Padilla led the way with little Elizabeth on his shoulders, followed by Christina and Maria, one pulling Mrs. Padilla's hand and the other pushing her from behind. The three girls wore a smaller version of their mother's *fiesta* dress — all homemade, as were her son's cowboy shirts. Having their own idea of where to go, Ricky,

Johnno and Joe-Joe fell out of line, but *Abuela* nixed that, herding from the rear with her flag. Crossing the street, the family settled on the corner near me.

"Ricky! Yoo-hoo!" Patricia had quit waving and was wildly flapping to get Ricky's attention. Patricia was boy crazy, always pining over this one or that one. Once she had even set her sights on Bucky, but I hadn't worried because Patricia's crushes never lasted long. By the time he figured out what was going on, she was mooning over someone else. Lately she'd been smitten by the eldest Padilla boy, but I doubted Ricky returned her affections. He ignored her yoo-hooing and went about setting up stools for his mother and grandmother.

"Hey, move over a bit and make some room," Melinda said, sneaking up on me.

"Do you think Patricia Simms is pretty?" I asked her as she sat down.

"She's got a pretty smile," Melinda said, taking in stride my unexpected question. Seldom did she say anything bad about anybody.

"Well, I think her face is too round," I huffed then added, "Where's Mrs. Mavrakis?"

"She's still baking, so I caught a ride with Miss Rebecca."

Whoa! This was news. I was just about to interrogate her when four gunshots announced the parade had begun. Murmuring swelled. Heads turned, but not in the direction of the oncoming parade. Our cluster of onlookers parted to make way for Rebecca Frick.

She was wearing a purple and green paisley crop top and the strangest pair of . . . pants? Baggy from waist to knee—which was also where the crotch hung—then skin-tight to the ankle, whatever the kind of britches, it looked as if she had dropped her drawers to make necessary and forgot to pull them back up.

Rebecca's piled-high hair, now platinum blond, was held in place by a sequined scarf. Golden hoops tugged her ear lobes down low. A dove medallion hung from her neck, and at least twenty bracelets adorned each arm. She also wore a few bangles on her right ankle. And she was barefoot! Her painted toenails were the same tortoise-shell red as her oversized sunglasses.

She carried beaded sandals in one hand and a cigarette in the other. Perched on her shoulder, wearing a little Uncle Sam's hat, was Francine, the African Grey.

Seldom were we exposed to a sight so exotic. Completely at ease with herself, Rebecca seemed to take our abashed stares as a compliment.

"Over here, Miss Rebecca!" Melinda called out, grabbing my arm to flag her down.

"Ah. There you are. Room for two?" she asked while politely navigating past the stupefied faces to our spot on the curb. "I am so glad y'all invited me." She beamed before kissing each of my cheeks and then did the same to Melinda. Then, in raspy splendor, she announced to those still gawking, "Francine just loves horses."

The bird corroborated this with a whinny-sounding *squawk*.

Hearing a rumble that meant the parade was almost upon us, I dashed into the street to get a better view of what was to come, then ran back to Rebecca and Melinda with a report. "About four blocks away," I told them.

Francine repeated her horse imitation.

The first to pass by was the VFW Color Guard, waving Old Glory and the blue-and-red buffalo flag of the wonderful state of Wyoming. People respectfully stood, and hats came off.

Next came the heroes of the past with General Custer and his unmistakable golden tresses leading the way. This year Morris Huxley, a prominent attorney, had donned the well-recognized ensemble—knee-high black boots, fringed leather jacket, yellow scarf and white hat. Custer was always popular, at least with the white folk. Sitting Bull, who only occasionally made it into the lineup, was a bigger hit with the Indians and kids of all kind.

Behind Custer came General Sheridan in his blue double-breasted general's jacket with its gold-tasseled bars. Almost the size of the pinto who carried him, the rider had a prominent nose and jutting chin balanced only by his bushy eyebrows and big black handlebar mustache. As he scanned the street from left to right, straight-backed in the saddle, the General presented a stalwart figure to all.

Then came Kit Carson in a wide brim hat wearing the same handlebar mustache as General Sheridan, only his was fake and falling off. Beside him rode Buffalo Bill, dressed in Buffalo Bill fashion. Both were smoking cigars and tipping their hats to the ladies.

Rebecca cupped her mouth when Buffalo Bill got within earshot. I couldn't hear exactly what she said—something to do with a six-shooter?—but it got his attention. He put his hat to his chest and bowed. His horse bowed, too. The crowd clapped and Francine went wild.

"What can I say," Rebecca said as he rode on, "I like a man in leather."

The next to pass was the American Legion Drum and Bugle Corps dressed cavalry-style in blue pants with a gold stripe, navy blue jackets, gold neckerchiefs, fringed buckskin gloves and the customary Stetsons. Slinging waist high drums and rat-a-tatting an infectious marching cadence, the Corps—with considerably more drums than bugles—was led by yet another Custer, this one a major who used his sword as a baton. When he got directly in front of us, he blew his whistle and all drumming stopped. Three buglers who had been in the rear ran forward, rang out revelry on Custer's cue, then retreated to the back again. After two swooshes of the sword and four short toots the drumming resumed. Melinda marched in place as the Corps carried on down the parade route.

"You like the drums?" Rebecca asked, more of a statement than a question.

"Oh yes!" Melinda said. "They're my father's favorite, too. Drums grab your heart and pound right along with it. The steadier the beat, the calmer the soldier. But make it harder, louder, and faster and you get someone ready for action. That's why the drums always prepared the way for battle. According to my father. All I know is I can't seem to sit still around them."

"They make her twitchy," I added, pulling her down to wait for the next attraction.

"I know what you mean," Rebecca agreed. "When Manny—that was my second husband—went through his beatnik phase he played

57

the bongos in a sweet little coffee house. What he could do with those hands!"

Rebecca gave a quick demonstration on my knee. "Zippity doo dah!"

Curious now, I asked, "Why'd you get divorced?"

She removed a cigarette from a concealed pocket and lit it, then took a long, thoughtful drag before answering. "Manny sure liked to beat on those bongos." She turned and looked directly in my eyes. "He liked to beat on me, too."

Uncomfortable, I sought refuge in Melinda's gaze, but she was puffing out her cheeks, clearly feeling awkward as well. I had never known anyone who had been beaten on, much less admitted to it. There was the time Old Man Braunski's wife kicked him in the behind and broke his tailbone, but that was because he had been drinking again and lost his paycheck gambling. Dad said he deserved it. Maybe not.

Francine brought us to our feet with an excited *squawk*. Coming our way were two big-eyed, big-horned oxen pulling a Conestoga steered by a beefy, bearded pioneer. They were followed by a team of draft horses and a mini mule train flanked by six women in peasant dresses and shawls. The pioneers were an indomitable lot. Not as swank as cowboys and a heck of a lot more pious, they represented the civilizing of the West, or at least an attempt at it.

The first flatbed float of the day was a canvas-roofed church with nine sod-busting Protestants holding hymnals and warbling "When the Roll Is Called Up Yonder" in their Sunday best. Atop the church was a wooden belfry with an attached rope that hung over the choir's pump organ. Every once in a while, the organist gave the rope an enthusiastic yank, adding to the clamor of an already unsteady ensemble.

Even with the bell, they were having a hard time competing with "Buffalo Gals" coming from the honky-tonk piano of the subsequent flatbed. Representing the infamous W. P. Mendel Saloon and sponsored by the county farm bureau, the float teemed with merry members partaking of spirits and a hot game of poker. I recognized my cousin Johnny at the table wearing a black bandana. Judging by his piled chips, Johnny would be in a good mood for the rest of the day.

Then came the ghastly beautiful Clemens hearse, and no one was laughing. Its intricately carved carriage of ebony shone brighter than Big Buck's impala after a Sunday waxing, and the fringed curtains on each side were half open to allow half-hearted viewing of the coffin inside. The hearse was drawn by a sleek black stallion who, despite his blinders, looked ready to race right through the gates of hell and out the other side. Beside the ghoulish driver sat Reverend Bauer looking as stoic as ever. On the hood of the hearse was the Clemenses' undertaker, a scary, gray-skinned man.

The whole effect was frightening. There were those in the crowd who had seen that very hearse take their loved ones to their grave, so all hats came off. A superstitious few turned their heads, not wanting to look upon the ominous carriage. Mrs. Padilla crossed herself, as did the rest of her family. Francine growled, and Rebecca covered the bird with her scarf.

More drums, more whistles, and the mood changed back to festive. The high school marching band was playing "Stars and Stripes Forever" while followed by a six-foot penguin perched on a diving board, its head shedding black crepe paper and exposing the chicken wire beneath. The float's sign read "Switch From Hot to Cool at Kramer's Swimming Pool." Although anchored to the trailer by six cables, the penguin swayed more than it should.

"I suspect our molting friend will take a nosedive before the parade's end," Rebecca remarked just as a giant red pointy thing careened past us—I counted eight pairs of legs—announcing the fireworks display at the All-Star Drive-In. "What kind of animal is that?" Rebecca asked.

"It's supposed to be a firecracker," Melinda informed her as a shabby ten-foot fuse slid past our feet, dragging manure and candy wrappers.

"That would explain its tail."

"Hey, Maggie! Heads up!"

A piece of salt-water taffy bounced off my nose. Three convertibles were passing by, and on the hood of the one in the lead was Bucky and his second-string partner, Michelle Fryer, a "Little Miss Snooty" whose father owned Fryer's Department Store. (In first grade she told everyone I'd borrowed my Christmas pageant dress from a mannequin because my parents couldn't afford to buy one). I couldn't stand her, and Bucky knew it, so he tried to make up with a shower of candy. Refusing his peace offering, I crossed my arms and stuck out my tongue. Michelle Fryer spied my gesture and tossed her hair — the only thing she tossed.

"Don't let her get to you, Maggie," Melinda said as she gathered the surrounding taffy. "Besides, it didn't look to me like he was having much fun."

"I have no idea what you're talking about." My stomach growled, reminding me that lunch was still a ways off. No doubt Bucky would be stuck with Michelle at the picnic. We'd have to come up with a way to ditch her.

Next up was the Sheriff's Posse Drill Team: twenty seasoned cowboys in white shirts and white hats all holding the Red, White, and Blue while riding single file. Upon a signal from the lead rider the line split and every other horse ended up on opposite sides of the street. After a synchronized turn, the two facing rows of ten did a pass-through and divided into four rows of five, two horses headed in one direction and three the other. Then they rotated like four pinwheels with the horses at the hub. More pass-throughs, more swivels, and the twenty were once again headed down the route. It had been a flawless routine. Amazing what a good rider could do.

Melinda and Rebecca were ecstatic, hooting and hollering along with everyone else. I even heard shouts coming from Doc Simms's balcony, but it was just the doctor shaking his fist and making a fuss because more than a few horses had left their calling cards near his reception stoop. Amazing what a good horse could do.

Three Indian chiefs in war bonnets headed towards us, which meant the parade was winding down. The first had feathers hanging as low as his horse's tail. He was big and wrinkled, fully decked in Indian finery, and he carried the American flag. No doubt someone of importance. The second's headdress was not as long but still grand, its beaded headband securing as many as twenty-five eagle feathers.

Attached to their tips was some kind of hair, maybe horse, maybe not. Hanging from the headband were long, fuzzy white animal tails, two on each side. Unlike the blond Custer wigs that were passed down from parade to parade, these headdresses were genuine; revered and well preserved.

The third rider was Johnny Redhorse, who I had met once with my father at Mr. Archer's barbershop. He wore a lone feather in his headband, and unlike his traditionally dressed tribesmen, was in combat fatigues. Having fought in Korea, Johnny Redhorse was damn proud of his war record. He was damn proud of his horse, and his horse was damn proud.

All three stared straight ahead, never acknowledging the crowd — no waves, no swivels. I wondered what they might be thinking. Even though I lived surrounded by battlefields, fallen forts and reservations, I didn't know much about Indians. No more than any kid who grew up watching Hollywood Westerns. I didn't go to school with any Indian children — Mom said most went to special agency schools — and so I didn't have any Indian friends.

An eight-wheeled, gear-grinding flatbed rolled by carrying a circle of men drumming and singing while several younger fellas danced beside them painted and bare-chested.

"I once went to a powwow," Rebecca told us as she ogled one handsome dancer. "It was in Oklahoma. There wasn't but a handful of us white people, and when it came time to enter the circle we were somewhat reluctant. Then this fine Potawatomi gentleman offered me his arm and I accepted."

"You danced with him?" I wanted to know more.

She chuckled. "Among other things."

"What was he like?" Melinda asked.

"He was a man. No better, no worse than most. But he certainly could lead a lady on the dance floor."

No better, nor worse. I liked Rebecca's demystifying point of view.

Another flatbed truck followed with Indian women and children. Some danced to the still audible drums and others sat on blankets and hides with their feet dangling off the edge. They were laughing and clapping and generally having a good time. I caught the eye of one little girl who grinned then shyly hid her head in her mother's shawl. When I was her age, my brother had teased me because of my suntanned skin, telling me I was adopted and that I really belonged to the Crows. At first I cried because I didn't want to be adopted, then I cried because I didn't want to be an Indian. I had heard people speak ill of "dirty-faced Injun babes" who went barefoot because their "no-account redskin" daddies drank their paychecks and couldn't afford shoes. But here amidst the beads and braids and blouses covered in shells, amidst the fringed dresses and embroidered moccasins and an occasional pair of sneakers, were regular happy people, celebrating just like the rest of us. Some things didn't add up.

Two patrol cars with flashing red lights crawled past, followed by the county street sweeper. The parade was officially over. Some of the watchers, including the Padillas, followed its tail-end. Eventually it would come to a halt at the Trails Inn near the train depot. There the floats would be dismantled, the horses would be loaded into their trailers, and the participants would disperse for the rest of the day's festivities.

The three of us lingered at the curb, on the lookout for my mother who was probably in the process of prying my father from the Bronco Saloon. Melinda eventually spied the two of them holding hands and heading our way. Rebecca bent down to fasten her sandals.

"I'll catch up with y'all at the picnic," she told us. "I have to ready myself for my rendezvous with Mr. Buffalo Bill. You know, change into something more appropriate for a gentleman of his stature." She gave me a sly smile. "And Francine is in need of her nap."

I had never seen a bird yawn, but I swear that was what it did. Rebecca covered it with her scarf then sashayed down the street.

•   •   •   •   •

The charcoal-fueled grills were aglow, and the food was on display: green beans, navy beans, pork and beans, bean salad, and potato salad after potato salad, each one slightly different and doted upon by a proud potato salad maker who much preferred hers (or his) to everybody else's. Ten tables were set aside just for desserts, and it took two pickup trucks to hold all the watermelon.

The Fourth of July picnic was always held in the middle of town at Kinder Park, our largest and most popular park, boasting giant cottonwoods, grassy nooks, a few bridges, and numerous benches and tables. Kinder Park provided not only the rudimentary park essentials, but also a fishing pond fed by the Little Goose and stocked by the county. The pond's murky waters had surrendered a first catch to countless young fisherman and also served as a favorite midnight dunking grounds for unruly teenagers.

At one time the park supported a zoo that housed a coyote, a bobcat and black bear; Jigs and Jasper, a pair of spider monkeys who got a kick out of peeing on spectators; a flock of Chinese pheasants; a small herd of buffalo; and Ralo the lion, arguably its most famous resident. Ralo's life in his eight-by-twelve home was boring, to say the least—pace, turnaround, pace, roar, turnaround, pace. One day Ralo stopped pacing and roaring. Then he stopped altogether.

There were those who wanted to replace Ralo. My father was not one of them. "What possible good does it do my soul to see a critter so unhappy it would just as soon die as to make it through another day trapped and gawked at, away from everything that's natural?"

Dad's way of thinking won over, and the emptied and debarred cages were now a playground for squirrels and pigeons. Today, only the buffalo herd remained, making their permanent home on the field with the barn that bordered the park's north edge. The herd was down to eight now: six females, an unweaned calf with a faint suggestion of a hump, and an enormous bull. The bull spent most of his time grazing at the top of the hill overlooking the park. Unless performing his seasonal duties, he seldom socialized with the females.

Melinda and I couldn't find the bull—he was probably out on loan—but we did catch sight of Bucky and Michelle Fryer standing along the fence near the buffalo barn, sharing the shade of an elm tree with the rest of the herd. Bucky was making obnoxious noises and generally making fun of the bearded beasts for Michelle's benefit. She was squealing, "Oh, Bucky" this, and "Stop, Bucky" that, and he was enjoying her pretentious protests entirely too much. Melinda thought likewise.

"Doesn't look like he needs rescuing after all."

"He's just showing off," I said, turning my back. "I hate it when boys do that."

"Boys aren't the only ones, Mags."

"What's that supposed to mean?" I shot back.

Melinda rolled her eyes.

"Are you saying I show off?"

"I'm saying that sometimes you're extra loud when you want attention."

"I am not 'extra' loud."

Melinda shrugged. "When you want to be noticed you talk louder, you laugh louder, and you usually do something reckless."

I quit listening to her because I was thinking of doing something reckless.

"Hey, Melinda, Maggie, wait up." Joe-Joe Padilla had spotted us. He was eating a piece of watermelon and wiping his juicy chin on the upper sleeve of his cowboy shirt. "Great picnic, huh? But where's Buckaroo? We're choosing sides for a game."

I folded my arms and pointed an indignant chin. "He's over there making an idiot of himself over Meee-chelle."

"Hey, Bucky!" Joe-Joe yelled. "Up for baseball? We're choosing sides."

Bucky chose to ignore Joe-Joe. Instead he continued wooing Michelle with a few choice belches and a rhythmic series of underarm farts.

"Hey, Bucky," Joe-Joe tried again. "We need you on first, man."

Still no response. Bucky was holding out for pitcher and Joe-Joe knew it.

Joe-Joe tossed what was left of the watermelon rind, then untucked two baseball gloves from his armpit and gave one to Melinda. "Whatcha say, Melinda? Wanna get in the game, huh?"

She slammed her fist into the glove. "Only if Maggie plays," she said, starting to back away so he could hurl a ball her way. After catching it without so much as a flinch, she drilled it back into Joe-Joe's glove.

"Geez. I don't know." He sent the ball back. "No offense, Maggie, but this is gonna be a serious game. Know what I mean, huh?"

I knew what he meant. I liked baseball. I really did. I could bat with the best and run the bases faster than most. But I could not throw a ball. I threw like a sissy. My dad tried to teach me, as did my brother Brian. Even Big Buck gave it a go, but by that time my bad habits had already set in.

"First off, you're not holding the ball right! Use two fingers, pointer and middle, with the thumb on the other side. That'll give it spin. You get snap by popping your wrist. And see there, you're standing all wrong. Left foot forward for a right-hander. You want leverage. Make sure your release point is the same every time. Nah, you let go of the ball too soon. Watch it! Watch it! You're releasing too far forward. There's no leverage on the wrist. Think about where you want the ball to go."

Even after Big Buck's instruction, the ball seldom went where I wanted it to go. At best, I could deliver one out of four throws. And that was without pressure. Put me in a game and forget it. If a ball actually found itself in my glove, I would get overly excited and inevitably toss it into the ground.

So yeah, I was pitiful at baseball, but he should have asked me anyway. I grabbed the ball out of Melinda's hand.

"I'll show you serious!" I took a windup and, by some miracle, pitched it squarely into Joe-Joe's glove.

"Strike one!" Melinda called out.

An astounded Joe-Joe threw the ball back to Melinda, and she tossed it to me. With exaggerated pitcher protocol, I looked to my left, and then to my right, laid bare some fancy footwork and hammered it smack-dab into Joe-Joe's glove, again.

"Strike two!"

"Hey, Bucky, did you see that?" Joe-Joe called as he ran to my side to grandly hand over the ball. "I think we've got a new pitcher, buddy."

From over my shoulder came a stingy "Yeah, right!" followed by a pesky giggle.

I spun around and threw the ball at Bucky, or maybe Michelle. It hit neither and ricocheted off the elm, going over the fence to strike the calf instead.

Bucky went into hysterics. However, Michelle was not amused. Nor was the unintended target's mother. She sniffed out the offending projectile, pawed at it, peed on it, then took flight along with her suckling and the other startled cows.

"Oh man! Why'd you go and do that for, huh?" cried Joe-Joe as he threw down his glove. "That's our only ball! Now somebody's going to have to get it."

"Yeah. *Somebody* has to get it," Bucky goaded as he strutted my way.

"Don't look at me," I said.

"Why not? You threw the stupid ball."

"Well I wouldn't have thrown the stupid ball if you weren't so darn . . . stupid."

Bucky stuck out his chest and got in my face. "Who you calling stupid?"

"Well, if the shoe fits."

"What do my shoes got to do with it?"

"Need I say more?"

"Oh, for crying out loud!" Joe-Joe yelled. "I'll go get it."

"You can't get it," Michelle blurted, pointing to a sign on the fence that read "BEWARE: Wild Animals. Keep out."

The four of us paid as much attention to her as we did the sign.

"How are you going to get it?" Melinda asked as Joe-Joe contemplated the problem. The six-foot chain-link fence had three strands of angled barbed wire at the top to enforce the sign.

"Can't you read?" Michelle demanded. "You can't get your stupid ball."

"She's right, Joe-Joe," I agreed to everybody's amazement. "You're not going to get it. I am." After all, it was the decent thing to do. I did throw the stupid ball.

"How?" Melinda asked yet again.

I took stock of my options. The fence was definitely out, but the tree had possibilities; although its trunk was outside the fence, several sturdy limbs hung over its border. I could easily climb one. Then it was just a matter of dropping down.

"Come on, Melinda," I decided. "I need a leg up."

We walked to the elm with Bucky and Joe-Joe close behind. Michelle stayed next to the sign, still certain its authority would prevail.

"I don't know, Maggie," Melinda said as she assumed the hoisting position. "Maybe you better think about this. How are you—"

"Quick!" Joe-Joe interrupted. "No one's looking. Go now!"

I placed my foot in Melinda's interlocked fingers and she boosted me high enough to grab a branch and get my belly over it.

Michelle was beside herself. "Make her stop, Bucky!"

Bucky made a lame attempt to do as she asked. "Come on back, Mags. You don't have to prove anything."

Too late. I had already dropped to the other side. Unfortunately, my right foot landed out of kilter and buckled beneath me. Before I could let out a yowl, Joe-Joe shook the fence.

"Stay down, Maggie. Someone's coming."

I wanted to tell him that staying down wasn't the problem here, but could barely keep from crying, let alone talk.

"Michelle!"

As I heard the not too distant voice of Mr. Fryer, I rolled over to a patch of tall weeds near the base of another tree. My hideaway must have been secure because he didn't make a stink when he showed up. At least not towards me.

"Your mother's been looking everywhere for you, young lady."

"I've been right here, Daddy," Michelle pouted.

"I can see that. What's going on?"

Michelle didn't say anything—no big surprise. She would be in big trouble simply by association.

Bucky answered for her. "Just getting together a team for a little baseball, sir."

"Well, if you want anything to eat, you better get to the tables now and save your game for later."

"We'll be right there," Melinda assured him, but no one budged. Suspicious by nature, Mr. Fryer clearly wanted his little girl to part company with the troublemakers.

"Michelle, say good-bye. Now. Your mother wants to take pictures."

"Yes, Daddy," she said.

Although they left with our mission still undetected, it was only a matter of time before Michelle would spill the beans. I had to act fast. Only I suddenly realized the ball's location was one small detail I had overlooked.

"Where is it?" I asked, wincing as I stood.

"There!" Melinda pointed to a spot twenty yards or so from the tree, about halfway to the buffalo barn.

I hopped to where she indicated; my ankle was beginning to swell.

"No, no. You've gone too far," Melinda said. "It's to the left about four hops back."

I pivoted and immediately hopped, hoping I was going in the right direction.

"Your other left," Bucky groaned.

I couldn't think straight. Like an ill-tempered knife, each jump delivered a malicious stab. At last I made it to the ball and bent to pick it up.

"For God's sake, Maggie," Bucky called out, "Don't move!"

I stopped mid retrieval.

"Take it slow and steady, Maggie." Joe-Joe was all business, speaking slow and deliberate. "And whatever you do, don't panic."

That only meant there was something to panic about.

Looking through my legs, I had an upside-down view of the buffalo barn. Something big was coming out of it. I slowly straightened, still balancing on one leg, and looked over my shoulder. It was the bull. He was looking at me, and he wasn't happy.

Weighing more than a ton, the buffalo was what Big Buck called "front-loaded." His huge, woolly head with its shaggy beard and his great hump littered with clumps of unshed hair didn't match his smaller rear-end equipment. "BEWARE: Wild Animals" indeed! With the exception of a shiny black nose that resembled the big button on Grandma's winter coat, there was nothing tame or friendly-looking about this fella at all.

As soon as he lowered his head and snorted a swirl of dust from his powerful nostrils, I panicked. I also let go of the ball. Joe-Joe, who had the most experience with bulls via his dad's rodeo clowning, took charge.

"Mags, listen to me," he coached, "Melinda's gonna slowly walk along the fence and try to get his attention. Don't move 'til I tell you."

I was petrified, so that was easy.

"Whatever you do," he warned, "don't piss him off."

Soon, Melinda was coaxing the bull with "Nice Mr. Buffalo" and "Over here, Mr. Buffalo," which only made the buffalo turn its head. She picked up Joe-Joe's discarded watermelon rind and poked it halfway through the chain link. "I bet you're hungry, Mr. Buffalo. What do they feed you anyway? How about a treat?"

The bull swung fully around, his menacing front end now aimed at her.

Joe-Joe raised a finger to his lips then pointed to the tree. Enduring what weight I could on my injured foot, I traversed the short but seemingly immeasurable distance back to the overhanging limb of the elm. It was nearly three feet above my head, another detail I hadn't considered before getting myself into this mess. Even without a twisted ankle, it would have been difficult to reach.

Taking advantage of Melinda's diversionary tactics, Bucky climbed the tree and scooted out on the branch. Locking one elbow around its thickness, he extended his other arm to me. "Quick! Take my hand."

I jumped as high as I could, but my one-legged leap wasn't powerful enough. Only our fingers touched. Determined to save me, Bucky increased his stretch, and we tried again, this time successfully making contact. He had me by the wrist, but try as he may he couldn't pull me up. I was dead weight.

Joe-Joe climbed the tree to help, reaching Bucky just as my hand slipped through his sweaty fingers. When I landed and unwittingly yowled, it regained the bull's full attention. In anger, he pawed the ground.

Joe-Joe jumped down and quickly pulled me to my feet.

"Get on!" he ordered, bending down so as to allow me to climb on his back. Holding his hands for balance, I placed my good foot on his shoulder and then somehow managed to stay on while he straightened his knees. With the extra height, Bucky was able to get a good grip on me as Joe-Joe shifted his hands to the soles of my shoes. When Joe-Joe executed an overhead press that took me even higher, Bucky grabbed the waistband of my shorts and hoisted me onto the branch and out of harm's way.

All the while Melinda tried to distract the bull, but he would have none of it, still out of sorts due to the annoying goings-on at the tree. My escape only made him madder.

Bucky repositioned himself on the branch. "Okay, Joe-Joe, your turn now."

Joe-Joe was about to jump, then stopped short. He had something on his mind, and we all knew exactly what it was — the ball.

"Joe-Joe, no!" Melinda cried out, but it was no use. After all the fuss, he wasn't about to leave it behind.

The bull glowered at Joe-Joe, and Joe-Joe glowered back. Eyeball to eyeball, they sized each other up. The bull knew he had the advantage, but he was wary just the same as Joe-Joe maneuvered closer to the ball with the grace of a ballerina, never breaking the bull's gaze. When he reached it, he pliéed, his fingers now able to clutch their prize.

"Honest, Daddy, I told them not to, but they wouldn't listen."

Michelle's whining came out of nowhere. But coming it was, along with a lot of other people.

Tempestuous rumblings came from the buffalo's throat as he unleashed a raging bellow. His head went down, and he gave it a mighty shake, sending a shower of snot as far as the sidewalk. The bull was going to charge and Joe-Joe knew it. There was no time to get back to the tree. His only chance was the fence.

"Melinda! Catch!" Joe-Joe threw the ball then made a beeline to the chain-link fence. With no time to spare he leapt on the fence, clearing four feet and scaling the last two. He was up to the barbed wire when the bull hit, propelling Joe-Joe over the spiked barricade and into the air. Joe-Joe executed a flawless tuck-and-roll and safely ended up on his feet on the other side.

The bull made a few more passes at the fence, putting a considerable dent in it, then gave a disgruntled snort and trotted off.

Melinda held up the ball for Joe-Joe to see as Bucky shouted, "Way to go, Joe-Joe!" A few hoots and hollers came from the bystanders, however Mr. Fryer did not share their enthusiasm. Nor did Mr. Padilla and the park policeman. We were definitely in trouble.

•   •   •   •   •

Six hours later, I sat in a lawn chair with my tightly wrapped bum ankle resting on a milk crate, a pair of crutches lying at my side. It was a pretty bad sprain. Doc Simms said I would be out of commission for at least a month, although it didn't matter because that was how long I would be grounded. Bucky was sentenced to two weeks. Melinda got by with a scolding from Mrs. Mavrakis (most of it in Greek) and a threat to call the Colonel if there was any more misbehaving.

Joe-Joe caught hell. The park policeman was not at all sympathetic to his reasons for disobeying the "Keep Out" sign and cited him for trespassing. Among those who had seen Joe-Joe airborne was Mr. Padilla. Proud of his son's performance yet nevertheless embarrassed by his lack of judgment, Mr. Padilla assured the policeman that Joe-Joe would pay for damages to the fence. Joe-Joe suffered further humiliation when *Abuela* conked him in the head with her purse. I didn't see it happen—I was being carried away by my father—but Bucky told me Joe-Joe looked like a whipped puppy. I'd have to make it up to him somehow.

The color was slowly leaching from the sunset, and the sky was transforming into a black backdrop. Fortunately, our punishment wouldn't go into effect until the next day, and we could spend our last night of freedom enjoying the All-Star Drive-In fireworks display. The best place to watch was from the vacant lot between the Padillas' house and mine.

The whole neighborhood was there. Mom was waiting on Mrs. Bales, topping off her hot tea and making sure she was warm. On one side of the grand lady sat *Abuela* tatting a doily, a task so second nature she could do it in her sleep. Mrs. Mavrakis occupied the chair on the other side. She had decided that *Abuela* needed English lessons, so the three matrons were passing words back and forth.

"Edah," Mrs. Mavrakis instructed as she pointed to her noggin.

"Etha?" *Abuela* answered back.

"Head," declared Mrs. Bales, correcting them both.

"Fudah."

"Futha?"

"Foot."

Sitting on the blanket beside her mother, little Elizabeth decided to get into the game. It was hard to tell who was leading who, but everybody was laughing and getting a kick out of one another.

Mr. Bales, Mr. Padilla and his oldest son, Ricky, sat close by on a tailgate, carrying on about democrats and republicans, topics I didn't have much use for. Instead, I was paying attention to my dad and Bucky, who were helping Big Buck set off his arsenal. Every year Big Buck spent what my father considered a fortune on missiles and doodads that went *boom*.

Dr. Simms disapproved of fireworks. "Do you know how many hands are blown off every year?" he asked no one in particular while pacing behind us. "I'll be getting a call from the wife or mother of some damn fool who lit too short a fuse or thought one of the damn things was a dud then found out the hard way it wasn't."

We got the same story from Doc every Fourth. And every Fourth he got his call.

Mrs. Majors and Mrs. Simms kept a steady supply of sparklers lit. Tommy and Billy jousted with the flaming swords while Bart the Fart, Patricia Simms, her brother Randy, and Maria and Christina Padilla drew swizzles in the sky.

Melinda grabbed a couple and brought one to me.

"Have you seen Joe-Joe?" I asked.

"Bucky said he's off somewhere sulking."

"I feel real bad about that, Melinda. It's all my fault." I waited for her to disagree, but she didn't. "I was thinking we should do away with the initiation test and let him in the club."

"Think he'll want to join now?" she asked.

It hadn't occurred to me that he wouldn't. "Well, maybe if we made him president, or something," I hinted.

President Melinda gave me a dirty look. So much for that idea.

Pop pop pop pop pop.

Johnno Padilla set off a string of firecrackers. *Abuela* scolded him in Spanish, no doubt reminding him of what happened the year before when he'd thrown a firecracker at a skunk hiding by his father's truck. It stunk up the place so bad we had to move across the street to watch what was left of Big Buck's show.

Other than Joe-Joe, the only unaccounted for member of our neighborhood was Rebecca. No sooner had I thought of her than a motorcycle driven by a hefty, longhaired fellow in a tank top pulled into our driveway alongside the sparkler brigade. Rebecca unwrapped her arms from her driver's waist, got off the bike, then took off an intimidating leather jacket and returned it to the man. He gave her a couple of *varooms* and went on his way.

"Martha, Mary Ann. Lovely night, isn't it?" Rebecca smiled as she removed her headscarf and fluffed her disheveled hair.

Mrs. Simms was tongue-tied. Mrs. Majors wasn't much more talkative.

"Sparkler?" she offered.

"How kind of you," Rebecca said as she retrieved a cigarette from her purse and lit up. She extended the pack. "Care to join me?" They both declined.

Rebecca puffed and sparkled on her own then excused herself. After paying respect to Doc and the ladies, she sat down on a blanket beside Melinda and me.

"I heard you had a run-in with a bull," she said eyeing my ankle.

I groaned. "Does everybody know?"

"Small town," she said.

I changed the subject. "How was your date with Buffalo Bill?"

"You might say I had an encounter with a bit of bull myself. And was he full of it. Now Chainsaw—the gentleman who escorted me home—he's a man of integrity."

Melinda's eyes widened. "Chainsaw?"

"He's an artist. Sculpts bears in wood."

My mother joined us on the blanket. "How were things in California?" Mom asked Rebecca, handing her a beer. "We heard you visited a spa."

"Actually, it was a nudist colony."

The women quit chatting, and Doc quit pacing.

"But I wouldn't recommend it, Myrna," Rebecca continued. "Some things are best left to the imagination."

Dr. Simms mumbled something about short fuses and didn't stick around to hear the rest of Rebecca's commentary.

"At first you're a little uptight," she told us, "but you eventually loosen up a bit and start looking around. You look at this and that. You look at a lot of *that*. It's kind of fun looking at *that*. But after a while *that* becomes boring and downright bothersome. You don't want to look at *that* anymore. And it's freeing. And then it's sad. I mean, I want to look at *that*. So I figured, 'What's the point?' and left."

While I had a good idea what *that* meant and was slightly squeamish, Melinda was bolder.

"You mean, you all were naked? All of you?"

"All of us, all the time."

I gasped. "Even during supper?"

"Even during tennis matches."

We all took a moment to think on that.

"I don't hardly know how you could play tennis naked," Mrs. Bales broke the silence. "With all that flopping about, who'd pay attention to the balls?" Then she burst into laughter, so tickled with herself she almost fell off her chair. Mrs. Marvrakis pretended to be shocked, but chuckled just the same.

"That's exactly what I mean," Rebecca replied with satisfaction. Mom was silent, but her body was shaking and her eyes were welling up, which meant she was in stitches. Even *Abuela*, who had no idea the ins and outs of what was going on, howled with the rest of us.

Our laughter continued until Big Buck's display of Roman candles, fountains, pop-bottle rockets, and starbursts came to an end. Then the big show at the drive-in began to light the sky. Dad turned on the pickup's radio and we listened to the local AM station's medley of patriotic songs. Supposedly they were timed with the All-Star's colorful explosions, although it was more a theory.

The last song of the program was "America the Beautiful," a moving rendition with lots of voices wailing and lots of cymbals crashing. Mr. Bales proudly stood behind his wife, his hands on her shoulders while the grand old lady sang along. The sky was ablaze with bursts within bursts of red, white and blue, the trails they left seeming to fall over the entire town.

From sea to shining sea.

The show was over and we applauded with exuberance. Smoke and sulfur thickened the summer air. The outside lights at the Simmses' came on, and Mrs. Simms summoned her husband. He had indeed gotten his call, officially marking the end of our July Fourth merriment.

Melinda held my crutches as Bucky helped me rise from the lawn chair. Out of the corner of my eye, I saw Joe-Joe in the street, illuminated by the Simmses' porchlight. He was carrying something in his hand. Something white. Something that looked like a plastic jug.

"Hey Maggie!" he hollered. "Look what I've got."

It was our clubhouse mascot, Hector the Clorox pig. Joe-Joe must have had him all along, the sneak.

"Ever seen a pig fly, Maggie?"

We watched as he ceremoniously struck a match, lit the fuse and dropped the explosive down Hector's snout before giving it a hefty toss and running for cover. The pig blew sky-high, going out with a bang.

Joe-Joe had gotten his revenge.

Of course, I would have to put up a fuss and pretend I was upset, but I couldn't say I blamed him. The pig was a small price to pay for my moment of hotheadedness.

CHAPTER 6

Every August, my father and his buddies fished the Snake River. Armed with beans, beer and bait, they'd load up the old jeep and hit the road for a weeklong retreat away from work and women. Mom didn't mind because it gave her a chance to catch up on ironing, her way of making extra money.

The going rate was two dollars a dozen, and Mom had plenty of customers. Seldom did our doorknobs not support the hangers of pressed shirts, nor was there a corner in our house that didn't have a tagged clothes bundle waiting its turn to be wrinkle-free.

My job as chief sprinkler seemed simple but required finesse. Using a large Coke bottle with a sprinkler head stuffed in its neck, I'd give each garment a few shakes—not too few, not too many—fold them then shove them in a plastic bag where they sat until they soaked up the right amount of wetness. Let them sit too long and they'd begin to mildew, which was what usually happened with our own clothes.

Most of my punitive time for the buffalo fiasco was spent helping Mom. I was walking again, although my ankle still smarted, as did my ego. On top of that, it had been two weeks since I'd seen Bucky. He was with his family on their annual summer vacation. The Majors had been almost everywhere—South Dakota, Idaho, Oklahoma. Last year they went to Canada to visit Mrs. Majors's sister. This year they drove all the way to California.

I hadn't been anywhere, really. Missoula. And Casper. Of course Yellowstone, but who hadn't been there? Even Grandma had visited the park, and she had no use for traveling after going back East once. "Too many damn trees," she said. Grandma liked wide-open spaces and was perfectly content to do her exploring in her own back yard. Dad was like her. He knew Wyoming and Montana, and that was enough for him. Mom, on the other hand, had a speck of wanderlust. She dreamt of coconuts and grass skirts, tiki torches and Don Ho. She was determined to get to Hawaii one day, with or without my father. Judging by the wistful look on her face, her mind was probably there now.

"Hang this up for me, will you, hon?" Mom handed me a perfectly pressed shirt then put down her iron and walked to the picture window. A dust devil was coming up the road. She raised her arms in front of the chilled air of the swamp cooler.

I hung the shirt on the nearest knob then joined her by the window. "Is it hot in Hawaii?" I asked.

"I suppose it is. But there's a big ocean to cool you off."

"How big is the ocean?"

"Big enough," Mom said as she ruffled my hair.

"When you go to Hawaii can I come, too?"

"Airplane tickets are awfully expensive. It might take us a while."

I reached into the sprinkle bag and handed her another shirt. Mom smiled and kissed me on the cheek. Then the phone rang, and she went to the kitchen to answer it, leaving me lost in thought. Of course you had to fly to Hawaii, it being an island, but exactly how far away was it? And where was it? I'd have to take a gander at the Colonel's globe.

"That was Mrs. Simms," Mom said, returning to her ironing board. "She's cleaning out closets and has a care package for you."

Great. Just what I wanted. More of Patricia's hand-me-downs. "I still haven't worn anything from that last bunch of goofy dresses."

"There might be something nice this time."

"They never fit."

"You're growing. Besides, the start of school's not far off and this could save some money."

A timid knock came at the front door. It was Randy, who was holding a brown grocery sack full of his sister's used garb. He dropped the sack and ran away. Randy was shy.

I took the bag and retreated to my bedroom, wanting to inspect its contents without my mother looking on. A pair of striped trousers — too big. A pair of yellow trousers — too yellow. A white sweater with red hearts — too girly. A pink dress with white rickrack — too Patricia. A checkered shirtdress that was actually okay. And at the bottom of the bag, two well-worn training bras.

I picked up the least weathered of the beginner brassieres and held it out for further inspection. Only the faintest indication of "AAA" remained on its label. A frayed little pink bow separated its tired cups. Its adjustable straps had lost their stretch and now depended on safety pins to take up the slack. Its sides were yellowed from Patricia's sweaty armpits. The eyelets on its nearest and farthest sets of fasteners had been pulled apart by the heaving force of Patricia's expanding chest. This breached "boulder holder," whose glory days were long gone, was to be my first bra. It was beautiful!

Melinda didn't have a bra. Mrs. Mavrakis bought her undershirts to tame her developing swells, but Melinda didn't have a bra. I did, and I couldn't wait to try it on.

I smuggled the bra into the bathroom — the only room in the house with a mirror — and locked the door. Cinching its remaining middle clasp, I slung my arms through the straps and slid it over my chest. It kind of hung there. Thank goodness for the safety pins. I tightened the straps. It still kind of hung there. I put my shirt back on, thinking that would make a difference.

Maybe after wearing it a while, my chest would get the hint and start growing. Maybe that's why they called them training bras. Maybe putting a little toilet paper in the stretched-out cups might help.

Not bad. I liked this new look, wondering if anyone would notice.

"Knock, knock. Can I come in?" Mom was at the bathroom door. I almost jumped out of my skin.

"No!" I yelled. "Can't a fella have any privacy around here?"

"Melinda's on the phone. I'll tell her you'll call back."

"No, I'll take it."

Flushing the commode for effect, I opened the door, careful to conceal my figure.

Mom gave a half smile and let me pass.

I grabbed the kitchen's wall phone and whispered, "Melinda, meet me in the clubhouse. I've got something to show you."

I was posing on the clubhouse bench when Melinda pulled aside the blanket that hung as our door. She took a moment to adjust her eyes, then sat down on her stool and gave me the once-over. "I don't know, Maggie. I think the left one's bigger."

I transferred a piece of toilet paper from the overstuffed cup to the understuffed one and refluffed.

Melinda smiled. "Now you're even."

Satisfied, I crossed my legs at the ankle in a ladylike fashion.

"I thought you thought bras were for sissies," Melinda said. "Why the sudden interest?"

"If you must know, I'm maturing."

"Well, 'maturing' is not necessarily what it's cracked up to be. Look at Patricia Simms. She can't keep her sweaters buttoned. The boys are always teasing her."

Melinda had a point, but how could she understand? She was pretty, in a soft kind of way, and round like a girl. She had always looked like a girl. There wasn't much to distinguish me from a boy — skinny, short-haired and scabby-kneed. A tomboy. So what if I liked to run and jump and get dirty and say my mind? Maybe I didn't like dresses because doing a cartwheel in one was no longer acceptable. That didn't mean I wanted to be a boy. I liked being a girl, and doing *some* girly things like playing jump rope and dress-up and hopscotch, or cutting out paper dolls. I wanted boys to notice me the way they did Patricia and Melinda.

"I think I'm rather vo*lump*tious," I bragged.

Melinda laughed. "Nice try, Maggie, but I think you mean *voluptuous*."

"Close enough."

Much of my vocabulary came from Melinda, at least the big words. Melinda had a voracious appetite for reading, and not just Nancy Drew and the like. She read important books, too, from cover to cover. Like *Jane Eyre* (which I couldn't get through) and *100 Years of Solitude* (which would have taken me 100 years to read).

Bucky and I were used to her big words, but unlike me, Bucky's ignorance didn't embarrass him. When Melinda would toss out something highfalutin, he'd just say "Huh?" and wait for her to explain. That's how we found out about words like "voluptuous" and "voracious." Of course, I'd claim to have known all along what they meant. My pretending backfired after Bucky, tired of being the dumb one, quit saying "Huh?" and I had to find out definitions on my own.

Mom wouldn't help. "Look it up," she'd tell me, even though half the time I had no idea how to spell it. Dad couldn't be relied on either, as I found out with "supercilious." Melinda had told me I had a supercilious laugh.

"Supercilious?" He pondered for a bit. "Sounds like 'simpleminded' to me."

Man, was I mad, and a little hurt. After stewing a couple days, I confronted Melinda.

"That's not at all what I meant," she'd told me. "Supercilious means 'prideful.' 'Condescending.'"

Not a flattering assessment of my laugh, but better than "simpleminded."

Melinda was still laughing at my malaprop—another fancy word needing explanation—when the curtain door flung open and Bucky appeared.

"You're back!" she shouted.

"You miss me?" Bucky asked as he threw himself on Aunt Sylvia's three-legged chair.

"Have you been somewhere?" I asked.

Bucky ignored my sarcasm. "You wouldn't believe California. So many gall darn people. And Disneyland! Man, we had to stand in line for over an hour just to get into the place, and once we were in, we had to stand in line for all the rides. I waited two hours to get on the Matterhorn. It's the most incredible roller coaster you've ever seen. Nothing like it, even at the State Fair." Bucky pulled a small box from his front pocket and handed it to Melinda. "Here. This is for you."

Melinda unwrapped a tiny Tinker Bell on a string.

"It's glass. I watched the man make it myself."

Melinda dangled the delicate trinket in a stream of light leaking through one of our rickety walls. "It's beautiful," she exclaimed. "Thank you."

"Wow, it really is," I said.

"Don't worry, Mags, I didn't forget you." From his back pocket, Bucky removed a rumpled Mouseketeer hat and handed it to me. "Sorry about the ear. That stupid Bart puts everything in his mouth."

"Thanks," I said with poorly disguised disappointment.

Bucky was oblivious. "I thought you might like it."

Wanting to shrug off my wound, I put on the blasted ears and performed a rousing rendition of the Mickey Mouse song. My performance abruptly ended on the *k* of Mickey's name when I remembered my stuffed chest. I quickly covered myself, hoping Bucky hadn't noticed.

"Thanks," I repeated.

"So what's been going on here?" Bucky asked. "Anything change while I've been away?" He raised his eyebrows and grinned.

I knew he knew. He knew I knew he knew. It was just a matter of time.

Not comfortable with how this might play out, Melinda cleared her throat to get Bucky's attention. "Well, Joe-Joe dropped out of 4-H." No reaction from her news. "*And* there was in an accident involving the Bales mutt."

Bucky wasn't listening. His focus was on me.

"Ah . . . ah . . . ahchoo!" he faux-sneezed. "Excuse me, Maggie. I guess I caught a cold on the trip. You got a Kleenex?"

As Bucky doubled over with laughter, Melinda sat silent, waiting for my reaction.

Feeling stupid and ugly, I started to cry. Not the put-your-head-down-on-a-pillow-and-let-it-out kind, but a choking, soul-shuddering cry with aching spasms and involuntary squeals. Unlike Melinda, whose tears needed little coaxing, or Bucky, whose waterworks could be provoked by a sappy television commercial, crying was not in my nature. In all our teasing and sparring, neither had seen me do so. Until now, and I couldn't stop. There was nothing to do but let the boo-hoo run its course.

As I wiped my runny nose with my hand, I caught a glimpse of my buddies. Melinda, of course, was also weeping. Bucky sat stunned. He knew he'd done something wrong and looked pitiful.

For some reason that made me feel better. It wasn't like they'd never done anything stupid. Once Melinda cut off half of her right eyebrow while daydreaming during Mrs. Plot's art class, and Bucky had to pitch a game in pink after he washed his baseball uniform with his mom's red terrycloth bathrobe. Hell, Bucky did something idiotic at least once a day.

Feeling better, I decided it was time to let my friends off the hook. Reaching into my shirt, I removed the toilet paper from the right cup and blew my nose. "Well, at least it's good for something." I said, passing the left cup's contents to Melinda.

Melinda's blow was loud and long and reminded me of an elephant seal I'd once seen on *The Wonderful World of Disney*. How could something so raucous come from someone so sweet? It made me giggle. She started giggling as well. About that time, the remaining back leg on Aunt Silvia's chair gave out from under Bucky. Suddenly everything seemed funny, especially poor Bucky, who brushed the dirt off his butt then decided it might be better if he just went home.

That night, under less traumatic circumstances, Bucky, Melinda and I reconvened in the open field behind my house for stargazing. Melinda had brought a couple of old woolen army blankets, and the three of us had assumed the contemplating position: arms behind our heads, heads cradled in the palms of hands, elbows wide and right feet resting on bent left knees. We looked like the set of novelty saltshakers Grandma used to have on her kitchen stove, plus one more.

The air was still and warm. A chorus of crickets sang in the background. All was well with my blanket-sharing friends. But the moonless sky's clarity and the "twinkle, twinkle" amid the Milky Way's smear triggered a new unsettling feeling.

"Tell us about the ocean," I asked Bucky, trying to shake it away.

"Well, it's not at all like swimming in Lake Smitty," he said. "Your skin tingles when you get out of the water, and little salt crystals form on your leg and arm hairs. The waves are the best thing. Pick you right up and tumble you over and over. I got pretty good at body surfing.

Better than Dad. He took a hit from this one wave and it nearly pulled off his trunks."

We all had a chuckle at the expense of Big Buck's exposed bottom.

"Man oh man, did I see some strange people," Bucky continued. "Lots of goofy-looking old farts strutting around and showing off their tan."

I could only imagine what the Californians thought of Bucky's white legs. I was going to make a comment, but decided to let it slide.

"It went on forever, Mags. As far as you could see and then some. I never knew there was so much water in this world."

"Interesting," I said.

"Yep," said Bucky

"Indeed," Melinda added. We fell silent.

Melinda pointed to a blinking plane overhead and traced its path with her finger.

"Where you suppose its heading?" I asked, more to myself than the others, thinking it might be going to Hawaii. It was hard to imagine being on a plane.

"Africa," Bucky answered matter-of-factly.

"It can't be going there," Melinda said. "It's flying north."

"Okay, hotshot," he said, a little less assured, "You tell us where."

"Alaska," Melinda wistfully suggested. "That's its final destination. There's a family on board. A mother and father and two children. She's an artist, and he's a professor of literature. They're going to set up a school in Alaska — for the Eskimos."

"Are they going to live in an igloo?" Bucky asked.

"Who would want to live in an igloo?" I wondered. Africa sounded good enough for me.

"Actually, they're meant to be quite warm," Melinda said. "Snowpack is a good insulator."

I shivered. Wyoming winter days were nasty enough, but according to a Johnny Horton song, springtime in Alaska was forty below!

"And why would anyone want to live in Alaska?"

"Because it's beautiful," Melinda continued. "And not a lot of people, so you have to look out for one other. The family on the plane—they're very close. The father and mother are blissfully in love, and they adore their children, both girls. When they arrive, the oldest daughter will be in charge of feeding and training the dogs for the sleds. Dogs are essential. She'll be very good at it and everyone, including the Eskimos, will come to her for advice. She'll make her father proud. When they get to Alaska."

"Okay, I'll go with Alaska," Bucky broke in, "but they're coming up from Africa, that's for sure, because that's where they got the diamonds."

I bit. "What diamonds?"

"The ones stolen from just about the largest diamond mine on earth! So many diamonds that the whole gall darn diamond world is in an uproar. The pilot's in on the heist. That's how they smuggled them on board."

"Who's they?"

"The Russians. Who else? They're going to make a big crystal ball that can reflect the light of the sun and melt the icebergs and drown everybody."

"Why do they want to do that?" asked Melinda.

"Because they're Russians. And there is this fella on board whose pretending to be a priest, but he's a secret agent. He's not too shabby. A good guy. People seem to like him. Anyway, they have his girlfriend and her dogs held up in some igloo along with the ice-melting machine."

"His girlfriend?" I asked, "And her dogs?"

"That's right. She trains them."

I was pretty sure I knew where this was heading and not so sure I liked it.

"*Anyway*," Bucky continued, "all they need is one more shipment of diamonds and bye-bye, Alaska. But don't worry. The secret agent will rescue her, her pooches and the whole gall darn world."

Melinda laughed. "Nicely put, Mr. Bond."

I shifted my focus from the sky to Bucky. He was smiling.

"How about you, Maggie?" Melinda asked. "What do you think?"

"I don't know," I sighed.

"Come on, Mags," coaxed Bucky. "You always have a story of some kind."

I switched my legs, making us no longer a set of three. "I don't know," I insisted.

Bucky was having none of that. "What do you mean you don't know? You always know everything."

"I do not."

"You think you know everything."

"We'll I don't know where the damn plane's going."

"Shush," Melinda said, gently putting a hand over my mouth and his. "It's gone now. Let's just watch the stars and listen."

So, we did, but the whole "plane thing" and its possible route had left me troubled. Where *were* we going? Destiny spoke to my friends; although they didn't know the particulars of its path, they knew its general direction. Melinda wanted a family, and Bucky, hero-bound, would be by her side. Where did that leave me? My future was as undeveloped as my body.

Suddenly I got queasy. Something told me I'd on my own when it came to figuring out my story, neither strapped to someone else's dreams nor their know-how. Wherever I was going, it would be away from my friends. Away from Wyoming.

I put my hands over my ears, choosing not to listen. Not now.

CHAPTER 7

September had snuck in. Its frost-sprinkled mornings were a little darker and its afternoon skies a little bluer. Both held the fragrance of the decaying summer.

The countdown to the first day of school was almost at its end. Bucky, Melinda, and I would be entering junior high. I was apprehensive. Not only would I have to break in seven teachers, I'd have to memorize a locker combination. And take showers in front of other shower-averse girls.

My birthday had come and gone—a meager celebration marked by thirteen candles on a strawberry angel food cake topped with whipped cream. There was no party, nor did I really want one. No way could I compete with the Majorses' forthcoming shindig.

Big Buck had been born on a Labor Day and all the Majors boys, with the exception of Bart, had birthdays in September. Mrs. Majors called them her "New Year's Eve toasts." To mark the occasion, Big Buck always sprung for a super-duper family gift. One year it was a camper. Another year, a color TV. Last year he bought new bikes for all the boys.

This year's surprise was an aboveground pool, eighteen feet around and holding eight thousand gallons of water, to be unveiled on the first Sunday after Labor Day, a late date for seasonal swimming, but Big Buck got a good deal. He hired my dad and Ricky Padilla to oversee the necessary construction for its installation, although he also gave them strict orders not to spill the beans and spoil the surprise, not even to his wife. Mrs. Majors was beside herself the morning Dad showed up with a backhoe and shoveled out a prime section of her lawn. Dad wasn't very good at lying, so he punted to Ricky, who calmed her down with a "trust me" and a wink.

The bulldozing of Bucky's backyard was the major topic of discussion at our No Name No Purpose Club meeting. Our list of possible reasons included: a barbeque pit, a basketball court, a five-lane bowling alley, a combination roller-skating/skateboard rink, a botanical garden with tropical flowers and exotic birds flown in from South America, a fully operational Swiss Family Robinson treehouse complete with water wheel, swinging ropes, hammocks, organ, and (oh, yes) an ostrich. We could have gone on, but Melinda had more on the agenda.

"Speaking of surprises," she transitioned, "my father is coming home!"

"When?" Bucky and I asked in unison.

"He didn't exactly say, but he's bringing me 'something special.' Those were his words."

The Colonel traveled quite a bit, but seldom brought anything back for Melinda other than Kewpie dolls. Not much of a gift giver, he let Mrs. Mavrakis do his shopping.

"What do you think it is?" I wondered.

"Oh, I've a pretty good idea. Last time we spoke I told him about the palomino I fell in love with at the 4-H fair. He asked a lot of questions and seemed very interested."

"So if you're getting a horse . . ." Bucky thought out loud.

". . . you'll have to put it somewhere," I said, completing his sentence.

Bucky struck his forehead with the palm of his hand. "Maybe that has something to do with the commotion going on in our backyard."

"Yeah." I did my own head thump. "Maybe your dad's putting in an arena."

Melinda was all smiles. "And some stalls. Maybe he's getting you a horse as well." Bucky wrinkled his nose. Of all our surmises, that had the least appeal. "Hmm. I doubt it."

"Well, perhaps that's just my wishful thinking," Melinda allowed, "but what else could my father's gift be? There isn't anything else I really want."

"Except for your dad to stick around a little more often."

I should have kept my opinion to myself because Melinda gave me a sour look. "I'm more inclined to go with the horse."

Bucky nodded in agreement.

"Anyway," I said, backing off. "We'll know soon enough."

And we would. It was impossible to keep a secret in our neighborhood, let alone one of such magnitude. When the big truck arrived and its installation experts unloaded boxes with the pool's redwood decking and turquoise liner, most of us had a good inkling of what was going on. The invitations instructing us to dress for the beach and bring a lawn chair confirmed our suspicions. The party was scheduled to begin at two o'clock, well after church and well into the acceptable beer-drinking hour.

For the most part, Sunday mornings in our neighborhood involved going to church. The first to head out for their weekly rendezvous with God were the Padillas. One come-on-we're-late honk for Johnno, followed by two you-better-get-your-rear-end-in-this-car honks for Joe-Joe, then all nine crowded into their 1963 baby-blue Rambler to make six thirty mass at the Immaculate Conception Catholic Church.

The Simms chose a more reasonable hour of devotion and left precisely at eight forty for the nine o'clock service at the First Methodist Church. An hour later, Reverend Bauer's black Lincoln Continental, driven by his lead-footed son Stephen, arrived at the Barn, whisking Mr. and Mrs. Bales and their seasonally appropriate hats to the First Presbyterian Church for ten o'clock worship. The Lincoln and its white-knuckled passengers sped past the Majors boys, who were always outside in their coats and ties ready to load up. They also attended the First Presbyterian.

About the time everyone was coming home from church, Rebecca Frick was getting out of bed. Although she had been raised Baptist, Rebecca had given up organized religion for health reasons. "All that Bible-thumping gives me a headache."

My parents just hit the prime times, Christmas and Easter. Like my mother, Dad had been raised Presbyterian. He found it a reasonably good affiliation, as churches go, especially because no one came down on him for his infrequent visits. Dad was comfortable with his relationship to the Almighty Father, although there was a time he questioned the beliefs of his own irreverent son. At age thirteen, my brother Brian announced he was an atheist. This disturbed my father. So when a door-to-door salesman-slash-missionary showed up one day peddling vacuum cleaners and the Book of Mormon—Dad took one of each—he agreed to an introductory lesson, insisting Mom and Brian also partake.

That evening, a couple of clean-cut guys showed up at the house with a flannel board and felt cutouts to explain their brand of worship. They also brought a list of dos and don'ts. Somewhere on the list of don'ts was tea drinking. Dad was a tea man. He drank it hot or iced, throughout the day and well into the night. If tea drinking was a vice, it was one of Dad's few and he'd be damned if he was going to give it up. He sent the missionaries on their way, but not before offering them a cup of Lipton.

After the Mormon encounter, Dad decided that the one true church was the great outdoors, and fishing was the best way to worship. Mom agreed, to a point. She figured it was too late to change my brother's mind, but she wanted me to know what was out there, just in case. She started me out as a Presbyterian.

I liked Sunday school. The Bible stories. Making up my own Bible stories. I liked the snacks. But mostly I liked to sing, and there were all kinds of fun, churchy songs like "Jacob's Ladder" and "Joshua Fought the Battle of Jericho" and "I've Got the Joy." One in particular, "The Birdy Song" (my title), was my favorite, although I never could figure out why Jesus wanted to take my birdies away, or why I would feel happy about it. Melinda eventually pointed out my mispronunciation of "burdens."

I probably would have stayed Presbyterian if it hadn't been for Mom's appendicitis attack. While the doctor was yanking it out, Mrs. Mavrakis was reeling me in.

Mrs. Mavrakis was Greek Orthodox, but its church was two towns away and not to her liking, so she settled on the Immaculate Conception. She'd talked the Colonel into allowing Melinda's baptismal — Melinda's mom had Catholic ties — and whenever home, he'd dutifully drive them both to nine-thirty mass then wait in his car reading a newspaper until it ended.

Although Wyomingites generally let folks be folks, some were suspicions of the goings-on at the Catholic church. The Sunday when Mrs. Mavrakis and Melinda first escorted me to the Immaculate Conception, I was skittish. My nerves were further agitated when Mrs. Mavrakis bobby-pinned what looked like a doily to the top of my head. Melinda got one as well. "It's the rules," explained Mrs. Mavrakis, she herself wearing a scarf.

Upon entering the church, Mrs. Mavrakis dipped her fingers into a dish with a sponge soaked in "holy water" and indicated I should do the same. Another rule. Melinda demonstrated the correct crossing procedure and recitation.

For the most part, a church is a church, but the First Presbyterian Church didn't have the *wow* effect of the Immaculate Conception. To the left of its entrance stood four wooden cubicles that I later found out were not phone booths but confessionals. Apparently, you had to confess your sins to the priest, especially those that had you so ashamed you wouldn't even tell your best friend. This had to be done before eating the Body of Christ.

Interesting.

Opposite the confessionals, in a cozy corner illuminated by five rows of candles, some lit, some not, was a curly-haired doll wearing a beautiful blue fur-edged cape lined in white satin and a crown. When I asked who she was, I was told *she* was a *he*, and he was the Baby Jesus. I had never seen the Baby Jesus in anything but a manger, and I certainly had never seen him dressed like that.

Fascinating.

Hanging at the front of the church on an enormous cross was a sorrowful, tortured-looking Jesus with blood trickling from his thorn-crowned head, his hollow chest, and his nail-pierced hands and feet.

Light from the blue-and-red stained-glass window danced on the altar that stood before him.

Humbling.

Before we settled on a spot among the pews, Mrs. Mavrakis did a quickie half-kneel and crossed herself again. So did Melinda. Once seated, she removed two beaded strings from her pocketbook and handed one to my friend. Both whispered little prayers while I thumbed through the hymnal waiting for the singing to begin.

Mass was mesmerizing. Bells rang. Incense wafted at us from a smoking ball on a chain. Alter boys chanted in a lyrical foreign language. The priest would say one thing and the parishioners would say another, back and forth, then in unison, with everyone knowing exactly when and how to respond. Up, down, up, down, from sitting to standing to kneeling. It was all so mystical. So awe-inspiring.

The priest gave a Biblical reading and sermon, which was pretty much like any other Biblical reading and sermon I'd heard—long and boring—but what came after caught my interest: his preparations for receiving the Body of Christ. I tried to get an explanation from Melinda, but Mrs. Mavrakis swatted us silent. When they stood with the others sharing our pew to join the Communion line, I figured I'd tag along. I didn't get far. Seems I was not worthy to receive the sacrament, and there were a whole lot of necessary steps I'd have to take before I became worthy.

For the next few months, I attended mass every Sunday. I learned the prayers. I learned when to kneel. I lit the candles. I illegally went to confession. I partook of the communion host—also illegal, but I was hungry.

On the road to conversion, I signed up for catechism classes and almost went, but something kept nagging me. This particular group of Catholics wasn't too keen on singing, and when they did what came out was as monotonous as their robotic responses to the liturgy. Come hymn time, I felt stifled. Sure, there was mystery here, but where was the passion? The *Joy, Joy, Joy*? As far as I could tell people were going through the motions out of some sense of duty; judging from the amount of watch watching, most would rather be someplace else. After a while, so did I.

So, I became a dabbler. A little here, a little there. When I was in the mood to sing, I'd go to church with the Majors. When I was in the mood to pray, I'd go with Melinda and Mrs. Mavrakis. And when I was in the mood to eat Mom's pancakes, I let my soul be damned.

The Sunday morning of their pool party the Majorses were opting out of church and Mom wasn't cooking, so I called Melinda to tag along with her to the Immaculate Conception. Mrs. Mavrakis answered the phone. She wasn't her usual cheery Sunday self.

"I think God will forgive us if we do not visit him today, Margaret."

"Are you sick?" I asked. "Is Melinda sick?"

"Today is not good. Good-bye."

"Wait a minute." Now I was concerned. "Does that mean Melinda will miss the birthday party?"

"I must go now. You see. Tomorrow will be better." With that, Mrs. Mavrakis hung up and left me hanging.

Melinda had been moody lately. Maybe it had something to do with her dad coming home. Or maybe she was having another visit from Charley. Great. That would certainly put a damper on the dwindling days of our summer vacation.

"Charley" was what girls whispered to each other when "that time of the month" came. I found this out from Patricia Simms one day when Bucky and Melinda weren't around and I wanted someone to ride bikes with.

"I can't go today because Charley is here," she whispered through cupped hands as we stood on her front porch.

"Charley who?" I asked.

"You know . . ." She looked to one side and then the other and cupped her mouth again. "Charley."

I figured he must be some wacky cousin. "Doesn't this guy ride bikes?"

"No. It's my Charley."

"You got a boyfriend?" Clearly I wasn't getting it, so Patricia sat me down on the stoop to fill me in.

Of course, I was well educated in the detail details, having seen The Movie at the beginning of sixth grade and read its accompanying pamphlet, "Growing Up and Liking It." Unfortunately, it didn't cover the ins and outs of communication protocol.

Patricia couldn't answer my question on why "Charley" had to be the code word. Why wasn't it something more girly like "Ethel" or "Eloise"? When I asked my mom, she said it probably had something to do with a "Charley horse" since the whole ordeal was a general pain in the "you know what." Mom didn't elaborate.

Although I was reluctant to have a Charley of my own, I felt left behind when Melinda beat me to the punch. During a clubhouse meeting at the beginning of summer she'd announced her menstruation status, taking my jealousy and Bucky's confusion in stride. She wasn't the least bit apologetic or embarrassed by us knowing her personal business.

Maybe Charley was visiting Melinda again. Maybe she'd feel better come party time, although it was doubtful she would swim. I decided to forgo church matters and bide the time in my room playing solitaire and listening to music.

Melinda hadn't been the only one with an unexpected summer visitor. My brother, Brian, showed up after my birthday and, in lieu of a present, sort of gave me his portable record player and LP collection for safekeeping. I was ecstatic about the record player. Unlike Mom and Dad's Philips, it had a stacking adapter so now I was able to play multiple 45s. I could also stack LPs, a sacrilege to Mom who took meticulous care of her albums, avoiding all fingerprints and scratches. Dad and I were forbidden to handle any of her personal favorites because we didn't have her light touch when it came to picking up the needle and setting it back down. Our impatience took its toll on the likes of The Kingston Trio and Marty Robbins, whose voices eventually crackled from abuse. Mitch Miller's sing-alongs had their share of permanent skips.

My very own LP collection consisted of six records: *The Monkees*, *More of the Monkees*, Garry Puckett & the Union Gap's *Woman Woman*, *Petula Clark's Greatest Hits*, *Let's All Sing with the Chipmunks*, and the movie soundtrack of *Oklahoma!*. With Brian's contributions, that number more than doubled to include Country Joe and the Fish, The Grateful Dead, Iron Butterfly, Judy Collins, Joan Baez, and Canned

Heat. I hadn't a clue who most of them were, and I hadn't a clue why he sort of gave them away.

Brian was a mystery to me. Nice enough—he always patted my head similar to how you'd pat a good dog—but not a talkative sort. I didn't know what made him tick, just what ticked him off. Mostly my dad.

Shortly after graduating from high school, my brother skedaddled, but not before my father stood watch as his only son—a One-A kid with no deferment cards up his sleeve—begrudgingly registered for the US draft. With that detail out of the way, Brian took his guitar and set off for the West Coast in a green, sun-faded Morris Mini-Minor; about the size of a toaster and with the same horsepower, it was an ignoble mode of transport for a young would-be man of fortune. Unfortunately, he never made it across the Northern Rockies. The Morris wimped out before the divide and left my brother stranded in Montana.

Brian stayed in Big Sky Country doing God knows what. Another thing only God knew was how he managed to stay under the radar of the United States draft. Periodically, when he wasn't happy with the direction his life was taking, he'd telephone my mom for a pep talk. Then Dad would get on the phone. "Sure, go ahead and play music, but don't think that's going to pay the bills or support a family. You need a real job." Brian would pretend to agree, and Dad would pretend his advice giving was not in vain. It was a strange dance, but one in which they both felt comfortable.

My brother left home with a ducktail and returned with a ponytail. Dad kept his thoughts to himself, but Uncle Willis, who happened to be at our house when Brian and his hair showed up, was more opinionated. "Why, he looks like a damn girl, doncha know. Might as well put 'im in a dress."

Dad may not have cared for my brother's hair, but he cared even less for Uncle Willis. The more Willis cussed and complained, the more my father defended Brian's ponytail. "A person's got a right to express the standards of their generation. It's what's natural. You think that Jesus Christ wore a crew cut?" Mom had to intervene before they came to blows. All the while Brian stood expressionless, hands shoved in his pockets, no doubt hiding the extended middle finger on verge of taking flight. Uncle Willis had driven away in a huff, which was customary after one of his visits. The unfortunate encounter turned out to be a blessing in that it created a temporary truce between father and son.

Dad was an early-to-bed, early-to-rise kind of guy. Brian, on the other hand, stayed out late and slept until it was time to stay out late again. So, when he rapped at my bedroom door well before ten o'clock, I was taken aback.

"What's up, hotshot?" he asked through a yawn.

"Old Man Solitaire's got me beat," I told him as I gathered my cards and shuffled. Brian threw himself on my bed and gave my humble décor the once over. I was in my purple phase: lilac walls, lavender bedspread, purple rug, purple lampshade. I don't think purple was Brian's color. He rolled his eyes and looked at me as if I was from another planet.

"Deal," he ordered. "Five-card stud, nothing wild."

Both Brian and I learned to play cards before we could read. Wicked at hearts and a master at cribbage, Mom made sure she'd have equally matched opponents. Meanwhile, Dad loved a good game of poker, so from an early age I had been allowed to stand behind his chair at poker parties if (and only if) I behaved myself. The first indication of bellyaching would send me to my room, so I learned to keep my mouth shut and observe. I got pretty good at judging who was bona fide and who was bluffing. Doc Simms was a lousy poker player, a "Nervous Nelly" as Dad called him, because of his good-hand butt-squirming and bad-hand finger-drumming.

"Read 'em and weep, kid."

My pathetic jack high had lost to Brian's two pair. He mussed up my hair then picked up my latest edition of *Teen Magazine* from the nightstand. After tossing it aside with a grimace, Brian got up and riffled through my stack of 45s. Another eye roll.

"So, what do you think?" he asked nonchalantly.

I wasn't sure how to respond. I couldn't remember the last time Brian asked me anything about anything.

He must have sensed my confusion because he laughed. "Don't hurt yourself. It's just a rhetorical question."

I frowned. Where was Melinda when you needed her?

"You need to broaden your horizons, little sister," he continued while looking through his discarded and my newly acquired records. "Here," he said handing me the Joan Baez album. "Give her a listen. I think you'll like her."

Then my brother went back into his room — now mom's sewing room — and shut the door. It was the longest conversation we'd ever had.

Although the day started out sweatshirt-cool, the afternoon turned to shorts weather and continued to heat up in more ways than one. By three o'clock Big Buck's party was in full swing. Cars and pickups lined both sides of Old Orphanage Road from the vacant lot adjacent the Majorses' to well past the frog pond.

Big Buck was in his element. Dressed in plaid swim trunks, a loud yellow shirt, and his favorite "Get 'em while they're hot!" barbeque apron, the three-handed wonder wielded tongs, dispensed chilled Budweisers, and did some unabashed imbibing of his own while chomping on a White Owl cigar.

Some of the men convened under the awning near the barbeque, while others mingled around the pool. A few had on their trunks but most wore jeans. Wyoming men were loath to show their legs, but the women, happy for this last tanning opportunity, sunned in lounge chairs scattered in various socializing configurations. Few grownups wanted to get in the water. The newly filled pool was too cold and too crowded with their rambunctious offspring.

Still a looker after having four kids, Mrs. Majors had her hands full playing hostess and keeping her boys in tow. Billy could tread water well enough to make it from one side of the pool to the other, but Bart hadn't yet learned to swim. He cried to be let in the water, and then cried to be let out. When Tommy wasn't chasing Randy Simms in an effort to pull down his trunks, he was splashing anything and everything. Bucky wasn't much help, so Mrs. Majors enlisted me as lifeguard.

When the doorbell rang I hoped it would be Melinda, but it was the three Padilla boys, all in cut-offs. As they made a beeline to the pool, Dr. Simms looked on with disapproval, grousing about the lack of swimming pool safety. "An accident waiting to happen."

Draped in a beach towel, Patricia Simms sat next to her mom hugging her own knees. She hadn't budged since arriving. Something looked different about her, but I couldn't put my finger on it. In mid-July she'd gone away to camp somewhere back east and had just gotten back. Tired of being the only girl in a boy-infested pool, I figured she could share mommy duty.

"Hey, Patricia. Come on in. The water's fine."

"Go on, honey," nudged Mrs. Simms. "Get in the pool."

Patricia reluctantly stood. After handing her towel to her mom, she twinkle-toed up the stairs to the pool's decking.

Holy schmoly! She had the same freckled face, the same uncontrollable red hair coaxed into a shoulder-length flip, and the same cat-eye glasses framing her squinty blue eyes. But what happened from the neck down? What happened to the pudgy part of her? She was a couple of inches taller and more than a few pounds lighter. Patricia didn't look fourteen, or even fifteen or sixteen. Standing before us in a pink polka-dotted two-piece was a stunning young woman, lean but well-endowed.

Johnno Padilla's tongue was practically hanging out.

"Patricia's been to a fatty farm," Randy Simms's voice rang out.

"Mom!" Patricia screamed in horror, only to fly off the stairs, grab her towel and storm into the house. Mrs. Simms shrugged her shoulders in apology then took off after her.

Bucky swam beside me. "Maybe you better see if she's alright."

I sighed. Normally, this would have been Melinda's duty. Handing Bart over to Bucky, I got out of the pool. After wrapping a towel around my little-girl body, I went in to see if there was anything I could do.

Patricia sat at the kitchen table, crying. Not having much luck consoling her, Mrs. Simms waved me over. "I'll just go outside and see if your father needs anything," she said giving Patricia a peck on the forehead.

Not sure how to cheer her up, I jumped in with the small talk.

"How was camp?"

"You mean the fatty farm?"

"There really is such a thing?"

Patricia could tell I was honestly unaware. "Sure, Camp Stanley."

Patricia had found out about Camp Stanley from an advertisement in the back of her *Heart Throbs* comic book. She showed it to her mom who showed it to Doc who had been concerned with his daughter's weight gain and lack of self-control. Her sudden display of self-initiative set Doc in motion. After placing the necessary calls and being satisfied with the program's reputation and results, he signed her up.

"I guess it wasn't so bad, although you wouldn't have liked it," she told me. "And nobody would have liked you. I mean, you being so skinny and all."

"Hmm." I didn't know if I should be insulted.

"There was horseback riding, badminton, fencing," she continued. "I even got pretty good at basketball. Bet you never thought that would happen."

"Hmm." When it came to shooting hoops, Patricia was one of the few neighborhood kids I could beat.

"It was kind of nice not being the heaviest girl for once." Patricia diverted her eyes to the soon-to-be-devoured chocolate birthday cakes on the counter. "They kept us really busy so we wouldn't have time to think about, you know, food."

"Did they starve you?" I asked.

"Oh, no. We got to eat pretty much everything that I eat at home. Just a lot less of it. I've got more clothes to give away now, if you want them. Nothing fits anymore."

"Hmm."

Rebecca Frick teetered in with an umbrella drink in one hand and a bottle of rum in the other. "Mind if I join you?" she asked as she set them both on the table. "I'm quite sure your conversation is more interesting than that political gabfest out there."

Rebecca flicked aside the skirt of her full-length Nehru cover-up (that didn't) to straddle the chair beside me, leaving her bikini's strategically placed flower petals exposed. A cigarette dangled from her lip as she emptied the remainder of the rum into her drink while giving Patricia the once-over.

"You seem to have grown up this summer."

Rebecca had always scared the hell out of Patricia. Panic-stricken, she opened her mouth but nothing came out.

"Well, that happens," Rebecca continued. "Sometimes a little too fast." She removed the umbrella from her glass and took a drink, but not before offering Patricia and me a sip we both declined. "I was about your age when I blossomed. If I only knew then the things I know now." Rebecca handed me the umbrella then indicated for us to move in closer, as if she had something very important to say.

"You are going to have all sorts of rascals sniffing around. Go ahead. Let them have a little *whiff*. But just a little. Oh, they'll want to get their noses right up there and take in all the fresh young sweetness you have to give. But then they'll leave you stinky, and believe you me, it takes a long time to wash that stinky off. Yes, ma'am."

"Yes, ma'am," we echoed.

"No, ma'am," she protested. "You just wait until you can fully appreciate the aroma of love." Satisfied with herself, Rebecca downed the rest of her drink then left us to contemplate our fate and the odors we unknowingly might be emitting.

Shortly after, Mrs. Majors entered the kitchen and announced that it was time for cake. "Girls, will you help me put on the candles?" As we arranged the various candles representing the ages of the birthday boys, the doorbell rang.

"That should be Colonel Thomas and everybody."

"The Colonel's home?" I asked.

"He came in last night. I'm surprised Melinda didn't tell you. Be a doll, would you, and get the door?"

Anxious to fill Melinda in on Camp Stanley and the "aroma of love," I hurried to the front door, but the everybody on the other side was not the everybody I'd expected. There stood the Colonel, stalwart as ever in his starched white shirt and high-waisted khaki pants, but to his right was someone I had never seen before. Someone as button-downed as the Colonel, but more vibrant. She looked like Annette Funicello with a widow's peak. They were holding hands!

"Good afternoon, Margaret," the Colonel said, as Melinda lingered behind him.

Used to feeling intimidated by him, I managed to squeak out a hello just as a chorus of "Happy Birthday" sprung from the backyard.

"I take it we're not too late?" the Colonel said, indicating I should probably shut my gaping mouth and let them in. As I moved aside, he gave the woman his arm and she gave me a warm smile.

Melinda kept her head down.

"What a lovely home," commented the woman as we made our way through the Majorses' front room, into the kitchen and out the back door.

"Thank you," I answered, not knowing why.

When we arrived at the patio, Big Buck stopped dishing ice cream and greeted the Colonel with a handshake. "Hey, Walt, good to have you back."

Heads nodded, acknowledging the Colonel, but all eyes were fixed on the petite dark-haired woman.

"Friends, ladies," he announced, "I would like to introduce you to my wife, Pamela."

The place was abuzz with back-slapping congratulations for the groom and ring-gawking compliments for the bride. Then conversations split, with the women whisking Pamela into their fold to find out the particulars of how the two had met and the men hovering around the Colonel to get his take.

Melinda watched the brouhaha from the sidelines. She looked shell shocked. Empty. Having similar ideas about intervention, Bucky and I brought her chocolate cake and ice cream. She wanted neither.

"Nice pool," she remarked with uncharacteristic sarcasm.

"Yeah. Surprise, surprise," Bucky said in Gomer Pile fashion.

"Is she supposed to be your surprise?" I asked.

"That's my surprise."

"She seems pretty nice," Bucky said.

Poor guy. He really was trying. But Melinda went bonkers.

"Nice? He came home with her last night. He didn't even tell me he was seeing someone. He didn't even ask me what I thought. He just did it. He just married her. And I'm supposed to like her? Just like that? I don't get a choice?"

She paused as if we might have an answer. We didn't.

"You know how he introduced her? 'Melinda, I would like you to meet your new mother.' My new mother? What about the old mother? What about Mrs. Mavrakis? What about me? Yeah, she seems pretty nice . . . and they can both go to hell."

Suddenly, adult poolside conversation rose fifty decibels as all hell broke loose.

"Where do you get off, thinking you're so smart?"

After flinging his chair aside, Big Buck's Brylcreem-haired chief auto mechanic, Roy McClure, was jutting his chest at my equally pissed-off brother. "Ease up, Roy," Big Buck said as he physically separated the two. "Brian was just making a joke."

"Well I don't think he's so funny," Roy snarled. "I think him and his hippie-dippie friends are a bunch of communists. Showing off their curls. Spitting on the flag."

"Ah, settle down, Roy," chided another of Big Buck's employees. "He's not bothering anybody."

"He's bothering me just by looking at him. Give me some clippers, Buck, and I'll make a man out of him."

My brother took a step toward Roy, but Big Buck's open-palm gesture held him at bay until my father could intervene.

"Back off, Roy. Brian, it's time we left."

Brian didn't budge. "Why, Dad? He's just an ignorant bastard proving my point."

"You worthless piece of shit!" shouted Roy, standing his ground.

"That's enough!" scolded Mrs. Majors from a safe distance, then added with a voice that meant business, "Buck, there are children here."

Big Buck tried to ease the tension. "Let's calm down, boys." Apologetically, he turned to my brother. "Brian, you know we were just ribbing you."

"Yeah, right. That's what it all boils down to, isn't it, Mr. Majors?" Not placated, Brian turned back to the mechanic. "So, you want to sheer me? Why not? I'm one of the flock now. Just a stupid-ass sheep doing what it's told. Standing at attention but paying no attention. Go ahead. Better yet I'll do it."

From beneath his windbreaker, Brian whipped out the bowie knife from the sheath attached to his belt. There was an audible gasp from everyone present.

Roy snickered nervously. "Hey, Buck, I do believe he's gonna scalp himself. I'll take a piece of that."

"Shut up, Roy." Big Buck grabbed Roy's shoulders and shoved him in a chair. "Nobody's taking a piece of anything." Then he turned to my brother. "Put the knife down, son."

"Brian," coaxed my mother, now beside my father in the center of the commotion. "Let's go home."

Brian ignored all but the mechanic. "You want it? Come on, big guy. And take my balls while you're at it. Take my legs, too. You might as well. They're going to be blown off pretty soon anyway."

Roy snarled, "Does anyone know what the hell he's yammering about?"

"Brian?" my father asked. "What's going on here?"

Brian snapped to attention. "Sir, reporting for duty, sir!" He saluted Dad, Big Buck, and the Colonel, his knife coming dangerously close to his forehead, before putting his hand down and addressing the rest of the partygoers. "That make you all happy? Another young man, trotting off to save the American Way for all you sons-of-bitches complaining about those 'worthless redskins' and 'lazy niggers' while they're getting their asses shot off just so you have the right to call them worthless and lazy. Well, eat me. And while you're at it, eat this."

The knife found its mark, and a perfectly severed ponytail bounced off Roy's greasy head and landed in the pool. As my brother Brian took off for parts unknown, the ensuing silence of his exit was broken when Roy opened his big mouth and spewed, "Goddamn hippie." The next sound was that of my father's fist hitting Roy's jaw.

I don't remember much of what happened next. I imagine Big Buck tried to smooth things over with good-natured joking and Mrs. Majors tried to reroute everyone's attention with more cake and ice cream. Someone must have picked up Roy, and someone must have run after my brokenhearted mother as she ran after her newly drafted and out-of-control son.

I do know at some point Bucky and Melinda walked me home, each tightly holding one of my hands. The arm around my shoulder was Bucky's, supporting me as he knocked on the door and my tearful mother answered, clearly hopeful her other child had returned. I had hoped both friends would stay until I could make sense of what had happened, but Melinda's spirit was still reeling from her father's surprise, and Bucky had to make a choice. What I didn't know was how binding that choice would be. With his arm now around *her* shoulder, they said good-bye and walked away.

For most of the neighbors, things went back to normal. But for me, something had shifted. Life outside my town had been only as real as television programs or photos from *National Geographic* magazine, and politics didn't go beyond who was making or breaking my parents' rules. I didn't know what a communist was. I didn't know where Vietnam was, figuring it and China and Japan were pretty much the same. I lived around the Indians of Northern Wyoming, yet not among them, assuming their point of view, values, and goals were no different than any other tribe in any other state. I had known all of three Negros in my life.

Something was happening, and not just in big cities but in towns like mine—towns not so small that you knew everybody's business, but not so big that you didn't know someone who did. Students were protesting. Bras were burning. The American Indian Movement was taking root, and Negros had had enough. It was an uncomfortable shift for the status quo. An uncertain ache not unlike growing pains.

At the precipice of adolescence, my friends and I were succumbing to changes from within and without, our childhood skipping away. We would never again be those first-grade babies, or second-grade tots, third-grade angels or fourth-grade snots. No longer the unripened peaches and pears of fifth and sixth grade. We would now be part of the big fat bears of society and, like it or not, kids no more.

On that September day of 1968, the slow, smoldering fuse of my social conscience was lit. Before going to bed that night, I turned on the record player and listened to Joan Baez.

THE WEDDING

She has timed the wedding just right, with the blooming of the lilacs. Teeming sprigs of four-petal flower-bursts grace each table, their delicate whiff holding the promise of something down the road. The celebration is in full swing.

Big Buck had sprung for the band. They are a mediocre yet versatile bunch who make up for their lack of musicianship with a varied repertoire, satisfying both the fogeys and the youngsters.

Hoots and howls are coming from the Elks Club dance floor where Mrs. Simms has twisted all 280 pounds of herself down, but not up. It takes Dad and Big Buck a couple of tries before they get her on her feet, but she makes it without skipping a beat. As big as she is, she's still one of the best when it comes to dancing partners. According to my dad, she could follow a hammered mule skinner with two left feet and still make him look good, and Dad knows his steps. It's nice to see him so lively again.

I am sitting at the head table, giving my feet a rest, when Bucky sneaks up behind me.

"Looks like your dad's having fun. Why aren't you out there?"

"I can't," I tell him, pointing to my feet. "Blisters. It's these damn shoes Melinda made me wear. Where is she anyway?"

"Taking a break from the spotlight," he says, then with the disapproving yet resigned look I've seen so many times before adds, "and probably getting a smoke."

•　　•　　•　　•　　•

"Where the hell did you get that?" Bucky whispered as we huddled in our latest secret hideout, a brush-hidden ditch just behind the Thomases' property on the other side of Sand Hill. Melinda ignored him and handed "that" to me, its loosely rolled—and very illegal—contents struggling to stay lit.

"Here," she said. "Take it and don't let it go out."

Not exactly sure what to do with it, I put it to my lips and took a tiny puff. It went out. "Sorry."

Melinda exhaled then took the unlit joint away. "Next time, Maggie, don't get it so wet."

"I didn't realize there'd be so many rules."

"Do you feel funny?" Bucky wanted to know. Unsure what I was supposed to feel, I looked to Melinda for guidance.

"Oh she probably won't get high the first time," Melinda said. "If you do, you'll feel a nice buzz, then suddenly everything becomes hilarious." Melinda went over her instructions again. "It's not like a cigarette. You don't just inhale then exhale."

Bucky and I looked at each other. We'd both flunked smoking a couple years back when Joe-Joe Padilla brought a pack of Winstons to our yet-to-be-torn-down clubhouse. It had been a rude introduction. Joe-Joe had the swagger of Dean Martin, and even though Melinda looked out of character holding a cigarette, she did a surprisingly decent job smoking it. Bucky and I sucked. My first tentative puff was executed well—head tilted back in contemplation, cigarette positioned in the vee of my index and middle finger—however after the second puff my lip captured the filter and the vee slid to the cigarette's smoldering tip, giving me a very nasty burn in a very tender spot. Bucky's one and only puff sent him on a coughing jag that lasted ten minutes and cemented a lifetime aversion to smoking.

"When you take a hit, hold it in as long as you can, like this." Melinda demonstrated then offered the relit joint to Bucky. He just shook his head and gave her that look. She shrugged and passed it to me.

•　　•　　•　　•　　•

"Are you going to join her?" Bucky asks, eyebrows raised.

"No, not my brand of poison anymore. But I wouldn't mind a beer." There's the unmistakable pop of a champagne bottle being opened at the bar. *"Or some of that. How are you holding up?"*

"Other than the monkey suit, I'm doing great."

"That was one fancy monkey. Anyone I know?"

Bucky grins as the band ends its Chubby Checker twist and slides into something slower. "You want to give it a go?" he asks.

I feel an anticipatory chill. "I'm not very good with the slow stuff. I might step on your feet."

"That's okay," Bucky says. "I know how we can fix that."

$$\bullet \quad \bullet \quad \bullet \quad \bullet \quad \bullet$$

"Put your arms around my neck and your feet on top of mine. If you're gonna step on them, you might as well go all out."

I was scared and embarrassed. I didn't know how to slow dance, only having tried it once at the seventh-grade sock hop with Gary Moss, a new kid from Wisconsin who had a crush on me. That had been a total disaster. I couldn't figure out where he wanted me to go and he couldn't move me without meeting resistance. Even the customary slow and circular slide-shuffle didn't work because neither of us knew where to put our feet, mine between his or one of his between mine. And where to put his sweaty and my cold hands? Hips? Shoulders? Did one go up and one go down? By the time we finally found a workable position, the song was over, which made us both happy.

I had sworn off slow dancing, but this was Bucky, and we were at his house party with the lights low and minimal parental supervision. At the request of Mrs. Majors, my time had been spent making sure her wide-eyed younger boys stayed away from the forbidden but inevitable make-out corners. Now I had the chance to dance. With Bucky.

"Come on, Maggie. It's real easy."

Had we ever been this close? Although we were both fourteen, Bucky was six inches taller than me. Doing as he asked, I put my arms around his neck and stepped aboard.

"Ouch," he teased.

"I'm sorry." I quickly got off.

Bucky laughed. "Honest, Mags, I was just kidding. Really, I can barely feel you're there."

Carefully, I once again placed my stocking feet on top of his sneakers.

"Look up here," he said. "It's easier when you don't watch your feet. Look at me."

I locked on to his sparkling eyes. So full of fun and mischief. So caring and kind. So maddening. He dipped and swayed with the rhythm, taking me right along. Never looking away. Never losing his smile.

"See, you're getting it."

I closed my eyes and laid my cheek on his chest, hearing his shallow breath, his beating heart. Melting into his body. He rested his chin atop my head, releasing a satisfied sigh. In that moment, I allowed myself to believe he was completely with me rather than worried about her.

．　．　．　．　．

Before I can turn down his offer to dance, Melinda returns from her bridal recess and blows Bucky a kiss from across the room. He is all smiles.

"There's my girl."

"With perfect timing, as always," I add, hiding yet another disappointment.

"Pretty near perfect, Maggie. It doesn't get any better than this."

"I'm guessing it doesn't."

"Yep. I'm one lucky son-of-a-gun."

．　．　．　．　．

"Hey, you lucky son-of-a-gun. When did the new wheels show up?" Pete Temple hollered from his beat-up Opal while waiting his turn to circle the A&W drive-in.

We were heading in the opposite direction, cruising in the latest Big Buck acquisition, a 1973 blue Datsun 240Z. Bucky revved the motor to the envy and delight of all the other driving-obsessed teenagers dragging Main Street and holding up traffic in their search for action.

"Ah, it's just a loaner!" Bucky yelled back, ignoring the honk from Steve Kenny who was behind us in a pickup truck hauling an empty horse trailer.

"Now that's a car you have to drive!" Pete said. "Hey, Mag-neato. Is that you in there? How'd you rate?"

Pete had the hots for me yet professed his feelings via merciless teasing like a six-year-old. I usually tried to avoid him, but now we needed his help given his goal in life seemed to be to know who was coming and who was going. I hoisted my upper body out the window and yelled over the hood. "Hey, Pete, have you seen Melinda?"

"How much is it worth to you, jock bait?"

"Come off it, Pete. Give."

"Saw her a couple times doing the loop, about an hour ago, I guess. She was with Dan Mazzone on his bike."

Not good, I thought as I slid back in my seat. Steve was getting impatient and again laid on his horn, so Bucky put the Z in first and we continued down Main Street.

"Want to circle Pogo's?" I asked, referring to another drive-in on the other side of town and my current place of employment. "I can score a free burger."

Bucky drummed a frustrated cadence on the steering wheel before answering. "No, let's just go home."

Damn. I played second fiddle to Melinda even when she wasn't around.

Our joyride was over. Bucky turned off Main, I turned up the radio, and we headed home.

PART TWO
Senior Year of High School 1973-1974

CHAPTER 8

By 1973, our No Name No Purpose clubhouse was long gone. Neglected then abandoned, its bedraggled contents had been pillaged and its rickety walls torn down and carted away. Other than that and some signage, not much had physically changed in the neighborhood.

The county had posted "Dangerous Intersection" near the bend where Old Orphanage Road met the back road to town, putting a damper on *whee*-bump thrill-seekers who took advantage of its long stretch of up and downs. And a set of four-way stops just off Old Orphanage and Bundy Lane showed up after Doc Simms plowed into Mrs. Majors (or, as Doc claimed, the other way around.) Mr. Bales pulled a few strings and the county placed "Ped Xing" signs within one hundred yards from the Barn, both directions, their effectiveness augmented by his handmade placard "Slow Down, Idiot." His wife was in the habit of sweeping the street and had her share of near misses.

Mrs. Bales took up her broom just after "the Accident." She started out with the walkway in front of the Barn, but as time progressed she moved into the street, eventually sweeping it from one end to the other. She liked to sing while she swept. Some of her songs were gibberish. Some were about the dog that had shown up on the Barn's doorstep one winter, half frozen and half starved. It was a mixed-breed mess, mismatched from front end to back end with squatty legs and big paws. Mrs. Bales took an immediate liking to him. She called him her "Little Stew Pot," or Stewie for short.

Stewie—a.k.a. "that damn Bales mutt"—thrived on trouble. He particularly liked to knock over Doc Simms's trash cans and take a dump in Doc Simms's front yard. His favorite urinal was Mrs. Padilla's concrete donkey statue with the flower baskets. His favorite digging spot was Mrs. Mavrakis's begonia bed. His favorite pastimes were chasing anything Big Buck happened to be driving, and barking at anything my father happened to be doing. But his number one preoccupation was propagation. There wasn't a neighbor within five miles that didn't curse "that damn Bales mutt" when their female dog came into heat. Stewie's reputation as a successful suitor could be attested by his many offspring, even after the Accident.

It's hard to tell whether the Accident caused Mrs. Bales to be confused or the confusion caused the Accident. It happened just before dawn. She heard a noise outside and called out to Mr. Bales, wanting him to check on the commotion, but he didn't answer. The water was running in the bathroom, so she figured he was taking a morning shower.

After hearing another rumble, Mrs. Bales was certain the sound came from the woodpile. The skunks must be back. She grabbed the loaded rifle that stood by the back door and went out to investigate. To her surprise a man was standing there with something in his hand pointed in her direction. Without thinking she raised her rifle and fired. The man fell backward into the woodpile, causing its contents to roll every which way.

Fortunately for Mr. Bales, his wife, a six-time champion at the shooting club, had only fired a warning shot over his head, otherwise he would have been dirt dead. He had been gathering wood for the fire, the one she had asked him to make. *She did?* He had pointed a finger, not a gun. *Really?* No, he hadn't been in the shower. He had turned on the shower for her, just like she had asked him to. *Funny. She didn't remember doing so.*

Little things. Little confusions.

Stewie, who had accompanied Mr. Bales to the woodpile in pursuit of visiting skunks, was not so fortunate, his right front leg having been crushed between two heavy logs. Mr. Bales put in a phone call to Doc Simms. Although Doc could be a stickler about not extending his services to animals, he never turned his back on a critter in pain. When there was nothing Doc could do to save the dog's leg, off it came.

For a brief period, "that damn Bales mutt" became "poor thing." Only "poor thing" didn't realize his physical handicap was supposed to slow him down. He kept carousing and getting into trouble, so we went back to calling him by his more deserved title.

While her dog had survived the Accident, the strain had been too much for Mrs. Bales and she'd taken to her broom "to clean the cobwebs out of my head." Five years later she was still sweeping.

Sure enough, as Bucky and I cleared the hill leading up to the Barn, there she was, Elizabeth Bales, all eighty-nine years and ninety-five pounds, with broom in hand and dog by her side. She had managed to sweep a considerable distance, almost to the frog pond. Wearing a Budweiser cap, mismatched gloves, Red Wing Boots, and nothing but a slip, the grand lady was oblivious to the October evening chill. Bucky stopped the car by the side of the road and we got out.

"Light she was and like a fairy, and her shoes were number nine. Herring boxes without topes, sandals were for Clementine," she sang.

"Evening, Mrs. Bales," Bucky said as he approached. "It's getting kind of late for cleaning up."

She stopped the broom and song. "Who are you?"

"It's Maggie Moore, Mrs. Bales," I answered, having been over this before. "And Bucky? Bucky Majors?" There was no hint of recognition in her eyes. "Remember, we live down the road. My father painted your house?"

Finally, something got through and she smiled. "Oh yes. Tell him I have a job. The kitchen faucet needs fixing. Have you seen Stewie?"

Stewie whimpered then barked. Mrs. Bales was getting more and more forgetful, but this was a first.

"He's right here, Mrs. Bales."

She looked at the dog then dismissed the notion. "That's not my Little Stew Pot."

"But it is, Mrs. Bales," Bucky explained. "He got into some burrs and you had to shave him. Remember?"

"Stewie, is that you?"

Little Stew Pot barked again and licked her glove.

"It's getting late, Mrs. Bales. Why don't you let us take you home?" Bucky offered his arm for support, but she gave him and our mode of transportation a dubious glance.

"You expect me to get into that hot rod?"

Fortunately, we didn't have to argue because Mr. Bales, still driving at the age of ninety, had arrived in his Chevy Bel Air.

"I'll take it from here, kids," he said as he got out. "Now Lizzie, how many times have I told you that you can't go out without your coat? It's not good for you."

"Have you seen Stewie?" she asked again.

"Let's go on home. Stewie will be waiting for you there." He gave us a nod before putting his coat over Mrs. Bales's shoulders then gently leading her to the Chevy. Stew Pot trotted behind.

Bucky shook his head as they drove off. I knew what he was thinking. It wouldn't be long before both of them ended up in the old folks' home.

Bucky was quiet on the short drive to my house. He had a lot on his mind. We both did. With homecoming week upon us, preparations needed to be made. And then there was Melinda.

"Do you suppose she's going to the dance with Danny Mazzone?" he asked as we pulled into my driveway.

"Maybe you should've asked her first."

"Right," he snorted. "Has she ever gone to a dance with me?"

"True." I tried to soften the blow. "There's always senior prom."

Bucky didn't say anything but his finger-drumming told me our conversation wasn't over.

"I don't get it!" he shouted with a simultaneous whack on the dashboard. The plaster cast covering his forearm made a loud *thunk*. "What does she see in him?"

"You mean other than the fact that he's Mr. Hotshot Quarterback?"

This didn't sit too well with Bucky. He'd broken his arm in the first quarter of the first football game of the season, and Melinda's attraction to Danny only made things worse. Actually, I didn't understand what had gotten into her either. She didn't usually go for jocks; her boyfriends were more the dark, brooding type, and always older.

Bucky whacked the dashboard again. His wince turned to a resigned sigh, and he changed the subject. "I heard Gary Moss was going to ask you."

"He did."

"Well."

"I told him I was going with somebody else."

"Oh yeah? Who's that?"

"You."

Bucky laughed so I hit him in the shoulder.

"Sorry, Mags."

I hit him again and got out of the car. As I walked away, he rolled down the window.

"I don't have to buy you a corsage or anything, do I?" he asked.

"God forbid!" I shouted over my shoulder.

"Good. Then you can go with me and Joe-Joe. Oh, and find out what gives with Melinda, will ya?"

"I always do."

After watching Bucky leave my driveway and pull into his own, I took a seat on my front porch. I had homework, and Dad was in the house fixing dinner—probably pork chops and macaroni given it was Wednesday—but I didn't want to go in yet.

The low light of the setting sun illuminated the golden cottonwoods lining the banks of the Little Goose and cast a burnt umber shadow on the prairie grasses in the distant foothills. Fence lines and telephone wires were beginning to fade into the ensuing darkness, as were the haystacks and uneven boxes of honeybee hives in the field beyond our row of houses. The still-visible stacks of the defunct sugar mill flashed red, announcing its presence to the occasional airplane that found its way into our night sky. Somewhere a dog was barking. And somewhere Melinda was on a motorcycle with Danny Mazzone, heading for trouble.

CHAPTER 9

In the spring of 1969 my Dad took a fall while repainting the dormers of the historic Fetterman Inn. Its high-pitched roof made for a tricky job, so Dad had rigged up a harness system much like a rock climber's, tying his safety rope to relocate from one anchor to another. Unfortunately, he disturbed a hornet's nest on the underside of the dining hall's chimney and in his enthusiasm to swat off the "seething bastards" lost his footing and took a three-story tumble. The Inn's sloped eave disrupted most of his fall, but he landed a hard six feet below it on the concrete sidewalk. The result was three cracked ribs and two broken kneecaps.

That pretty much put an end to my father's painting career. He suffered through the pain, taking jobs whenever he could, but the frequent bending and kneeling was more than he could handle. His monthly earnings fell to almost nothing. To make up for lost income, Mom left her part-time job at Fryer's Department Store for a full-time position at the Sew-N-Save. I covered my extraneous spending by babysitting and working in the school cafeteria. Eventually, I became a waitress.

Always a gadget man, Dad let his "o-matic" obsession grow once Mom became the chief breadwinner. If it sliced and diced, he bought it. Most of his time-saving devices were time-consuming when it came to cleanup, a chore he left to Mom and me.

Dad detested doing dishes. Maybe that was why he was so smitten by the Majorses' automatic dishwasher. We really didn't need one for just the three of us, but he insisted our lives would be improved by the used GE Mobile Maid he bought for a mere ten dollars. After Dad replaced its missing top rack with refashioned wire hangers, it was good to go.

Mom hated that thing. It ran louder than a dairy pump, and leaks perpetually sprang from its finicky faucet hose and underbelly. Given it used twice as much water as handwashing and took twice as much time, she couldn't figure out why Dad was so adamant we keep it, but we did.

Generally a go-with-the-flow kind of gal, Mom was definitely uptight when it came to loading the dishwasher. Things had to be lined up just right to maximize space. She could position fifteen dishes to my haphazard five. And Mom rinsed every dish before putting it into the machine. This baffled my father.

"You know you don't have to do that," he'd tell her. "That's why they call it a dishwasher."

"More like a garbage can," she'd argue. "There's nothing worse than opening up this smelly thing with festering leftovers."

"The machine takes care of the leftovers."

"The heck it does," Mom would say. "It just splashes everything around then bakes it on."

"Well, if you gave the dishes some space for the water to work instead of packing them in tighter than a hair in a biscuit you might get a different result."

"I might also get the urge to throw this blasted thing out the window and you right along with it."

Round and round they'd go. I learned to stay clear of the clamor, but when caught in the middle I also learned it was best to do things Mom's way.

Twice a month, on payday, Mom went grocery shopping. Dad liked to go with her, only he seldom put anything in the basket that we could turn into a meal. He was more into purchasing extras; fancy sauces and such. We often had more condiments in our refrigerator than actual food.

Always on the lookout for a sale—buy one, get one free—and a sucker for a gimmick, particularly towels in detergent boxes, Dad considered himself a bargain hunter, which is why no one should have been surprised by his next livelihood.

Well into the second year of his unemployment and domestic service, my father got a curious phone call from Dick Masterson, the same fishing buddy who had sold Dad the infamous pink aluminum house siding. Dick had since become a go-between for local ranchers and out-of-state sportsmen. When he claimed to have an "exciting opportunity," Dad pressed him for details, but Dick insisted they discuss the matter face-to-face in the lodge room of the Elks Club at seven p.m. sharp.

My father spent the rest of the day thinking up all kinds of scenarios, finally concluding that Dick wanted to hire him as a fishing guide. That wasn't the case. Dick wanted Dad—along with six other men who had also been offered the same "exciting opportunity"—to sell Happy Solutions.

It wasn't that Dad didn't like the company's products. He had bought a box of soap from a Happy Solutions door-to-door salesman and it had done a decent job despite being overpriced and lacking a free towel. And it wasn't that Dad didn't respect door-to-door salesmen. It was the conniving way Dick set about roping him in that Dad couldn't abide. "More back-door than door-to-door." He walked out precisely at seven twenty, not even bothering to finish his beer or sample the Elks' free Swedish meatballs.

Disappointed by the meeting's outcome, Dad sat in his pickup and considered what he had thought the opportunity was to begin with: the fishing guide thing. Perhaps he could make a go of it on his own? Who else knew where to find the most generous spots on both private and public land, not to mention whose palms to grease while traipsing there? Plus, he had the temperament necessary to put up with the Texan bigshots and the whiny dudes from back east. In the end, Dad decided fishing was his pleasure and he didn't want it to become his job. He'd have to figure out another way to pay the mortgage and feed his family.

One Saturday morning during breakfast, Mom decided it was time to do something about my father's being out of work. She drew a center line down a piece of paper then handed it to him with the pen, instructing him to make a list of his strengths and weaknesses. Starting with the plus side, he wrote as she dictated: "hard working," "loyal," and "trustworthy." I contributed "curious" and "good at reading people." Dad added those to the list along with "knows a bargain." Mom and I weren't sure if he put that tidbit in the proper column.

Dad's minuses included: "doesn't like to take orders," "doesn't like to listen to advice," "has a problem with authority," "can't stand being cooped up," "intolerant of stupidity," and "has a tendency towards sarcasm." Mom was getting a carried away, so I led us back to plusses: "has a good sense of humor."

"Have you thought about going back to school?" I asked my father.

"Not sure where it would get me," he answered before crumpling the list. "Not sure if this old dog can learn a new trick."

Dad was down, and our well-intended meddling only made things worse. Even a face-lick from Oscar Doggie, our miniature dachshund, couldn't cheer him up. Oscar was supposed to be my mother's dog, a birthday present from my father when my brother went missing, but Mom wasn't keen on having Brian replaced, so Dad and doggie bonded, sticking together like Velcro.

Wanting to get out of the house, Dad took the pooch for a drive then happened upon a flea market worth checking out on the north side of town. With Oscar Doggie on his leash, Dad meandered through rows of odds and ends and castoffs, marveling at the stuff people were willing to part with and the prices people were willing to pay. At one table, he found a rusty Singer Sewing Machine sign bruised by a couple of bullet holes, its red "S" still vivid. Pictured on the sign was a seamstress in a yellow dress who reminded Dad of my grandmother. He offered two dollars and bought it for three.

On his way back to his pickup, a woman stopped to ask where he got the sign. She went on and on about how it was exactly what she'd been looking for and she just had to have it. Dad was about to give her the damn sign just to shut her up when she offered him ten dollars, more than triple what he'd paid. He considered selling it for that price as punishment for her chattiness, but decided it wouldn't be fair.

Instead he settled on three dollars above cost plus a buck for the inconvenience of carrying it to her car.

When Dad came home, he had a four-dollar profit in his pocket and the beginnings of a new career.

The junk business was slow at first. Inventory was low and Dad had a hard time parting with what little stuff he had accumulated, but he eventually got the hang of it. Accompanied by Oscar Doggie and his trusty pickup, a metal detector, and an occasional extra pair of willing hands, Dad became a twentieth-century treasure hunter.

A lot of his finds came from back-road trash heaps or abandoned shacks scattered throughout BLM land and the national forests. Oscar Doggie's digging helped him root out the loot. Sometimes Oscar came in handy just by being cute. Dad did a fair amount of door knocking, and a man with a tail-wagging dog opened a few doors. Most folk were happy to let him cart away their unwanted, unsightly clutter. Some he kept, some he took to the dump. My father's junk hunts led him to all kinds of Western paraphernalia—railroad ties, barbed wire, tin cans, cow skulls—and when "cowboy rustic" became the hot ticket, he had a hard time keeping up with demand.

Not having a storefront, my father often sold his goods right out of the truck. He and Oscar were permanent fixtures at the weekly flea market, as well as various community festivals. Dad also traded with the Crow Indians on their reservation. That's where he rescued his first outhouse.

Cast aside in favor of indoor plumbing, this one-holer was lined with pin-up cards and posters, some dating back to the turn of the century. He figured someone would see its usefulness. "Good riddance" was the only comment of its previous owner, who not only accepted Dad's offer of cash but helped him pluck it from its roots and load it into the pickup.

His second outhouse came from the Beecher estate off Bundy Road. The old farmhouse was being razed for a new grocery store and Dad stopped by to see what he could salvage. His booty included a claw-foot tub and another privy, which meant Dad now owned a pair of outhouses. Once you have two of something, the third is not far behind. And once you have three of something, you have a collection.

At last count, we had fifteen outhouses scattered behind our garage and along the sides of our house.

Needless to say, Doc Simms wasn't too happy about the accumulating junk in my family's environs, particularly "those damn Moore crappers," but lately Doc had more pressing worries. His daughter, Patricia, nineteen and hot to trot, was in love, again, with the eldest Padilla boy, again, only this time she meant business. Patricia had gone to the University of Wyoming in Laramie her freshman year but downright refused to go back after Ricky returned home with an honorable discharge from the United States Army. Now attending the local junior college to please her mom, she pleased herself by attending to matters of the heart. Doc was not pleased at all.

As if his daughter's foolhardy romance wasn't enough to prey on Doc's mind, his son, Randy, was spending more and more time with the Padilla girls, not because he fancied them but because he fancied their toys and clothes. It didn't help matters that Mrs. Simms was now selling Avon and had an endless supply of makeup samples with which her son could experiment.

Then, there was the campaign, which in Doc's eyes turned out to be an eyesore.

Mr. Padilla was running for a spot on the Board of County Commissioners on the platform that the town needed to be more accessible to outsiders. Of course the neighbors supported Candidate Padilla. "Vote Padilla for Progress" signage sprouted from our fields and our lawns. Even the Colonel allowed a few on his property, although he was not home to see them, nor would he be home in time to vote. Melinda's father was off again with his wife, Pamela, this time to Nova Scotia.

Colonel Walter Esmond Thomas had retired from the United States Army the same year he married Pamela Mae Derian. Neither newly acquired status did anything to curtail his travels. Soon after making the necessary introduction to his daughter, the Colonel took "the trollop," as Melinda called her, on an extended honeymoon. Melinda would see neither of them again for six months, although she did receive weekly updates from "the she-devil," another of Melinda's favorite stepmother monikers, via "fastidious" postcards.

As the new lady of the house, Pamela Thomas had the good judgement not to try to take over Mrs. Mavrakis's duties. She did try to reach out to Melinda, but was not successful by any standard.

I didn't have a problem with the new Mrs. Thomas. She was kind and thoughtful and did her best to fit in without being pushy or presumptuous. The neighborhood moms liked Pamela Thomas as well. She routinely placed Avon orders with Martha Simms; she hosted a surprise baby shower for Mary Anne Majors after her fifth child and only daughter, Julie, was born; she attended at least two of my mother's Tupperware parties; and she participated in lighthearted gossip, told stories on herself and even supplied a few missing details concerning the Colonel's life.

"Wally," as Mrs. Thomas referred to him, had been abandoned shortly after being born, then orphaned at an early age when his adoptive parents died in the 1918 flu epidemic. He spent the remainder of his youth at the Masonic Home for Children in Oxford, North Carolina, where his proclivity for metalworking and electronics eventually lead him to the Signal Corp of the United States Army at Fort Monmouth, New Jersey. In 1938, he was instrumental in developing the U.S. Army's first radio-based aircraft detection and ranging system—or radar. Ten years later he met Evelyn Godfrey, Melinda's mother.

Evelyn was a free spirit from California whose dreams of becoming a freelance photographer landed her on the East Coast. Like the Colonel, she had no family and had been on her own since her mid-teens. They met at the dedication of the New York International Airport, where he, a stiff dignitary, and she, a bouncy documenter, collided on the tarmac. Six months later, after she succeeded in pulling the Colonel out of his stodgy shell, they were married, and nine months after that Melinda was born. Evelyn never did like East Coast high society and had been resolute in not raising Melinda to be a snob. A head-on car collision made certain she'd never get the chance.

After her death, the Colonel visited a friend in Wyoming and found it a good place to park his daughter and his troubled mind. He was sure the late Mrs. Thomas would approve.

In the five years that Pamela had been a part of the family, she did her best to connect her distant husband with his obstinate daughter. The new Mrs. Thomas walked the fine line between pushing and backing off, extending too much or too little affection. She remained hopeful that Melinda would come to accept her, or at least tolerate her. But Pamela's first duty was to the Colonel, who couldn't seem to stay put. She traveled with him everywhere, never leaving his side, and Melinda was always left behind.

Melinda grew more and more resentful of the woman who wanted to be her mother, and by the autumn of 1973, our senior year of high school, she had succeeded in turning that indignation on herself. Like my father's tumble off the Fetterman roof, Melinda's fall would knock me off course.

CHAPTER 10

"Jesus, Bucky! Take it easy!" I screamed from the back seat.

Bucky ignored my plea. Hell-bent on reaching the "B" at the top of the hill before it could be destroyed, he shifted into low and floored it for the run.

"Go, go, go, go, go!" coaxed Joe-Joe, who was sitting shotgun. The Blazer groaned as it crawled higher, sage and sand spinning from its wheels.

Located on the northeast side of town on a highly visible knoll in the middle of nowhere, the "B" announced to all that our one-high-school town was ruled by the Broncos. Its yearly restoration had become a homecoming tradition.

Mother Nature along with rivals from nearby towns routinely took their toll on the monogram, and its sprucing up took sizable annual effort given the road leading to the letter didn't amount to much. Many ill-suited cars got stuck in sand or high-centered along the way. Those who made it to the "B's" base often had to hike the one-hundred-foot ascent while hauling rocks and buckets of whitewash.

Because his broken arm took him out of the game, Bucky had been particularly zealous of this year's refurbishing, doing what he could to help the Riot Squad, our school's male equivalent of a pep club, by providing transportation to and from the site and convincing Big Buck's Cars and Trucks to provide refreshments—although someone else had seen to the acquisition of beer.

The "B's" annual facelift was one of the many traditions of homecoming, an entire week of spirit-filled activities that fueled the town's excitement for our football team. The maroon-and-gold Bronco banner spanned the entrance of Main Street and merchants painted their store windows with catchphrases of support like "Proud To Be a Bronco" and "We're Number One." Naturally, there was a homecoming parade featuring the Bronco marching band and drill team, class float competitions, and the Court of Honors, where the senior king and queen and their lower-class attendants all rode along in stylish convertibles.

Homecoming royalty was announced at the Come One Come All pep rally held on the eve of the parade in the stadium stands. The well-attended pep rally's finale was often more anticipated than the game itself. After the customary pomp and call to victory, a human chain of arm-linked chanters snaked its way off the field to the dirt parking lot for a bonfire of pagan proportions and the burning of our opponent's mascot.

Preparations for the bonfire fell to the sophomores, who began collecting fuel a full month before the big game, routinely ransacking grocery store dumpsters and picking through the city landfill's least disgusting trash. If it was made out of cardboard, it was a candidate for the bonfire. The bigger the box the better.

All these combustibles had to be secretly stockpiled somewhere, because the juniors' job was to seek out and steal the boxes, ensuring the bonfire in the making would not be so big as theirs had been the previous year. Thus, the box raids. Some eleventh-grader would catch word of the latest hiding place then call his classmates, and pickups would spring into action, transferring the stolen cargo to a new locale, usually some ditch. It was all in good fun, but nevertheless the raids elicited more than a few fistfights. The boxes would eventually be found and piled upon their pyric altar.

Some years' bonfires were better than others. My sophomore year's had been a particularly good one because the new Sears had just opened and folks were clamoring for discounted refrigerators and other big-boxed appliances. Lacking in school spirit, this year's sophomores barely managed to stack twenty feet. Their parade float also sucked.

In fact, this year's whole homecoming whoop-de-do sucked thanks to a light but cold rain that had made the bonfire more smoke than flame. The drizzle continued into the parade day, and while the chill didn't seem to affect the marching band, the drill team, of which I was a member, had to put up with over-exposed knees, soggy pompoms, and treacherous puddles. After a high-step slip, our co-captain, Twyla Harper, limped a full block before retreating to the curb in tears.

The class floats didn't fare much better. Constructed out of chicken wire and tissue paper, they were more in need of flushing than floating. The only good thing was that the convertibles' raised tops meant Michelle Fryer, head cheerleader and major pain-in-the-ass, didn't get to show off as queen.

The game was also a major disappointment. The only players catching Dan Mazzone's passes were on the other team. We lost 31 to 6. Then, despite me actually looking forward to the dance—I bought a dress and everything—Bucky informed me that we had to leave because he had heard through the grapevine that tonight there would be a raid on the "B." Bucky planned to stand guard and he wanted Joe-Joe as backup.

I'd be damned if I'd let him leave me behind to dodge Gary Moss, who had figured out that Bucky was more of an escort than a date, so I went with them. I would have asked Melinda to come with us, but she wasn't at the dance, nor had she been at the game. Melinda wasn't into football, thinking it imbecilic, but I'd figured she'd be there supporting Dickhead Dan.

"Give it all it's got, brother," hollered Joe-Joe as he lurched forward on the dash. "Jerk it! Jerk it!"

It was no use. The Blazer couldn't climb higher which meant we were going to have to back down. In the dark.

Bucky stuck his head out his window to get a better view of what was behind us. "Jesus, I can't see a thing," he said, then turned off the headlights and idled the Blazer until our eyes adjusted. With no moon to help, Joe-Joe grabbed a flashlight from the jockey box and got out to coach us through the descent. Praying we wouldn't roll over, I offered what guidance I could, as inch by inch Bucky backed down the wet hill to level ground. I had to hand it to him, Bucky could drive about anything in any direction.

"Close call." Joe-Joe jumped back in. "Try her one more time, huh?"

"Oh, that's a swift idea," I said, not wanting to go through the ordeal again.

"No way, man," said Bucky. "If I can't make it up, nobody can."

"Yeah. You're probably right," Joe-Joe agreed. "Doubt if anybody's coming out here tonight, anyhow."

"Ya think?"

Joe-Joe shrugged off my sarcasm. "Looks like the rain's outta here, huh? 'Cause there's that kegger happening up the Choke Cherry."

"You up to it, Mags? Or do you want to go back to the dance?" asked Bucky. No longer in the dancing mood, but not eager to go home, I agreed we should check out the kegger. Joe-Joe popped Elton John into the 8-track and we headed to Choke Cherry Canyon.

There were two popular nearby spots where kids our age gathered: one was along the shores of Lake Smitty and the other was up on the ridge of the sandstone bluffs that overlooked Choke Cherry Canyon. Both were favored make-out destinations, but Choke Cherry was the place to let loose. Easily accessible but tucked away, the canyon provided the illusion of authoritative absence and the freedom to party.

The kegger wasn't hard to find, as whoever had organized it had brought enough dry wood to get a fire going. A crowd of my fellow schoolmates, some who had already graduated, stood warming their backsides with beers in hand.

I didn't recognize the older guy working the keg. Bucky called him "McGregor" and gave him three bucks for three plastic cups, each of which McGregor skillfully filled with just the right proportion of beer to foam.

The three of us stood together by the fire sipping our beer and listening to various conversations percolate around its flames. Other than a few "we needed you on the field" comments directed at Bucky, there was surprisingly little mention of the game. The girls mostly talked about guys. The guys mostly talked about hunting. Both brought up past parties and compared notes on who drank what and puked where.

Missing from the fireside chat were the pot smokers, who preferred more secluded spots not because they worried about their illegal behavior, but because they didn't want to share. The unmistakable aroma of marijuana floating in from nearby tweaked Joe-Joe's nostrils.

"Hey, uh, I'm gonna split. Got a date with a doobie." Knowing Bucky wouldn't be interested, he bumped me with his hip. "Want to come along?"

"No. I'm good." I bumped back. "Isn't pot off limits?"

Joe-Joe's eyes twinkled in the firelight. "Not yet."

Joe-Joe was barely making it through high school. He was smart enough, he just thought school was dumb and didn't have much to offer, with one exception. Wrestling. Being a wiry guy, it appealed to his catch-me-if-you-can nature. Known to be devious, Joe-Joe could evade any opponent and slip out of any situation. He had been state champion in his bracket for two years in a row and planned on a third. Joe-Joe didn't give two hoots if he failed his classes and racked up detentions, but during wrestling season he pulled the grades he needed and was on his best behavior. That meant no fighting, no drinking, and no smoking. Tonight, he informed us, would be his last hurrah.

After Lori Chandler chastised Dave Davis for spitting his chew a little too close to her shoe, followed by a chorus of disgusted ewws when he removed the round can of Skoal from his back pocket and offered us girls a dip, I decided it was time to look for a different spot as well.

Bucky took our cups for a refill while I moved to a flat outcrop of sandstone about twenty feet away from the fire. It was pretty chilly and my windbreaker did little to keep me warm, but it was nice to get away from the smoke. When he returned, Bucky asked me to hold the beer, then—in a gesture that took me by complete surprise—removed his letter jacket and handed it to me as he sat down.

"Thanks, but you don't have to do that," I told him.

"I've got thicker skin than you."

Draping the jacket over my bare legs, I put my arms through its leather sleeves then hugged my knees, feeling the weight of Bucky's warm back against mine as we wiggled in close to use each other as lean-tos, something we had done since we were kids. Like a game of follow-the-leader, I responded to his every movement. When he lifted his cup, I took a drink. When he adjusted his rear end on the damp sandstone, I wiggled as well. When he breathed, I breathed. It was the first time I had been alone with my so-called homecoming date, and I let myself believe that the butterflies in my stomach were also in his. A temporary illusion.

The voices from the fire had merged into a sibilant hum punctuated by an occasional laugh and shout. Then came a distinct sound, distant at first then ripping through the darkness. Soon the headlights of McGregor's pickup—our designated lookout—flooded over a motorcycle. Melinda un-straddled and slid off as Dan Mazzone put down the kickstand and signaled "kill the lights." Then he went one way and she another.

Danny Mazzone was not a nice person. I knew this from firsthand experience. In the summer between my sophomore and junior years, I had finally developed a pair of boobs and the curves that went with them. Emboldened by the new me, I foolishly approached Danny on the first day of school and flirted. "Why, Mr. Mazzone. You're looking good," I said, to which he replied, "Why, Maggie Moore. You're looking better." I was crushed. It took the rest of the year to get beyond his backhanded compliment.

Danny Mazzone wasn't nice, but he was an excellent athlete. He and Bucky had been teammates in a myriad of leagues. Both were ace pitchers, and baseball had room for more than one top dog. But small town football? There could only be one quarterback, and the guys settled that matter in junior high when Danny's arm outshined Bucky's. Bucky, the faster of the two, became a wide receiver.

They made one a hell of a pass-catch combo, but Danny never liked Bucky to best him, especially when Bucky was selected most valuable player in ninth grade. He started to throw to Bucky less and less. Danny was in it for Danny. If that meant being an asshole to get what he wanted, he'd be an asshole.

Danny went through a lot of girls, and even though he wasn't a kiss-and-tell kind of guy, everyone knew when a Mazzone romance was over. He left his heartbroken exes with no phone call and no explanation. Just a dismissive look that said, "I win. See ya later."

Melinda sat in front of Danny in American Humanities. Intrigued by her aloofness—Melinda couldn't care less about Danny's elite jock status—Danny also knew that Bucky had a thing for her.

She turned down Danny's first and second offers, but decided what the hell after he scored some badass weed and suggested they ditch class to smoke it.

According to Melinda, Danny was on the boring side of dull. He did very little talking, which was okay because when he did open his mouth he had very little to say. He was a lousy kisser, a tongue-thruster with about as much finesse as a jackhammer. "So why go out?" I'd asked. It turned out Melinda liked being pursued by someone with a playboy reputation. She knew it was all a game. She also knew that the only way to stay in control was to play hard to get. The more she held him at bay, the more he came at her (and the better the pot).

To Melinda, the back-and-forth had become a turn-on, but she eventually passed into Never Never Land, believing that when it came to successfully taming a bad boy she was the exception and not the rule. She was wrong. When Melinda got off Danny's motorcycle, he gave her the Mazzone "I win. See ya later" look. I saw it, Bucky saw it, and so did everyone else.

Through the diffuse light of the fire, Melinda found us on our sandstone perch. She grabbed my arm and said, "Come with me. I've got to pee." We left the light and wandered into the protection of the scrub cedars.

"Where have you been?" I asked as we squatted. She hesitated before answering.

"We went to John Peyton's house."

"Oh. Okay." Enough said.

John Peyton, well into his twenties, was the go-to man for underage kids wanting to purchase alcohol. Although he didn't directly sell pot, his one-bedroom house was a convenience store for those who did. It was also a love shack.

I had been there once, with Melinda. A night from hell. Every time someone knocked on the door, I jumped out of my skin. We sat in the living room on John's squishy couch, stoned senseless, listening to the wailing guitars of some psychedelic band while watching God knows what on a soundless television set. At least the TV was a distraction from the horny twosomes carrying on in full view. Every so often a couple would respond to some "it's vacant now" cue and untangle themselves enough to head to John's bedroom, a mating scenario that played out three times that evening. I couldn't get out of John's place and into a hot shower fast enough, and I swore I'd never go back.

"Can I get a ride back with you guys?" Melinda asked as she buttoned up her Levis.

"Sure."

"Can we go now? I really want to go home."

"I'll round up the troops."

I didn't need to tell Bucky we wanted to leave. As soon as he saw us coming out of the brush, he put his head down and told us he would wait in the Blazer. Melinda hung back while I approached Joe-Joe, who had returned to the fire and was on the make for Susan Weston.

"Bucky's ready to leave," I lied.

"What for? We just got here."

"He just is. Maybe you can get another ride."

"Ah, man." Joe-Joe sized up his chances with Susan. We both knew nothing was going to happen.

"Yeah, it's probably time to go," Joe-Joe said.

Danny Mazzone remained in the group huddled around the dwindling fire. Melinda tapped his shoulder and told him she was going home with us.

"Suit yourself," he replied, then turned his back and continued his conversation.

Bucky had the engine running and heater on. Melinda took a seat in back. I climbed in beside her in the bench seat and let Joe-Joe have the front.

"Pretty good party, huh?" Joe-Joe said.

Nobody responded.

"Heya, Mags. Remember last year's homecoming?" he said, oblivious to the strained surroundings.

How could I forget? Joe-Joe had gotten his hands on four jars of homemade sangria. "Don't worry," he'd told us. "It can't get you drunk. Less kick than beer and goes down like soda pop." I spent eight hours puking my guts out and two days recuperating.

"Must I?"

Joe-Joe ignored that. "Man, I got the munchies. Anybody else hungry, huh? I could go for a cheeseburger. How about the Truck Stop, Buckaroo? Melinda, you in?"

Melinda was looking out the window, not responding to Joe-Joe's steady stream of verbiage.

"Wow, did you see that? Did you see them eyes? What was that? A coyote? Yeah, I think that's what I saw? Did you see that, Mags? Huh? Did you see that Bu—"

"Shut the hell up, would you?" Bucky snapped, but the ensuing silence was even more unbearable so he softened his blow with, "No offense."

"None taken, brother."

Poor Joe-Joe. As much as he and I butted heads, he was one of us. He knew when things were off, and things were off. I reached for Melinda's hand and gave it a squeeze. She responded likewise, then quickly pulled it away, withdrawing into her despair.

Respectful of the mood now, Joe-Joe riffled through the selection of tapes strewn about the front seat and popped in a favorite. Cat Stevens took us out of the canyon and back to our respective houses. Our senior year homecoming was over.

CHAPTER 11

I didn't see Melinda in the days following homecoming. Not on the bus, not in the school hallways, and not in concert choir, the one class we shared. Two weeks passed before she finally returned my many phone calls.

I could tell by her shaky "Maggie, I need a favor" that something was off, and my suspicions were confirmed when she asked, "I know it's early, but would you call Bucky and have him meet us at your house? I have an errand to run."

Before I even had a chance to tell Mom and Dad good-bye, Melinda was standing in my driveway. Within minutes, Bucky pulled up in the Blazer. She opened the door and lifted the seat to crawl in back, not waiting for me to engage in our customary argument over who got shotgun. When Bucky gave her the "Where to?" shrug, she whispered, "Just drive."

We drove along Old Orphanage Road in silence, passing the frog pond, passing the Barn. It wasn't until we reached the bend that Melinda spoke. "Take me to the Rexall. The one on far side."

Bucky didn't ask any questions. Neither did I.

Fifteen minutes later we arrived at the drugstore's parking lot. Bucky turned off the engine and the three of us sat in silence. Finally, Melinda started talking.

"I've got the crabs," she told us.

At first I didn't understand. *Crabs? Like seafood?* I glanced at Bucky, whose scrunched brow indicated he was also drawing a blank.

"I found one," she continued matter-of-factly. "Well, more than one. In my pubic hair."

Holy crap! Those crabs! I was familiar with head lice. In third grade there had been an outbreak at school, and Mrs. Watson gave us a lecture on eradication dos and don'ts. (I still got the willies when resting my head on a seatback at the movie theater.) But crabs were in a whole different category. Something out of a porno magazine.

"I was going to the bathroom," Melinda continued, "and I looked where one looks, and I saw a small mole. Only I don't have any moles in that area. I scratched it with my fingernail, and it came off. At first I thought it was a scab but then . . . its legs started to wiggle." Melinda was getting increasingly upset, her breath beginning to catch. "Then I saw another one. Actually four. And some eggs. I was mortified!"

She devolved into full-on sobs. Bucky and I were useless, temporarily paralyzed by thoughts of cooties.

"Well, don't worry," Melinda said between gasps, "they're not going to assault you." Bucky gave her his hanky, and she tried to compose herself. "I did some research about . . . *phthirus pubis* . . . in our encyclopedia. There's a special shampoo I need." Her sobs returned. "Oh, Bucky, please. I can't go in there. I just can't do it."

Bucky didn't blink. He didn't hesitate. He got out of the Blazer and went into the drugstore, leaving me to console Melinda. I didn't want to make light of an uncomfortable if not downright embarrassing predicament, but all I could think to say was a favorite phrase of my Uncle Willis: "Well, shit fire and hold the matches."

It did the trick and I got a chuckle out of Melinda, but then I got worried.

"Jesus, Melinda, I thought when you called . . . I mean . . . do you think you could be pregnant?"

"No. At least I'm not that stupid. I'm on birth control pills."

The pill? This was news to me. When did this happen?

"I've been on the pill for a while now," she said as if reading my mind.

"How'd you get that past Mrs. Mavrakis? I thought birth control was a big no-no with the Pope."

"Catholicism isn't my thing anymore, and what Mrs. Mavrakis doesn't know won't hurt her." Melinda blew her nose then scrunched it as if smelling something foul. "I used Pamela, okay? I convinced her that taking the pill warded off a bad complexion."

"And she bought that?" Melinda's skin was flawless. If she had a zit a year, I'd be surprised.

"Well, I had my doubts, but she called the doctor and *voilà*, prescription."

"Interesting. Maybe I can use that logic on my mom and kill two birds with one stone," I said, although at this point I'd prefer getting rid of pimples to having sex.

"Besides," Melinda continued, "I just got my period. That's why I . . . how I found . . ."

". . . your little friends?"

"So to speak."

My attempt at humor was no longer having the desired effect. Melinda withdrew, pulling at the splits in her long hair.

"Melinda, it's going to be okay. It's not that bad, really. Sure, it's gross, but they're just bugs."

"I also read that they're often accompanied by venereal disease. There's a clinic in Casper that I can go to, but they're only open on Thursdays."

This was sounding scary. People could go crazy from VD. People could die. I grabbed Melinda's hand in a panic. "I'll go with you."

"What about school? You'll have to ditch."

"Done it before."

As she gave my hand a squeeze, her eyes welled again. "Hell of a way to lose my virginity."

"Are you going to tell Danny?"

"It's not as if he won't figure it out on his own. But I'll have to tell him if . . . if it's more serious."

Bucky came out of the drugstore then, looking from side to side as if he'd just pulled off a robbery. Still red-faced, he opened the Blazer's door and handed Melinda a stapled white bag along with three loose packages of rubbers.

"These were on the house," he said, straining to mask any emotion. When Melinda waved her hand, indicating she didn't want them, Bucky exploded. "Goddammit, if you're going to be screwing around you can at least make sure you don't get knocked up."

It was the angriest I'd ever seen Bucky. He held Melinda's startled, clearly wounded eyes until he could bear their shame no longer.

Softening, he said, "Take them, Melinda. Please."

Melinda remained hesitant.

"Good Lord, give them to me." Having had enough tension for one day, I grabbed the packages and ripped one open. It was the first time I had ever seen a rubber. "How do you put this thing on?" I said more to myself than to my unamused friends. I unfurled the oily prophylactic to its full extent, wondering if it was one-size-fits-all. Just how big could this thing get? Maybe it was cliché and unimaginative, but I had to blow it up, and it made one hell of a balloon. I handed it to Bucky. "Tie this for me, would you?"

"Jesus, Maggie, grow up."

No one talked on the way home, but the voice in my head wouldn't shut up.

Grow up.

The ultimate insult, much easier to dish out than take in. Bucky said it to my face. In front of Melinda. He didn't even try to make it better. So much for my feelings.

When Bucky pulled into my driveway, I barely waited for him to stop before opening the Blazer's door, slamming it after I got out, not bothering to say good-bye to either of them. Not looking over my shoulder to see if Melinda transferred to the front seat when they backed away. Let him deal with her. Who cares?

It wasn't even ten o'clock, and my Saturday was ruined.

Grow up.

Two in the morning and I was still fuming, preoccupied with listing Bucky's many un-grownup shenanigans. All the "pull my finger" pranks. The farts in a bottle. All his daredevil stunts with Joe-Joe. Like when they smeared heat balm in the crotches of their Fruit of the Looms to see who could stand torture the longest, then raced back and forth from one end of the neighborhood to the other, screaming to high heaven. Or the time he purposely ran over a dead cow in Burton's pasture with the dune buggy. Its back wheels spun out on the cow's not-yet-rotten backend and spewed yellow decomposing cow gunk all over us. Not to mention the torn-off leg that almost hit me in the face, nearly putting my eye out.

"Grow up," indeed. I must have told Bucky to "grow up" a hundred times. But now that he was a high-and-mighty eighteen he thought himself some paragon of maturity? I wasn't supposed to make a joke?

Okay, maybe my timing was off. I could have been a little more sensitive. This had to be killing Melinda.

Dammit all—I should have kept my mouth shut. It was always getting me banished to the hall or sent to the assistant principal's office to atone for a smart-ass remark. The kids in class took it for granted that I'd comment on unreasonable assignments and suffer the consequences. I was always the one to point out idiotic actions, whether they came from a teacher or a classmate. To "tell it like it is" and say what everybody wanted to say but didn't have the guts to say. Well, I was tired of being everybody's mouthpiece. Let someone else be the jester.

It was time to make a few changes. From now on I would be quiet. Demure. Polite and non-contrary. I would raise my hand to speak, and then only if I had a question. Hell, I would stop asking questions altogether. I would be all niceness—sugar and spice. Yes, ma'am. No, sir. The epitome of a mature young woman. Dammit, if a grownup is what Bucky wanted, then that's exactly what he'd get. Him and everybody else.

The following Thursday, rather than feign illness, I maturely asked my mother for permission to take the day off from school. When she asked why, I told her the truth: Melinda needed to see a doctor in Casper and I needed the car to drive her there. After reassuring her that Melinda was not in any immediate trouble, Mom handed me the keys.

We spoke little on the drive. I let Melinda decide what to tell me, which wasn't much. She did say that the examination room had been freezing and the old battle-axe of a nurse had been very condescending. "They're called *stirrups*, sweetie, and you're going to have to relax if you want me to get this duckbill in for a looksie."

Melinda came by our house a week later and called for her test results while my mother discreetly made herself available, just in case. Melinda was in the clear. I refrained from any inappropriate remarks.

• • • • • •

Being on my best behavior at school wasn't easy, especially since everyone was chomping at the bit because of the upcoming holiday. Tuesday before Thanksgiving, the senior social studies and humanity classes loaded up on two busses and headed to Montana for a field trip to Custer's Battlefield.

Melinda was a no-show and Bucky was on the other bus. Under normal circumstances I would have sat with one of them and led everybody in song. Instead I settled for a spot a couple of seats behind Mr. Heinz and Mrs. Lemmon, our teacher escorts, so I could brood in peace. Martin Yazzie chose to sit beside me.

Martin Yazzie was an interesting fella, half Spanish—Spain Spanish—and half Navajo Indian. His father had been a lawyer on the Navajo reservation in Arizona before moving his practice and family to our state.

I met Martin the first day of our sophomore year, catching him in the stairwell between classes—literally. He was going up and I was going down when the spiral from my notebook snagged the sleeve of his knitted sweater. It took a couple of steps before I sensed a pull and discovered who was on the other end of the yarn: a boy with intense brown eyes that oddly combined twinkle with scorn. He was lean and tall, and didn't dress like the other kids. Instead he wore a white shirt and tie under his sweater, which thanks to me was now unraveling. It took some time to disentangle, as I was both apologetic and a little giggly. It took longer to gain his trust.

Martin's astute sense of bullshit wouldn't let me get away with anything. One day in humanities class, after a discussion on the famous World War II code talkers, I'd felt the need to embellish my ethnicity with Native American blood.

"Really. You're Indian?" Martin challenged, dismissing my usage of the now appropriate *Native American* identification. "What tribe?"

"Cherokee," I proclaimed, then sheepishly added, "Somewhere in there." It could have been true.

Martin skewered me. "Why is it that white people claiming to be part Indian go with Cherokee? Why not Arapaho, or Paiute? Or Ponca, or Chippewa? Next time, Maggie, say you're Kootenai and I might believe you."

Lesson learned.

Monotonous chatter mingled with the wheels of our bus as we jostled down the highway. We were well past the Wyoming border before Martin put down his book—he always had a book—and acknowledged my silent presence. His shrewd eyes sized me up.

"What's wrong with you lately?" he asked.

"What? You don't like the new me?"

Martin shrugged. "Stick with the old you. For some reason, it works."

He went back to whatever he was reading, and I went back to the world outside my window.

It was a cloud-covered day. A brown day. The trees along the gullies, stripped of all but a few fallow leaves, were waiting for the winter. Up on the hills, the yuccas and sagebrush, even the evergreens, were now sepia-toned, muted by the preseason cold that had already settled in. A few antelopes popped up here and there, grazing amidst the cattle. The countryside was big and beautiful, but a lonely place to be alone. To die.

I had been to Custer's Battlefield twice. Too young to remember the first, I'm told I referred to it as the "Custard Stand" and was disappointed when there was no pudding. There was the Seventh Cavalry horse cemetery, and my mother had to lead me away in tears. My brother Brian also went away unhappy because he was denied permission to dig up any damn area he pleased in search of memorabilia. Brian never did pay attention to signs or fences.

My second visit was more recent. I was returning from a scavenging trip with my father when he decided to pay the monument a spur-of-the-moment visit. It had been raining hard all day, but just as we drove through the battlefield entrance a double rainbow appeared over the purple-green horizon, giving the site an ominous glow.

We climbed to the top of Custer's Hill. On the sloping land below, scattered every which way, were white markers indicating where Custer and his men were found dead after their out-numbered and ill-fated encounter with the Northern Cheyenne and several tribes of Sioux. Custer's prestigious remains ended up somewhere back East, but he left behind those of over two hundred soldiers. Initially buried where they fell, they were reinterred in a mass grave marked by a stone memorial.

"Where are the Native Americans buried?" I asked.

Dad told me they had carted off their own dead to deal with them as they saw fit. Dad wasn't sure how many of the five thousand or so warriors lost their lives. Some say as little as thirty. Others claim it was more like three hundred. Knowing the ways of history, the truth was probably somewhere in between.

My father knew a lot about the Indian Wars, having been fascinated ever since finding his first arrowhead. "Custer was an arrogant SOB," he told me. "He underestimated the Indians' intelligence and fortitude, and pretty much got what he had coming."

Dad was sympathetic to Native Americans, but he was also a realist. "Can't blame them for trying to hold on to what they had. Still, there's no ignoring the persistent needs of civilization when it comes knocking wanting to borrow this and that. Custer lost the battle, but the Indians lost the war."

As our bus drove past the Crow Reservation I could still see the effects of that loss. Propane-fueled houses more shack than home, with questionable roofs and precarious antennas. Flimsy, weather-beaten trailers perched on cinder blocks. Junk cars and junk piles. Fallen fences and scattered garbage. Lots of litter. In a different season it all might have looked better, but that day, one hundred years since the end of the Indian Wars, things looked forlorn.

"My mother never did like to go on the reservation, but I used to fantasize about living the old ways and what it would be like," Martin said beside me.

His uncharacteristic personal disclosure took me by surprise. His usual frankness did not. Wanting to hear what he'd say next, I kept silent.

"One day, my father took me to meet his sister, Aunt Irene. All I knew about her was that she helped missionaries translate the Bible into Navajo. Aunt Irene and my three cousins lived near Window Rock, Arizona, in the middle of nowhere. They didn't have much. A barn with sheep and a corral made of whatever they could scrape together. Still, it looked like a good life to me. She lived in a *hogan*, sort of the Navajo version of a tepee. It was round, mostly made out of mud and stone. It was surprisingly roomy inside. Big enough for the woodstove, a small bed and my Aunt's loom.

"My cousins lived in a trailer next door. My father bought it for her — well, them — but she wouldn't have a thing to do with it except use its toilet. One cousin, he was about my age. Harry. I made a comment like, 'Nice place you got here,' or something like that. I meant it, too. He thought I was an idiot. Said that's what he'd expect to hear from an Apple."

"What did he mean by that?" I asked, still looking out the window.

"Red on the outside, white on the inside."

Wanting to understand more, I turned to Martin. His coal-colored eyes told me nothing of his feelings, challenging me to come to my own conclusions. But shouts coming from the restless bus riders interrupted, indicating we were nearing our destination.

As we drove through the entrance gate, Mr. Heinz stood up and went over the field trip rules again: stay with your assigned group; stay on the trails; no rough-housing; no smoking; no bad language; be respectful; learn something.

After the teachers herded us off the bus, we huddled in assigned groups — Bucky in group four, Martin and I in group one — until the historical guides took over. Ours was a clean-cut, stiff-backed park ranger who looked more drill sergeant than tour guide. He sounded like one, too.

"My name is Ranger Bicks. You are at the scene of the last important battle in the war between the United States government and the American Indian."

Martin leaned into me and whispered in my ear, "Oh brother. This is going to be an us-them kind of guy."

Ranger Bicks carried on. "Today, you will hear the telling of the Last Stand of General George Armstrong Custer and the five troops of the Seventh Cavalry under his personal command. It is the story of how, on a hot day in June of 1876, our heroic soldiers, faced with hopeless odds, were overwhelmed by the sheer number and savagery of the attacking enemy and met defeat and death."

You'd have thought Ranger Bicks had been there himself, reloading his carbine and standing alongside Custer. I suddenly felt very uncomfortable for Martin, who would undoubtedly be cast as "them." It wasn't fair that he had to be on one side or the other, or that anybody here did for that matter. Some of these kids' grandparents, one of mine included, weren't even in this country until the 1900s, but we would still be an "us." Shouldn't Martin be an "us" as well? I wondered if he wanted to be.

Ranger Bicks extended a straight arm, indicating it was time to march up Custer's Hill. Not feeling the need to follow him, I told Mrs. Lemmon I had a headache, which wasn't far from the truth. Opinion-squelching had taken its toll. Knowing my nature, Mrs. Lemmon said I could wait for everyone inside the museum. On the way, I caught Bucky's attention as group four was getting their briefing. It had been well over a week since we'd last talked. He nodded acknowledgment, but that was it, essentially giving me the cold shoulder. A dart to my immature heart.

The battlefield museum wasn't very big. It had a small souvenir counter run by a not-so-small and not-so-pleasant woman who *shushed* me when I walked in and warned me not to touch anything. Other than her, I was the only one there. Man, was she going to have a cow when the rest of the kids showed up.

Making sure to keep my hands to myself, I viewed the Last Stand diorama. Even though its cob-webbed miniature solders looked like they had seen better days, they still brought out an urge to maneuver them into a scene of my own making. But sensing the evil eye of Counter Lady, I moved on. Mixed among historical documents and diagrams were artifacts recovered from the site. There were guns and cartridge cases, pocketknives, buttons, even a few wedding rings.

Custer's personal display was quite the shrine thanks to his devoted widow, Elizabeth, who spearheaded the polishing of his tarnished reputation and kept his legend alive. Along with photos depicting various stages of his military career—augmented by his actual uniforms, hats and accoutrements—Mrs. Custer had also donated many items of an intimate nature. Among them were a lock of his famed yellow hair and the hair brush he used to comb it; his toothbrush, made of horse hair and so big I wondered if it was also used on the horse itself; and a razor, a razor strap, a shaving mug, and a brush.

Then I saw it, yellowed and sweat-stained, coiled between his soap and his canteen. At first I thought it was suspenders, but attached to its leather straps was a cup-like protuberance that made me suspect it was meant to provide support to a different part of the male anatomy.

Oh, what to do when you've got an oddity aching for comedic commentary and no one to share it with? No Bucky to pepper with the multitude of possible wisecracks. No Melinda to ask, "What the hell was Elizabeth Custer thinking?" I considered engaging Counter Lady, but figured she wouldn't appreciate my brand of humor. There was nothing to do but hold this hot potato until someone showed up. I found an inconspicuous spot close to the target of my esprit and waited.

Two women entered the building, both elderly. They paid their respects to Counter Lady and asked her a few questions before donning their glasses and going about the museum in tandem, basically taking the same route I had. As one lingered reading a page from Custer's personal diary, the other began to study his stuff. With gleeful anticipation, I followed her progress. The hair, the hairbrush. Now the toothbrush. Back to the hairbrush to whisper something to the other woman. The razor. The razor strap. The . . .

"Sweet Jesus, Milly, they've got his jockstrap in here!"

Milly—short, stubby and looking ever so grandmotherly—took off her spectacles for a closer gander. "I declare. They sure do, Martha."

Without skipping a beat, she added, "But I'm more impressed with the size of his toothbrush."

Well, that was it. Milly started giggling. I burst out laughing. Martha and Milly, surprised by my presence, laughed even louder. Counter Lady *shushed* us, but I started snorting between guffaws. Martha became so hysterical she couldn't catch her breath. Milly doubled up from laughing so hard that she ended up sitting on the floor. After an eye-roll that said she'd seen it before, Counter Lady decided to give up.

Nothing raises spirts more than a good laugh. I decided it's not necessary to grow up to be a grownup, and vice versa.

• • • • •

It felt good to get back to my normal self. Starving my immature instinct undoubtedly left me wiser, but also ravenous, and Thanksgiving could not have been better timed.

After last year's nasty confrontation with Uncle Willis regarding the ins and outs of carving the turkey, Dad had decided to bow out and go fishing instead. Every time my mother tried to guilt him into coming, he'd counter with, "I'm going to see those people at Christmas, why should I have to put up with them now?" So Mom made her apologies to the family, and sent her regrets as well. "I'm never going to hear the end of this," she told me, "but I'm tired of coming to your father's defense. Let my brother stew on that."

Having lost our dinner, Mom set about trying to finagle an invite from the neighbors.

The Padilla option was out. Successful in his run for County Commissioner, Mr. Padilla was eager to begin his service to the community and had volunteered his family to feed the hungry at the soup kitchen. Mrs. Padilla had made nine matching aprons and hats for the occasion. We considered going with them. Seeing Ricky, Joe-Joe, and Johnno—who was now embracing his Chicano roots and going by Juan—dressed as pilgrims would have been worth signing up, but Mom figured there would be more than enough help and we should do our do-gooding on a less popular do-gooding day.

The Simms would be in Billings feasting with Doc's in-laws, and Mrs. Mavrakis would be gone as well, tending to a sister in St. Louis who was recovering from back surgery. The Colonel saw no need for Pamela to make a big fuss over cooking and had made dinner reservations at the Country Club. For Melinda's sake, he invited us to join them. The problem was so did Mrs. Majors.

Mom and I discussed our duo-invite dilemma. Should we get decked out and go to the swanky Country Club for fine dining knowing the experience would be usurped by the tension at the table? Or should we clean ourselves up a bit and take pies to the Majorses'? We opted for the latter, especially after Melinda assured me she could handle "an evening in the doldrums" on her own, thanks to some speed she had scored.

After sleeping in on Thanksgiving morning, we took our time gearing up for the hectic pace that would take over once we entered the Majorses' household. Mrs. Majors had begun her cooking a full week in advance, and she and her sister-in-law from Casper would be setting out a steady stream of edibles. No doubt Mom and I would be part of the maid brigade once we arrived because all of the menfolk would be sitting on their butts in front of the television set watching the football game.

It was close to four o'clock before we decided to leave. I was carrying the pumpkin pies and Mom had the apple. Just when she opened the front door, the phone rang.

"I better get that," Mom said. "Just in case."

I waited by the door as she went to answer it.

A *splat* came from the kitchen then Mom cried out, "Thank God, you're alive! Oh, honey, it's you."

Running in to see what had happened, I slipped on an aluminum plate, apple-covered side down. Both pumpkin pies shot out of my hands. One soared off behind me and the other hit Grandma's cookie jar. I landed on my ass.

My mother was bent over, clutching the phone with one hand and holding her stomach with the other. The color had drained from her face. I crawled to her, took the phone from her hand and brought the receiver to my ear.

"Mom? Mom?" It was a voice I hadn't heard in a long time. "Are you okay? Mom?"

"Brian?" My brother was on the other end.

CHAPTER 12

Brian had always been a loner, never belonging to a group, not because he was particularly shy or quiet — Brian liked the company of others — but because he always got overlooked. The "Who's that?" kid in class photos, my brother learned to be satisfied with his own company.

That all changed in boot camp.

In the fall of 1968, Brian had dutifully reported to Fort Lewis in Washington for basic combat infantry training, having resigned himself to serving his country. He was apprehensive, as were most of his fellow draftees who had no desire to kill or be killed.

After being collectively bussed, sheared, outfitted, tagged, and tested, Brian was tossed into a platoon of motleys made better by their blending: a gung-ho group balanced between chest bangers and mama's boys, fat boys and frat boys, brothers and honkies. By the end of the third week Brian had made more friends than he had over the course of his entire life. By the eighth, the recruits had thoroughly bonded, becoming a whole that would have gone to hell and back for any one of its parts. Although he was still dubious about America's involvement in Vietnam, this new camaraderie gave Brian something to sink his teeth into. At least now he understood his purpose — watch out for his fellow soldiers and help keep them alive.

As soon as the platoon passed their combat proficiency tests and Basic was over, military occupational specialties were handed out. Brian had been assigned to advanced infantry training at Fort Polk,

Louisiana. So had two of his favorite buddies, Jim Powell and Richard Brown.

On the evening of graduation, the newly trained soldiers, along with a few parents, girlfriends, and wives, gathered for one last party. Amidst the beer-drinking and story-swapping, Brian took a turn on the community guitar. Accustomed to being background music, this time he was center stage, playing for an audience whose applause validated his existence.

The platoon's proud task master, Drill Sergeant Davis, put in an appearance as well. He brought along First Lieutenant Stickler, a hard-nosed army medical officer looking to make captain. They sat down directly in front of Brian. First Lieutenant Stickler was particularly observant of my brother's strumming technique. His curiosity suddenly changed to concern.

"What the hell is wrong with that soldier's finger?"

• • • • •

Brian's right index finger was a placeholder at best. It couldn't bend. It couldn't straighten. It had no feeling. It was a wonder the finger was there. Like the various body parts of many a child, it had fallen victim to our town's unofficial junkyard.

Nobody ran the junkyard, although it was just off the railroad tracks next to Little Goose Creek on property owned by Old Man McKinley. Years prior, the county had deposited the shells of abandoned cars and trucks along the banks of the river to hold back erosion, and their placement had inadvertently made a nice swimming hole, attracting kids in need of a break from the heat. Unfortunately, unwanted wreckage kept showing up, eventually accumulating outside the water and spilling onto McKinley land. As rusted vehicles were piled three, four, sometimes five high, it created jagged metal teeter-totters, another attraction for bored kids who couldn't resist the temptation to jump from one car to another. A romp through the treacherous playground was a definite parental no-no, and the tell-tale signs of rust-stained pant legs and slashed shirt sleeves tattled on those who defied the "keep out" signs. My brother had been warned, more than once, to stay away, but swats from Dad did little to deter him.

One day he was tailing the Henderson twins, trying to keep up as they went from heap to unsteady heap. The top car in a stack of three was still groaning from the weight of Billy Henderson's last jump when Brian alit on its front hood. The car gave way and took a nose dive. Although Brian successfully jumped sideways and avoided being pinned between its grill and the ground, when he put his hand down to brace his fall the middle car lurched forward and the break drum of its tireless wheel hub sliced through most of his finger, leaving only a sliver of skin intact.

After Bobbie Henderson determined Brian's finger might need some attending and Billy bound my brother's hand with his used hankie, the three boys had no choice but to face the music and seek help.

The finger was reattached, but was useless from then on. Still, Brian wasn't going to let a little thing like a bum finger get in the way of growing up; his four-digit hand relearned everything it had known up to then and moved on from there.

After a while, Brian seemed to forget about his supposed affliction. The rest of us forgot as well. So, when the United States Army came calling, it never occurred to my brother or my parents to bring it up. It wasn't until First Lieutenant Stickler spied its idle behavior in a strum that the finger became a factor. As unbending as his name, he was furious at Brian for somehow slipping through the process and made sure Brian was immediately handed his walking papers along with a full medical deferment.

My father was glad the army had no use for his son—he had lost his only brother to World War II and had seen his share of friends go off to Korea—and Mom was ecstatic. But Brian was unsettled. Being a lucky son-of-a bitch who beat the odds was one thing, but being a spoke without a wheel was another. He took no joy in his dismissal. No satisfaction in not accompanying his best friends to Vietnam. And when Jim Powell was killed by a booby trap and Richard Brown died from an accidental explosion of a white phosphorus grenade, the guilt of not going became too much.

Brian took off, phoning home from time to time to check in. Including one morning on July 21, 1969.

"Did you see it? Did you see it?" he asked Mom, an unnerving excitement in his voice.

"Where are you, honey?"

"I'm on the moon!"

A telling silence came from both ends. Again, Mom asked, "Where are you?"

Standing beside my mother, Dad and I struggled to hear Brian sobbing at the other end of the line, "I don't know, Mom. I'm drifting. Don't worry. I'll call you when I get back. When I land."

•   •   •   •

Five years later, Brian called on Thanksgiving to tell us he had landed at a laundromat in Shawnee, Oklahoma.

His phone call had been brief. He was well. He was employed. He had spent the last year living in Oklahoma, but now he was ready to leave. He was also out of coins. Mom pleaded with him to call collect, and two weeks later he did, to let us know that he was thinking of a Christmas visit. A week after that he called again, this time from Albuquerque, New Mexico, where his car had broken down. He had considered hitchhiking to Wyoming, but it wasn't a good time of year for that, so he planned on catching the bus.

Now, if all went according to Hoyle, he was supposed to be home today, on the eve of Christmas Eve. That seemed doubtful. Even though the snow wasn't piling up in our neck of the woods, it was pummeling the Rockies and the roads between here and there.

Mom had been jittery all day, not trusting he would show up nor certain how long he'd stay. While she browbeat the local Greyhound dispatcher for the latest updates, Dad busied himself making fudge, something he always did this time of year and something he was really good at. Dad made fudge the old-fashioned way. "You can't have good fudge without beating the shine out of it." Devouring the bowl scrapings left in the aftermath had always been a favorite of mine, and the licking of the wooden spoon had always been Brian's. I caught Dad tucking the spoon behind the milk carton in the fridge. "For Brian," he said as he winked at me, then we all headed off to the station.

Three hours later, the bus still hadn't arrived and Mom had grown restless. It was too cold to window shop on Main Street, so we decided to wait it out at the Woolworth's counter.

Mom had her worry face on. Come to think of it, she had worn a variation of the same expression since Brian had been out of touch.

"You know, that kid has always been late," Dad said, reaching for Mom's hand to stop her fingers from drumming on her coffee mug. "He came into the world late."

Mom shook her head. "Stubborn little fella."

"Well, he made it, just the same. Biggest boy in the nursery."

Mom gave him an indifferent glance, then spoke into her mug. "That was the last time he out-weighed anyone."

There was a ten-year gap between me and my brother, and I didn't know the difficulties surrounding his birth, Mom being the private sort. In fact, it wasn't until Mrs. Majors gave Bucky a new little sister that I found out Brian and I weren't Mom's only children. There had been two boys in between, two years apart. One she miscarried at seven months and the other died shortly after delivery. Of my own beginnings, I knew I hadn't been the easiest thing to carry around. When I wasn't making Mom sick, I was kicking her. Dad had been fishing when she went into labor, and Mom had to drop Brian off at Grandma's before driving herself to the hospital. I was born ten hours later.

Not eager to go through heartbreak again, she had done what she could to prevent another pregnancy. I was an *oops*. Once I plopped out, she told her doctor that she wanted her tubes tied. She'd had enough of worrying about unborn babies. But the doctor wouldn't do it without permission from my father. Permission! Mom called the doctor everything in the book and did the same to my absent dad. Exhaustion won out, on both accounts, and when Dad finally showed up he was informed that his crying baby girl in the nursery would be the end of his blood line.

"Was Brian a fussy baby?" I asked as the counter clerk topped Mom's coffee.

"He was a sleeper," she said. "You'd hardly know he was there."

It was dark when the bus finally arrived. We caught our first glimpse of Brian in its headlights. His hair had grown out from the boot-camp buzz and was now back in a ponytail. He was skinny and underdressed for the cold, but he had always been skinny and underdressed for the cold. He didn't have much with him, just a duffle bag and a grocery sack. There was a fatigue in his eyes that suggested more than a tiring bus ride. Still, he was smiling just the same.

Mom couldn't help herself. She put him in a bear hug and wouldn't let go. Brian seemed to be okay with that and gave her one in return.

Dad threw my brother's stuff in the back of the pickup and the four of us cozied into its cab. Brian didn't want to go straight home, so I suggested we drive past the Blue House and check out the Christmas decorations. Dad was happy to oblige. Second to making fudge, driving around looking at lights was his favorite yuletide ritual.

The Blue House on Banner Avenue near the outskirts of town belonged to Raymond and Modette Hunter. Their old two-story wasn't much to speak of, but at Christmas time when most people decorated in red and green, it was the only house edged from top to bottom in nothing but blue. On winter evenings when the ground was covered in white, the blue sparkle enticed wonder and quiet reflection.

Dad pulled off the road and turned off the headlights. There it stood. Even without the snow, no illumination bridged the gap from darkness to light like the color blue. Nobody said anything. We didn't need to.

Dad broke the silence with a family-favorite story, a dialogue he and my mother had performed for my brother and me numerous times before.

"Remember when Brian discovered Santa on the toilet?" he asked.

"I remember you were supposed to convince him that Santa was real. Brian was just a little thing, too little to quit believing."

"He let us know in no uncertain terms that he was going to sleep on the couch all night, so if the ol' boy did show up, he could catch him in the act."

"You brought home that shabby suit from the Elks Club. God knows how many Christmas parties that thing had seen. It reeked of whiskey and had rabbit fur sticking out every which way."

"Boy howdy! The plan was for you to wake him up in time to see me running across the lawn."

"Instead, he saw you in the bathroom with your pants around your ankles hollering for toilet paper."

"Yep. You tried to convince Brian that even Santa needed to use the facilities every once in a while."

"He waited on the other side of that bathroom door for a long time before I could talk him into heading to bed and letting Santa go about his business."

That was Brian's cue to add, "Santa's 'business' sure did stink!" and my cue to follow with laughter.

A jolly good performance by all.

Mom's Christmas cheer was unleashed by Brian's homecoming, and now she wanted to go all out. First on her to-do list was the tree. For the last four Christmases we'd had an artificial one that Dad had bought secondhand from Fryer's Department Store after it had served its purpose as a store display. Our fake tree was supposed to look real, only it didn't. It wasn't bad, once all the lights were on and it was decorated, but after many put-ups and take-downs its wire boughs were a bit on the sparse side. When Mom found out Brian might be coming home, she absolutely would not let Dad rouse the imposter from its yearly slumber on the coat closet's top shelf.

Filled with the spirit now, we headed to Burns Tree Lot. Mr. Burns sold Douglas firs harvested from the Bighorn Mountains, and they were the best trees in town, but this late in the game the pickings were slim. Even so, Brian went for a slightly off-centered, sort of misshapen one that had been passed over by those who could not see its potential. It went in the truck, and we went home.

Our own neighborhood decorations looked good, albeit with each home lit according to the nature of its occupants. Our house was intentionally understated — the mailbox blinked red, as did two of our outside evergreens, but that was it. Dad enjoyed looking at lights, but he was impatient and didn't particularly like setting them up, although he did ready our new tree on its stand as soon as we got up the next morning. After arguments about how to place it in our picture window for optimum outside and inside viewing, Dad did his part, then got out of the way.

Mom and Brian were kindred spirits when it came to tree decorating.

Light stringing came first. The lights had to circle the tree in a seemingly random yet methodical fashion, not haphazardly like Dad's hodge-podge on the ones outside. They also had to be strategically positioned to avoid too many like colors being next to one another. And, finally, a prominent spot up front needed to be reserved for Grandma Lane's bubbling candle bulb, the only remaining workable light from the string that had once graced her tree.

I had first plug-in honors. Both Mom and Brian stood back and looked at the tree from various angles, readjusting the bulbs until it was pronounced good to go, then we moved on to the ornaments.

For whatever the reason, my family tended to be hard on Christmas ornaments, which meant the survivors of Christmases past fit in five shoe boxes. Mom favored the handmade ones, and most of those were in pretty sad shape. Brian's Santa with a macaroni beard and his popsicle-stick Star of Bethlehem both needed regluing every time they came out of the box. Meanwhile, my earliest attempt at ornament making, a lima-bean Baby Jesus glued into a walnut-shell manger and swaddled in a shredded A&W napkin, was downright embarrassing. But it held a soft spot in Mom's heart, so much so that she always made a point to find it the perfect nook within the branches.

Grandma Moore's angel was the last to go on. Spun-glass rays jetted out from around a paper angel whose red hair was the same color as Grandma's had been. One of her golden wings was torn, but other than that she had aged well.

Then came the tinsel, which Mom and Brian had the patience of Job when it came to hanging, because they put it on one strand at a time. My one strand turned to ten and so on, until I finally just threw a glob of it at the tree hoping it would stick somewhere. Mom and

Brian were not pleased, so I handed Mom what was left and told them I was more suited to setting the table.

We had decided that our Christmas Eve dinner would be simple, but that didn't mean it wouldn't be festive. While Dad was tending to the Christmas music, I removed the plastic cloth from our kitchen table and replaced it with a fancier poinsettia version.

After hunting down four matching china plates, I opened the knickknack cabinet and took out Mom's good silverware. Her silver-plated set had been a wedding present from Dad's Aunt Sylvia. It lived in a walnut box lined in white satin and purple felt and slotted to hold a myriad of utensils, most of which were never used. I had learned proper table setting in Home Economics but my family never cooperated. Dad only used one fork for the entire meal, and it was whichever one he happened to grab.

The "which and why" of table manners didn't matter to me, but the silverware did; because its formality and elegance graced us only once, maybe twice a year, it was an important part of marking special occasions, of taking us away from the feeling of the everyday. I gave each place setting two forks and two spoons, liking the way it looked.

"Hey, Maggie," Brian's voice rang over Dad's chosen Christmas album. "Come look." I joined my family eyeing the decked-out tree. "It's beautiful," I admitted.

"Couldn't have done better myself," Dad said as he grabbed my mother's hand and placed it in his left. "Let's dance." Mom didn't protest, swing-stepping with Dad around the couch to Elvis singing "Here Comes Santa Claus" until remembering a detail she'd missed.

"The presents!"

This time Mom did the grabbing. "Jack, come help me." She led him toward their bedroom, leaving Brian and me by ourselves for the first time since his arrival. Brian picked up a fallen tinsel and fiddled with it, avoiding my eyes until he broke our awkward silence. "So, little sister, when did you grow up?"

I chuckled, then suddenly felt angry. Seeing Mom so happy was wonderful, but Brian's disappearance was what made her unhappy in the first place. His non-communication had been downright inconsiderate.

"That's what happens," I said, giving him and indignant shrug. He lowered his head as my parents came back into the living room laden with presents.

Five Christmases had come and gone with no Brian, but not a year had passed without Mom buying him a gift in the hopes that he might show up. Now my parents laid them under the tree along with this year's addition, plus two for me and one for Dad, wrapped and ribboned in Mom's meticulous way. Dad, a notorious last-minute buyer and equally notorious sloppy wrapper, added his packages to the pile. I had a few of my own and would put them out later.

In my family, we didn't have Santa gifts on Christmas morning. Those stopped coming as soon as a surly teenage Brian had informed six-year-old me that the old man was a figment of the collective capitalistic imagination and a ploy to guilt poor people into spending money they didn't have. In reality, he was just mad that he wasn't going to get the pool table he'd circled in the Montgomery Ward catalog.

We did continue the tradition of allowing ourselves one present to open before the big day. This year, we decided our Christmas Eve picks would be those Brian brought home. With the prospect of presents, I couldn't stay mad at him for long.

Brian had changed. In the past our house had just been someplace for him to eat and flop. Now it seemed he really wanted to be home, and he really wanted to be with us. When we sat down for Christmas Eve dinner, he raved over Mom's pot roast. He showed concern about Dad's bad knees and offered to move some of the heavier pieces of junk accumulating in our garage. He asked me about school, my friends, my job, and he wanted to know what I thought about college. He told Mom not to worry about cleaning up after dinner because he would do the dishes, and he did them Mom's way. The old Brian would have rinsed them, foregoing the soap, and left them in the drainer 'til the cows came home. But what he didn't do was tell us anything about himself. That came later.

It was around eleven o'clock, well past my parents' bedtime. Dad was sitting in his reclining chair with Oscar Doggie on his lap, their jointly claimed living-room territory. Mom was curled up on the couch wearing her favorite powder-blue housecoat, last year's Christmas present from Dad. A new one was under the tree awaiting its turn to keep her warm. No doubt there was one for me, too. Bathrobes were a standard Dad present.

I was lying at the other side of the couch maneuvering my cold feet between Mom's folded legs. We didn't have a fireplace, but the off-and-on cycle of our wall heater provided the necessary warm blast to keep out the chill, and the seductive twinkles coming off our tree drew us in to the Eve's magic.

Brian had just passed out his unwrapped gifts: For me, a turquoise bracelet that he picked up in New Mexico. For Dad, three colorful fishing lures dating back to the 1930s that he found in a discarded tackle box. And for my mother, a beautiful silk shawl with embroidered flowers. He had one more gift for all of us, but especially Mom. After retrieving a bottle of bourbon from the kitchen, he poured himself a shot, downed it and poured another, handing the bottle to Dad for safe keeping. Brian stood facing the three of us, his eyes watering.

"I'm sorry."

He put his glass on the coffee table without drinking his second pour. "I owe you all an explanation of where I've been the past five years."

• — • — • — • — •

The loss of his army friends had set something off in Brian. Yucky feelings he didn't understand and didn't want came out of nowhere and smacked him down. This made Brian retreat to his old haunts in Montana, hoping to regain some peace of mind. But peace didn't come, only angst thanks to the naive accusations of his peers and the blind patriotism of the older generation.

Then we landed on the moon. The moon! Surely, this enormity would budge him from his numbing idleness. Thrust him out of self-doubt and towards a purposeful existence. For the six-plus hours between Apollo 11's landing and Neil Armstrong's "small step," Brian was awash with possibility. Then . . . *smack!* The yucky feelings raced back in, taking hold of his soul and sucking it dry.

Tired of self-pity and just plain tired of being Brian, my brother was convinced that the only way to rid himself of "him" was to leave everything he knew behind, including us. He called home to say good-bye.

Brian went to Mexico and hung out along the Baja, where he eventually learned enough Spanish to get a job on a chartered fishing boat. After a failed relationship — Brian left out most of the details — he went back to the States and started working as a part-time landscaper, part-time jeweler. There he took up with another girlfriend, this one from Vermont. When she grew tired of the desert, he followed her home. That girlfriend didn't work out either, nor did East Coast living. Much like my grandmother, Brian needed his vistas.

Brian drifted westward, ending up in Shawnee, Oklahoma, where he found a decent-paying job. One that would allow him to save up a bit before continuing on into Texas.

Brian didn't like Oklahoma. First of all, it was inhabited by too many Baptists, one of which was his next girlfriend, a receptionist at a small seminary college. Although she was of age, she wasn't allowed to dance or drink or dally in anything fun. (Except she did, because much like every other Baptist woman, she wanted to dabble in sin while she was young enough to enjoy it and far enough away from her date with judgement.) Baptists or otherwise, the people of Oklahoma were just too damn slow, even for laid-back Brian. Laziness had nothing to do with it — in fact, my brother admired their hardworking, stick-to-it nature. But Oklahomans were more tortoise than hare, and Brian was somewhere in between. Oddly enough, it was a hare that would change the course of his life.

Brian worked for a wholesale company delivering over-the-counter pharmaceuticals, cigarettes and candy to various mom-and-pop stores in the Shawnee region. One day while driving on the back route to Stillwater, a jackrabbit ran in front of his truck. Brian swerved to avoid it and his truck went catawampus. After some quick correcting, Brian got his wheels back under control, but it had been a close call, so he pulled over to regain his composure, then figured he'd take a leak while he could.

Just as he was zipping up, a fella in a Rambler sped past him at seventy-five, minimum. (Seems driving was the exception to the Oklahomans-are-as-slow-as-molasses rule.) Brian watched the car as it tore off into the distance. Suddenly, there was a kick-up of red dust. Thinking that couldn't be good, he jumped in his truck and headed toward the commotion.

The Rambler had rolled several times before hitting a telephone pole. Brian found its ejected driver in a ditch some fifteen feet from the car. He was conscious but in bad shape; from the man's odd position, Brian guessed that his neck was broken.

Brian's delivery truck was equipped with a CB radio so he made the necessary emergency call and was told an ambulance was on the way.

The early morning sun had yet to heat up the chill, so Brian grabbed a blanket from his truck. He knew better than to try to move the injured man, but given the ambulance was a good thirty minutes out, he needed to make him as comfortable as possible. As Brian was tucking the blanket in place he felt a wallet in the shivering man's back pocket. Brian carefully removed it and looked inside.

The man's name was Harry Lange and he was fifty-three years old. Along with his driver's license and four one-dollar bills, he carried three photos. One was of a woman in her graduation cap and gown, dated as 1965. In another the same woman, only slightly older, was holding a baby girl, who was possibly the same girl missing her front tooth in the third photo. Written on the back of that picture was "Katie 1st Grade."

"Your granddaughter?" Brian asked. "Katie?" Harry's shocked, unfocused gaze sharpened a bit, his eyes answering yes.

"She reminds me of my sister at that age," Brian continued, trying his best to engage Harry's dwindling spirit. "I bet she's a pistol."

Harry was fighting to keep his grip on the present. *I'm not ready!* Harry's eyes told Brian. But he slipped back into traumatic despair.

It was the fear in Harry's eyes that Brian would never forget. Fear of being alone. Of dying alone. Brian didn't have any doctoring skills, so he couldn't fix Harry, but he could do his best to make it better, even if that just meant giving a damn.

Brian whispered into Harry's ear, "I'll tell Katie you love her." He took Harry's hand, transferring every ounce of empathy he could muster, and waited. Brian didn't leave Harry's side, not until the ambulance arrived and the paramedics declared him dead.

My brother kept his word, and after locating Harry's daughter he told her and little Katie that Harry's last thoughts were of them. That was on Thanksgiving Day, the same day Brian had called us from the laundromat. The same day that Brian had been struck with divine inspiration.

He had found his calling. Brian was going to become a nurse.

CHAPTER 13

Mom announced Brian's decision to become a nurse at the Lane Family Christmas get-together, and it went over surprisingly well. Uncle Willis made none of his usual commentary about my brother's long hair, nor were there any derogatory remarks regarding Brian's choice to pursue a traditionally female profession. Cowmen and ranchers, my uncles and aunts were practical people who believed that medical training came in handy regardless of title. Cousin Johnny said it best: "This is America, where a man can be what he wants to be, even if it means wearing a funny hat."

My brother spent the weeks following his return formulating a plan. In doing so, he did a most un-Brian-like thing: he asked for help. Only Doc Simms told him to forget the whole nursing thing and set his sights on a medical degree. "Sure, it's more schooling. But in the end, you're in charge. And believe me, the white coat makes more money and gets more respect than the white hat."

Brian considered Doc's point of view as our neighbor went over the list of doctors-do-this and nurses-do-that, emphasizing that he considered the "this" list a much better deal. Trouble was, Brain identified more with the "that" one.

"Well, if your mind's made up, I don't see much point in trying to change it," Doc relented. "But they won't necessarily make it easy for you. Most nursing schools in the country close their doors to men."

Brian hadn't considered his sex being a roadblock. Fortunately, both Montana College of Nursing and the University of Wyoming didn't discriminate. Westerners were, indeed, practical people. Now all he had to do was apply.

My reacquainted family spent the first month of 1974 getting used to our new living arrangements. As we only had one bathroom, schedules needed to be arranged and household duties had to be adjusted. Brian helped out with the cooking. He also pitched in when Dad needed a strong back and offered unsolicited advice regarding my father's business prospects and inventory management.

With me back in school and Mom working all day at the Sew-N-Save, Dad and Brian spent a lot of time together, enough that soon they were starting to get on each other's nerves. Tensions came to a head when Dad wore Brian's "best" white tennis shoes to retrieve the morning newspaper and left them covered in brown mud splotches. According to Brian, his "best" white tennis shoes were meant to be worn inside, not outside, in the mud, by sweaty feet that were not his. Dad balked at being on my brother's shoe shit list. Both wanted an apology. After a day of sulking, followed by a day of uncomfortable avoidance, Dad acknowledged his offence and Brian admitted he went a little overboard.

They had worked it out, a first for my father and his so-like-him son. Still, things got much better after Brian took a job fertilizing Charlie Burton's alfalfa fields. Between days spent mucking and loading manure and nights spent taking classes at the junior college, little time was left for father and son to rub each other the wrong way.

Meanwhile, I was having my own relationship problems, given Bucky, Melinda and I hadn't completely patched things up since the Mazzone incident, largely because Melinda had moved on from her less than pleasant "first" by seeing a guy she'd met while babysitting the Rochensky boys during their parents' cocktail party.

Richard was a philosophy professor on loan to our junior college, and had wandered into the den where Melinda was watching TV with "Thing One" and "Thing Two." Dressed in loafers and smoking a pipe, he'd reeked of sophistication. He was also well into his thirties while Melinda was only on the verge of turning eighteen.

Bucky didn't think it an appropriate match and had let his opinion be known on a drive home from school. "What do you see in that dirty old man?" he'd asked her, eyes darting from road to rearview mirror.

Huddled in the back of the Blazer, Melinda had pulled her overcoat's fur-trimmed hood in tighter, hiding most of her face. "He can hold an intelligent conversation. And he doesn't judge me."

After that a silent wedge had worked its way in. I couldn't figure out why Bucky let himself be hurt over and over again. Why couldn't Bucky just let her do her own thing? Melinda wasn't his girlfriend. And hey, yoo-hoo, what about me? He certainly had no problem with my romances, inappropriate or otherwise. It didn't bother Bucky that Carl Roach, a notorious playboy, had put the moves on me in the bleachers. Nor did it bother him that Carl was probably going to ask me out and I was probably going to accept. Instead Bucky said that Carl's reputation was exaggerated and I could do a lot worse. Not the reaction I had wanted.

So the three of us took a hiatus from each other, which was a good thing all around. Melinda didn't have to explain—once again—about the order of Socrates and Plato to her unenlightened friends, and Bucky didn't have to lie—once again—about Melinda's whereabouts to Mrs. Mavrakis or Pamela Thomas. As for me, I could focus on making money, because I desperately wanted my own car.

I had been earning some portion of my keep since age four, when Mom paid me a penny a hankie to help her iron. After Dad gave me a potholder loom for my eighth birthday, I went into manufacturing and sales, peddling my woven wares door-to-door—fifteen cents for one, twenty-five cents for two. That kept me in candy until fifth grade, when I started earning lunch money by working in the school cafeteria. Standing in our white aprons and hairnets, me and two other students plopped our assigned *dish de jour* onto silver trays while the head lunch lady, Mrs. Kielstrup, an imposing woman with a face set to permanent frown, barked orders. "Keep the line moving." "Easy on the meatloaf." "Don't scrimp on the spinach." "One piece of cake ONLY." Seldom pleased with her underlings' abilities, she'd have one of us in tears nearly every afternoon.

Still, as threating as Head Lunch Lady Kielstrup could be, she didn't hold a candle to my current boss, Pogo DeMille.

A tall, skinny hash-slinger from way back, Frank DeMille owned a restaurant next to our only indoor mall. It was called Pogo's Place, a name its sign spelled out in neon next to a stick-figure french fry holding a cup of coffee in one hand and a plated hamburger in the other. Part drive-in, part diner, each table and parking spot at Pogo's provided a lit menu and telephone. When customers were ready, they simply picked up the phone and ordered.

Pogo was a fitting nickname for a man who was always in motion, a compressed coil of potential energy ready to spring from one "ticket on deck" to another, flipping burgers on the grill and operating the fryer all at once. However, when Pogo lost his cool, which happened daily during the noon rush, he went off like a loaded pistol, and everyone working with him was his target.

Unattended switchboard calls and undelivered food set him off the most, and when the order-taker wasn't fast enough to suit him, or, God forbid, forgot to include a table number, Pogo's tirade commenced. He'd snatch all the trays lined up on the counter and stack them up in one pile. "You imbeciles can't manage to do two things at once without screwing it up, so for now on this is how we're going to do it. One tray, one order at a time."

Kitchen mishaps weren't his only triggers. It wasn't unusual for Pogo to grab a tub and go after a dirty table that hadn't been bussed thanks to whatever smock-wearing employee he believed was not doing her job. This often included his wife, Claudette, our peppy manager. Claudette liked to fraternize with the costumers while refilling their coffees. When Pogo had one of his episodes, he'd pull her off the floor and put her to work behind the line, yelling at her and everybody else to get the hell out of his way.

Why Claudette put up with her temperamental husband was a mystery. Funny thing was, when his tantrum was over and the dust settled, Pogo would go back to being his likable self, forgetting what made him mad in the first place.

I began to work for the DeMilles the summer before my sophomore year, after Mom had mentioned to Claudette I was looking for work during one of my parents' Tuesday-night bowling dates. Claudette told her to have me show up at eleven the following Saturday and she'd see how I handled myself. My very first time delivering an order I spilled a chocolate shake. The damn thing slid off the tray. Too horrified to do anything about it, I stood petrified, watching ice cream ooze across the table and into lap of the booth's lone occupant. Claudette came to the rescue with a wipe-down and an apology for the costumer along with a pep talk for me. "Everybody does that at some time or another. Aren't you glad you got it out of the way?" Then she whisked me back to the counter and helped me set up another tray. Pogo never knew it happened, and I was hired. Two weeks later I received my first honest-to-goodness paycheck and paid my first income tax.

Now, in my senior year, I was working one shift every weekend, but I was hoping to pick up an extra day, maybe even a night.

It was mid-day Saturday, one hour to go before my shift was over. Lunch had been a killer; we got slammed at eleven thirty and didn't come up for air until well past two. Pogo's son, Simon, had walked out after his dad threw a chef salad at him for going overboard with the dressing, and Claudette had taken over his precarious spot at the pantry, leaving me to do double duty running trays and the register.

Although Simon had come back with his tail between his legs and was now in charge of the grill, he was taking a break, reading the latest *Muscle and Fitness* magazine—Simon had high hopes for a different body and a different life. Just he and I were left to run the restaurant until four o'clock when the dinner crew arrived.

The booths were mostly occupied by old-timers who liked to drink coffee and eat pie. I'd come to like these regulars even though they seldom tipped more than a quarter. I was making my coffee refill rounds when in walked Carl Roach, Danny Mazzone and (could it get any worse?) Michelle Fryer.

Carl spotted me immediately, feigning a start as if surprised. With a stick up her ass, Michelle sashayed to a round booth—the only table I hadn't yet cleaned—and sat down, scooching to its middle. Danny flopped on one side and Carl the other. Reluctantly, I grabbed a bus tub and a rag.

Danny, being his usual stuck-up self, barely acknowledged me clearing his table, but Carl was all charm.

"Hey, Maggie. I thought you might be working today." He stacked a couple of dirty plates, hoping to make my job easier. I put them in the bus tub then wiped down the table. Michelle quickly put me in my place. "You missed a spot here."

I made an exaggerated sweep with the rag as she gave me and my yellow polyester smock the once-over. Michelle's closet was her father's entire department store.

"What a shame to not have your weekend off," she said to the boys. "I'm glad I don't have to work."

"Well I do," I said, not playing into her social one-upmanship. "So, what can I get you?"

Michelle picked up the phone, indicating that was how she preferred to place her order even though she knew full well I'd be the one answering her call. I refrained from rolling my eyes. "You can just tell me what you want."

"One large order of fries for us to share," Michelle instructed as if speaking to a child, "and three medium Pepsis."

"Gimmie a large coke," grunted Danny.

"And I'll take a Sprite," added Carl.

"So that means only one medium Pepsi," Michelle corrected, making certain I understood.

"Got it," I assured her. "Anything else?"

"Extra ice in my drink, please."

It was 38 degrees outside and Michelle needed extra ice. Probably to replace the cubes in her veins.

"And see that the fries are fresh," she added as I walked away. "Last time I was here I was served cold leftover fries."

I bypassed Simon and filled their order myself, making damn sure the fries were hot and the drinks were cold. Then I promptly delivered them, hoping they'd promptly eat up and get the hell out. Sidled up to Danny as if making her claim, Michelle gave me a half-ass thank-you that really meant "move along now."

Carl touched my hand, stopping my retreat.

"So, Maggie. You've been threatening to go out with me for a while now. How about tonight? You up for a movie? The Kinder's still showing *The Exorcist*."

Michelle stopped mid french fry. "But you saw that with us when it first opened," she whined. Ignoring her, Carl continued.

"What do you say, Maggie? I don't mind seeing it again, if you haven't."

"It's goddamn freaky," Danny interjected with a yawn, bored by the company and the conversation.

Before I could ponder my response, Michelle scooted Carl out of the booth and excused herself for the bathroom, but not before saying, "Could you bring me another bottle of ketchup? This one's disgusting."

I could understand Danny's attitude. To him, I was inconsequential. But Michelle? Why did I upset her apple cart? If I had a more accommodating nature, I would have blown her off. But I didn't. "Sure," I answered Carl loud enough for her to hear. "Why not?"

Carl smiled. "Great. I'll pick you up at seven."

• • •

Dating wasn't something I did often, largely because I seldom got asked out. Including Carl's offer, I could count my dates on one hand. Maybe I emitted an unapproachable vibe. Maybe I was uninteresting. Although Amy Hanks's out-of-state cousin hadn't thought so.

She had introduced me to him at a baseball game the summer before I started high school. A stocky guy from San Diego whose mischievous eyes reminded me of Bucky's, he had a cool way of talking that I didn't completely understand. When he told me that I was "a real turn-on" and added, "Can you dig it?" I had no idea what he meant. Was that code for "Do you want to go out?" Or did it mean something more physical like "Do you want to make out?"

Embarrassed by my ignorance, I took a chance it meant the former, and when in the course of our conversation he repeated, "Can you dig it?" I answered, "I don't know. Maybe. When?"

"What?" he asked.

"What you said," I answered.

"What'd I say?" he asked.

"Oh, never mind," I answered.

"I can dig it."

"What?" I asked.

"What?" he asked.

"I might. I'll have to ask my mom first."

Totally confused, he left me to join Amy at the concession stand and I never saw him again.

My sophomore year, when I was no longer flat-chested, a senior took a shine to me. Randy Cole. We'd pass looks between classes in the science hallway. I knew he was building up the courage to ask me out, and when the spring dance came around, sure enough he did. I liked Randy, but I wasn't interested in pursuing a romance. My heart belonged to Bucky. Still, it was flattering to get asked out by someone older, so I said yes.

Mom was more excited about my first date than me. She fussed over what I should wear and even offered to treat me to a new outfit from the Young Miss Closet, our mall's hippest boutique.

I needed a back-up plan, just in case things didn't go too well, and Mom helped me cook one up, suggesting a curfew, even though I didn't have one. When Randy came to our front door, she laid down the law as rehearsed. "Now, Maggie, I want you in by eleven thirty and no later." I rolled my eyes for Randy's benefit.

It was an okay date. We had fun. But I didn't like the awkward do-we-kiss moment at my front door. When he asked me out again, I turned him down. It was for the best.

My evening with Carl started off in the same manner, only now Brian played the curfew cop. "Get her home by eleven thirty sharp! Not one second later!" No eyeroll was necessary.

We did a quick drag of Main Street in Carl's Dodge before parking in the theater's lot and joining the rest of the moviegoers lined up at the box office. I offered to pay for my ticket, but Carl insisted it was his treat, making it an honest-to-goodness date. He wouldn't even let me pay for the popcorn.

Named after Oliver Kinder, a wealthy town founder, the Kinder was our region's oldest and grandest theater. Originally touted "The West's Finest Picture Palace," the Kinder started her pre-talkie career gilded in gold and decked in boudoir-red. Bright stencils of peacocks and other plumed beauties decorated her walls and ceiling, and live canaries in oriental cages hung in her lobby. Her outsides were redressed to Art Deco in the 30s and soon after, Western-themed murals replaced her painted birds. Mounted buffalo heads came to dominate the lobby until 1941 — the same year my father eagerly paid his twenty-five cents only to make it midway through the feature before running out in terror of the Wicked Witch of the West — when the Kinder was given more seating capacity and a modern-day, neon-encrusted face lift. That was how she looked in 1964 when I plopped down my dollar to see *The Blob* and exited in the same fashion as my frightened father had.

That was also how she looked when Carl and I took our seats in the Kinder's balcony, the hot place for teenagers. Accessed by a stairwell in the lobby, the balcony split into two sides with the projection room standing in between. It was an unspoken rule that smokers sat on the right side, but not everyone followed it. I preferred the left.

Minors weren't allowed to smoke, but only a few ushers enforced the rule. Bossy Bessie was one of them. Once her keen sense of smell zeroed in on the offender, she'd immediately make him or her put it out. She could also detect any illegal substance, be it pot or booze.

A skinny little thing no taller than your average ten-year-old, Bossy Bessie proudly wore the red usher's jacket embellished with gold epaulettes and brass buttons above a black pleated skirt that hit at the knees. She had an enormous head and an equally big vocal capacity she wasn't afraid to use when making her flashlight rounds looking for feet on the seatbacks—her particular pet peeve. She also didn't appreciate anyone making out on her watch, and if she caught you, on went the flashlight, followed by a loud "Keep it clean!" that elicited snickers and sometimes applause.

The Exorcist didn't lend itself to romantic notions, and there wasn't much smooching going on, just a lot of hand-grabbing and head-hiding to go along with the screaming. Some of it from me.

So far Carl was behaving himself. More so than Jeffry Taylor, who'd been making moves on Susan Weston in the seats in front of us. Susan would give him an elbow and he'd back off for a while, then creep back in for whatever feel he could get.

Between the bed-bouncing demon on the screen and the scene playing out right in front of me, things were getting intense. I didn't want to miss anything, but desperately needed to go to the bathroom.

"Better hurry," Carl whispered as I got up and climbed over him. "The best part is coming up."

Making my way past an aisle of legs, I dashed downstairs to the ladies' room in the lobby. Its waiting area served as a cry room. It had speakers and a glass window, making it possible for mothers to watch the movie while tending to their babies and unruly kids. After taking care of business, I paused in front of the window just in time to see the demon-possessed child on the screen projectile vomit ghastly green bile smack-dab in the face of her horrified priest. Then a hand came down on my shoulder.

"Maggie."

"Jesus Christ!" I screamed, nearly jumping out of my skin. I swung around expecting to see the devil himself. Instead it was Joe-Joe.

"What the hell are you doing in here?"

"I saw you come in. Pretty scary movie, huh?"

Joe-Joe was being fidgety, even for him.

"What are you?" I asked. "Some kind of pervert?"

"Yeah, well. I need your help. With Bucky."

"Bucky?"

"He's, ah . . . kinda sick."

"What do you mean 'sick'?"

"Let's just say the girl in the movie's not the only one barfing."

"Is he here?"

"Yeah, and he's kinda drunk."

"Bucky? Bucky doesn't get drunk."

"Well he is tonight. We saw Melinda and the old guy going into Mendel's Bar."

"When did she get a fake ID?" I wondered out loud.

"Maybe she doesn't need one with Gramps. Anyway, it set him off, and when Joel MaCrae passed around a bottle of Southern Comfort in the balcony Bucky hit it pretty hard. I need you to help me get him out of here without anyone noticing before we both catch hell."

"Where is he?"

"In the bathroom."

I poked my head out to check the lobby. Not a soul, not even at the concession stand. A testament to the movie's seat-gluing power. I followed Joe-Joe to the men's bathroom and waited by the door while he made sure Bucky was the only one inside.

"The coast is clear, but we gotta hurry."

I ventured in. Sitting beside a urinal with his head in his hands, Bucky looked up with a lopsided grin. "Maaaaggie," he warbled. "Maaaaggieeee."

I couldn't help but laugh. "You're sloshed."

"This ain't funny," Joe-Joe said, darting beside Bucky as he kept one eye on the door. "Help me get him up."

"I'm good. I'm good," Bucky insisted as he struggled to stand, but it took the three of us to make sure he could. I steadied Bucky while Joe-Joe carefully opened the door and peeked through.

"Shit!" he mouthed, closing it and creating a barricade with his body. "It's Bossy Bessie taking a cigarette break."

I panicked. "That'll take forever! We need a distraction."

"Yeah. Go tell her something."

172

"I can't let her see me coming out of the men's room."

Joe-Joe gave me a shrug. He had nothing.

"You go," I insisted. "Tell her you . . . you lost . . . I don't know, something. Your keys! Get her to look for them. Then I'll take Bucky outside and we'll meet you there."

Joe-Joe liked that plan. He slapped his face, twitched his neck then crouched low, jumping from foot to foot as if preparing for a wrestling match. Sufficiently psyched, he opened the door to take on his opponent.

It didn't take much finessing. Always eager to put her flashlight to good use, Bossy Bessie snubbed out her cigarette and followed Joe-Joe back to his seat to hunt down the keys in question.

I guided Bucky as he stumbled through the deserted lobby, and we successfully exited the theater's double doors without being seen. Fortunately, the cold temporarily sobered Bucky, and I didn't have to worry about him falling over. It wasn't long before Joe-Joe joined us.

"Worked like a charm. Got her upstairs, and what do you know? My keys had been in my pocket all along. Then she went apeshit on Billy Chambers and a whole row of guys for having their shoes on the seatbacks." Joe-Joe took off his jacket and tossed it my way. "You stand here with Buckaroo and I'll pull the Blazer around."

"No. I can walk," Bucky protested. I wasn't so sure, but he managed to make it around the block and to the Blazer without too much conspicuous staggering.

I stopped Joe-Joe before he got behind the wheel.

"Wait a minute. Maybe I should drive. How much did you drink?"

"Come on, Maggie. Cut me some slack, huh? You know I've got the state tournament coming up."

I had to hand it to Joe-Joe for his dedication. When he wanted something, he did what was necessary to make it happen.

I flipped the passenger seat up and poured Bucky into the back. "I'm going to sit in the back, too," I told Joe-Joe, "Just to make sure he's okay."

Bucky didn't protest when I told him to lay his head in my lap, and I didn't protest when he grabbed my hand, using my arm as a drape for his shoulder.

Joe-Joe talked the entire way home, but I didn't pay attention. Nor did I notice the cold. I was only aware of Bucky and what it felt like to be so close to him. To have the heft of his curled-up body within my reach. His warm breath on my hand. His silky, yet slightly oily hair between my fingers. The rise and fall of his chest on my thigh. The rush of his beating heart, and the sweet ache in mine. Even in his current state I wanted more of him. More time to explore.

The ride home was too short.

Joe-Joe pulled into the Majorses' driveway and cut the engine. "Okay. Now we have to get him in without getting busted. Suppose we could ring the bell and run?"

"Don't be an idiot," I snapped just as Bucky sat up, trying to get his bearings.

"I think I'm going to be sick," he announced.

Joe-Joe opened the passenger door and lifted its seat just in time for Bucky to make it out of the Blazer before upchucking in the front yard. Bucky wiped his mouth with his shirt sleeve, experiencing the momentary relief that comes after tossing one's cookies.

"I'm okay," he assured us. "I can maintain."

We followed him to the front door with outreached arms, on alert in case he stumbled. Bucky grabbed the door handle and steadied himself before leading us into the house. We paused in the entryway. So far, so good. No voices. Only the sound of the television set.

Joe-Joe nudged me. "Let's sneak him into the bedroom."

We made it through the front room and into the hall before getting caught by Tommy, who was coming out of the kitchen with a bowl of Cheerios. Tommy pointed his spoon at his brother. "What's up with him?"

"Bad hot dog?" Joe-Joe replied.

Tommy shrugged.

"Where's your mom and dad?" I asked.

"Out." Tommy took a bite of cereal. "They left me in charge of the kids." After scrutinizing the situation, he added, "Don't worry. Your secret's safe."

As Tommy headed back to the rec room and its TV, Bucky staggered down the hall leading to their bedroom. When his little sister Julie was born, Bucky had had to give up his privacy. Now he shared a room with Tommy, one marked by a skull and crossbones sign to ward off their youngest siblings.

I had often wondered what Bucky's bedroom looked like. Two shelves dominated the room's pine-paneled walls. One held Bucky's trophies and model cars and the other supported Tommy's passions, model airplanes and various rocks. All very "boy," including the blue checkered bedspreads on their unmade twin beds.

Bucky plopped onto his while peeling off his shirt, but had trouble getting it over his head. I stepped in to help, freeing the shirt's neck-hole from his chin.

"Peekaboo," he giggled.

I cradled my head, trying not to laugh. When I uncovered my eyes, Bucky was looking at me in that cocksure way boys do when they like what they see. He was checking me out!

"Maaaaggie."

I couldn't move.

"Come on. Come on," urged Joe-Joe, who was trying to take off Bucky's shoes.

"Maggie, you smell so good. You always smell so good."

"More than I can say for your feet," Joe-Joe said, snorting as he tossed Bucky's sneakers in the corner.

"I love your hair. It's so . . . don't ever cut your hair, Maggie. Maaaaggie. Have I ever told you. . ." Bucky's head hit the pillow in mid-sentence.

"Told me what? Bucky?" I shook his shoulders "Told me what?"

Bucky was out, his disclosure left unsaid.

"Nighty night, Buckaroo. You're going to be in a world of hurt tomorrow." Joe-Joe tugged on my arm. "Come on, Mags. Let's get while the getting's good."

Joe-Joe drove us home and walked me to the door as I chewed on what had been about to follow that "Have I ever told you . . ."

"Jeez. It's awful early to be home, huh?" Joe-Joe said looking at his wristwatch under the porch light. "The movie's just getting out."

"Crap! I forgot all about Carl," I groaned. "He's either going to hate me for ditching him or be worried sick."

"I told you I squared it with him."

"What?"

"When we were driving home? I told you I told him that I saw you coming out of the bathroom and you wanted to leave. Remember?"

"Why did I want to leave?"

"I said you didn't like the movie."

"And he was fine abandoning me and letting you drive me home?"

"I don't know. Yeah?"

That kinda sucked. You'd think he'd at least try to convince me to stay.

"Well, it doesn't matter anyway. It's for the best."

Joe-Joe looked at his watch again, avoiding my eyes. "I wouldn't make too much of what Bucky said, you know what I mean?"

I took off the coat that he had lent me and tossed it in his face. He put it on then sniffed at the collar. "Damn, Maaaaggie. You do smell good." Then he gave me a thumbs-up and took off running.

Damn Joe-Joe, anyway.

CHAPTER 14

That March was the coldest I remembered. It had been relatively warm, hovering in the 50s, then Old Man Winter belched an untimely arctic blast and temperatures plummeted. For three days, the thermometer read no higher than four degrees and got as low as minus thirty. The sun blazed in the noon sky but the air could be cracked, just like the sidewalk's ice puddles. It was the kind of cold that stuck your nostrils together when you breathed in, and where your steamy exhalation was the only evidence that heat existed.

It was definitely too damn cold for a funeral.

The visitation had also been cold due to a shoddy heating system. Taking place the previous day, it had been held at the First Presbyterian Church in two rooms separated by a curtain. On one side were benches for mourners to sit and pray while they waited to pay their respects. On the other was Elizabeth Bales in her casket.

It wasn't my first viewing. On the eve of my grandmother's funeral I had sat with family and friends waiting to make the trip around the curtain and say our goodbyes. We were supposed to be praying and crying, but I could do neither. I was too mad at God for taking her and too mad at Grandma for letting him. So when my Aunt Sylvia and Uncle Bob came from around the curtain, both weeping, and my father took my hand saying, "We're next," I dug in my heels like a kid being dragged to the dentist. I refused to go with him. To see her "that way."

Now, eight years later, I willingly saw what the dead looked like.

Mrs. Bales looked good. At least that's what everybody said. According to them, Mr. Clemens, owner and undertaker of Clemens Funeral Parlor "sure has a way of making them appear natural."

This being my first time, I had to take their word for it. Her snow-white hair, gathered in its usual tight bun, appeared natural enough, but to me that was the only thing that did. Her skin's color seemed off, a bluish-pink mixed with shades of orange and gray. Her sunken shut eyes off-set her brow and the bridge of her nose, making them both seem coarser than they had actually been, and her pursed lips, artificially tinted red, showed no hint of a smile. There was no tenderness in her face. It had settled into a stern version of itself that only partially reflected how Elizabeth Bales had lived her life.

She was wearing a pink chiffon nightgown and its matching robe, a peignoir set she and her sister had picked out years ago for just this occasion. "Damned if we're going to wear fussy dresses for all eternity. No siree, Bob. A nightie will do just fine. And for heaven's sake, put me in slippers!"

Without a doubt, there was a comfortable pair under the crocheted lavender afghan tucked around the lower half of her body. Her blue-veined, age-spotted hands were crossed on her abdomen with the thumb of her left hand grasping that of her right. She wore her wedding band. And a watch. I didn't recall her saying anything about the necessity of telling time in eternity, but she had said she wanted a grand casket, preferably black, lined with white satin, and possessing big brass handles to ensure she wouldn't be dropped when carried to her grave. One more substantial than the cheap wooden coffin her sister had been buried in. She had gotten her wishes on all fronts.

Elizabeth Bales had died on the last day of February, two weeks shy of her ninetieth birthday. Her peaceful passing happened shortly after lunch as she and her husband watched their favorite game show, Let's Make a Deal, in the living room. When Monty Hall offered his customary trade to a sexy female contestant dressed in a sailor suit and Mrs. Bales didn't yell out, "Take the box, stupid!" Mr. Bales knew something was wrong. She had died in her La-Z-Boy with her dog, Stew Pot, at her feet.

The details of her dying were known only to close friends. The story of her life was legendary, recapped in her obituary and bandied about before her memorial service by the many movers and shakers with whom she'd surrounded herself.

Bred from can-do people, Elizabeth Watson was a native Wyomingite whose mother, Pearlie, a hardheaded suffragette from New Jersey, had moved to the Wyoming territory in the 1880s primarily because it was one of the few places where she could vote. That right, placed in the determining hands of the individual states then systematically revoked across the board, passed into Wyoming law in 1869, making the not-yet state the first in the country to grant suffrage to women, more than fifty years before the ratification of the Nineteenth Amendment.

Another reason Pearlie traveled out west was that she wanted a reputable husband, and with six men for every woman she figured she had pretty good odds. It took less than a month to grab the attention of Jack Watson, a bright, ambitious land surveyor, and less than a year after that to give birth to her first daughter, Elizabeth.

Jack Watson and his new bride not only shaped the infrastructure of our fledgling town but were in on the ground floor of statehood. In 1889, Jack was elected to serve the constitutional convention in Cheyenne, and Pearlie, with little Elizabeth and a suckling infant in tow, was by his side making sure he and the rest of the entirely male delegation remembered what side of the equality fence they were on when drafting the Wyoming State Constitution. She also weighed in on matters concerning religion, labor, and education.

Little Elizabeth keenly observed her mother's well-crafted influence. Like her mother, she would advantageously use her intellect and wit in both politics and business for the rest of her life. Mrs. Bales had been a fountainhead in our community, lending her support—sometimes financial, sometimes in the form of sweat—to numerous charities and organizations. Her pet project had been the Historical Society, and its entire membership (at least those who weren't at death's door themselves) were on hand to pay their respects to the woman who had been the lifeblood of their archival cause. Elks,

American Legionnaires, and Odd Fellows also vied for seating among the church's overflowing pews.

More than four hundred people showed up for her memorial service in spite of the weather. Most of the town's dignitaries, past and present. Mayors, sheriffs, fire chiefs. Even a former state representative flew in to pay his respects. The business community was also well represented. Her guestbook read like a who's who from the Chamber of Commerce.

The Reverend Bauer, pastor of the First Presbyterian, had been tending to Elizabeth Baleses' soul for over forty years and was in his element eulogizing from the sanctuary's pulpit. Mrs. Bales had specified that she wanted no droning at her funeral. No carrying-on by anyone, no matter how well intentioned. "Make it short and sweet." Reverend Bauer's sober tribute was neither. He extolled her virtuous Christian leanings at length and left out her colorful boorish parts. In between lengthy readings and prayers, he led us in singing hymns as stodgy as his one-sided testament to a many-faceted lady.

Mr. Bales had little say in his wife's memorial given she had always called the devotional shots. He would just as soon be thrown in a cardboard box and buried in a potter's field when his time was up. But to please his wife, Mr. Bales had purchased a double plot at the Eternal Mount Cemetery where he was obligated to eventually join her.

The brutal cold had deterred only the frailest mourners. Most had followed the Clemens hearse to the cemetery and were now huddled in groups as close to graveside as possible. The casket had been carried without incident by Mrs. Baleses' pallbearers—my father, Big Buck, the Colonel, Doc Simms, Mr. Padilla and Ricky Padilla—where it hovered over its hard-earned hole. (The frozen ground had had to be heated before a backhoe could dig down the necessary six feet.) A simple wreath of red and white carnations topped the casket's gleaming black lid and spears of sunlight reflected off its brass handles.

Whether he was hungry or just didn't like the cold, Reverend Bauer wasted no time initiating Mrs. Baleses' final send-off. One prayer, one blessing, now drop her, boys. As the lowering device eased the casket down, the Reverend folded his arms and tossed an impatient nod in my direction. That was my cue.

Mrs. Bales had specified two songs be sung at her funeral. The first was the hymn "Our God, Our Help in Ages Past," which had been warbled by Reverend Bauer and the church's elderly choir as the pallbearers fetched her casket and loaded it into the hearse. The second was unconventional and, in the Reverend's opinion, only marginally acceptable funerary fare: "Little Joe the Wrangler," a Western ballad to be sung by me at graveside.

Mrs. Baleses' favorite song, "Little Joe the Wrangler" was a real tearjerker. One of those multi-versed cowboy poetry songs steeped in hardship and tragedy, recited and sung around campfires — or, in my case, in front of my grandmother's furnace.

It was an ominous tale from its very first line — *Little Joe the Wrangler will wrangle never more.* Although the song disturbed me, I would beg Grandma to sing it, and as I sat on her lap with my head pressed against her chest, I would listen to her scratchy yet tender voice tell Little Joe's sad story while hoping for a different outcome.

Life at home for Little Joe was not easy. His real mother had died, then the mom after that, and *his new ma whipped him every day or two.* So, one day he saddled his old brown pony and set out with hopes of learning how to *paddle his own canoe.* Soon he came upon a round-up camp, weary and looking like a disheveled stray, and even though Little Joe *didn't know straight up about a cow*, he asked for a job. The wranglers, including the boss, took a shine to the gutsy little fella and made him feel welcome. They taught him how to work the horses and other wrangling necessities.

Things went along pretty well for Little Joe until one night, while camping along a bend in the Red River, *a norther commenced to blowing* and spooked the herd. Everybody had to do their part to keep them in line. Even Little Joe.

The cattle stampeded *like a hailstorm, long they flew,* and the wranglers tried to get to the front and turn them. But one horse, Old Blue Rocket, was ahead of them all *tween the streaks of lightning*, and riding him was Little Joe *with his slicker 'bove his head* doing his darnedest to catch the leading agitators and slow them down.

At last the cowboys got the herd quieted and they all headed back to camp, but when they got there someone was missing.

Next morning just at sunup we found where Rocket fell,
Down in a washout twenty feet below.
Beneath his horse, mashed to a pulp, his spurs had rung the knell
For our little Texas stray – poor Wrangler Joe.

There was a silence when I ended the song. A finality. Even the wind stopped blowing. No one moved. Not even the Reverend. As we stood in perplexed suspension, a pair of black crows flew overhead, their back-and-forth *caw caw, caw caw* penetrating its harsh frigidity.

Was it over? Were we done? Apparently we were, because the same Eternal Mount Cemetery worker who had pushed the lever to lower Mrs. Baleses' casket into the ground started tapping on his wristwatch. In a not-too-subtle voice, he directed the Reverend to "move these people out. Got another in a half hour."

Mr. Bales stood up from the folding chair that had been placed graveside for him and walked to the hole that had swallowed his wife. "Well, my dear. It's time to get out of the cold."

Then, like a restless herd, the rest of us followed his lead towards warmer environs, making room for the next in line.

CHAPTER 15

A blue funk descended upon Old Orphanage Road after that. Perhaps it was lingering grief. The death of Elizabeth Bales, the matriarch who had packaged our seven families and tied the bow on what became our neighborhood, had really knocked us for a loop.

Of course, we were worried about Mr. Bales. "I've seen it happen time and time again with old folk," Doc Simms warned us. "One passes, the other shortly follows. He won't last long." Even though the old guy let it be known he had no intention of dying just yet, we kept close tabs on him. Mrs. Mavrakis and Mrs. Padilla did most of the hovering, making sure he was well fed. Mom made sure he had clean clothes. And Dad popped in daily with his tool kit.

Between morning coffees at the Pancake Alley with Mr. Padilla and daily visits from a myriad of checker-uppers, Mr. Bales fared reasonably well for a newly widowed ninety-year-old. He had his health, his wits, and he could still enjoy the occasional cigar and glass of bourbon.

On the other hand, Stew Pot, the Bales mutt, was going downhill fast. His rambunctious lifestyle and estimated nine people years had taken their toll, and all three of Stewie's legs were riddled with arthritis. He spent most of his days curled up in his bed and only ventured outside to relieve himself.

Or maybe the weather put us in a foul mood. Although the calendar read spring, we were still in winter's grasp. The novelty of snow had long worn off. Unlike the wet stuff that could be shaped into snowmen and compacted into snow forts and snowballs, the season's-end flurries were dry and unmalleable, making outdoor activities of all stripes, chores or otherwise, not fun. Five inches of anemic powder fell on Good Friday.

I had hoped that the Majorses' Easter morning egg hunt would cheer things up, as Mrs. Majors always delighted in playing the Easter Bunny, finding the perfect hiding spots within the confines of her shrubbery for her own goodies and the neighbors' pre-delivered contributions. She could be quite a tricky hider, and stumbling upon an errant egg long past Easter wasn't unusual. Along with dyed hard-boiled eggs, her bunny deposits included multicolored plastic eggs, each holding a candy treasure or hard cash, the latter being the best insurance that older kids would take part. Mrs. Majorses' only rules were you had to have a basket and you had to pose for the Easter photo. A small price to pay.

But sadly, for the first time in our neighborhood's ten-year history, the hunt didn't happen. Partly because Big Buck's car sales were in a slump and partly due to Mrs. Majors being "just too damn tired." They compensated for the cancellation by delivering chocolate bunnies to each doorstep along with an invitation to join them later at Kinder Park for the annual Chamber of Commerce Eggstravaganza. I declined. My egg-hunting days had come to an end.

Mrs. Majors wasn't the only one lacking *oomph*. Dad's knees had been giving him fits and he spent weeks in bed. My father was not a good patient. Mom did her best to put up with him, but she had her limits and turned over nursing duties to Brian, thinking that if my brother could handle Dad's bellyaching he stood a good chance at attaining his nursing goal.

On down the line the moping continued. Fed up with refereeing his three younger brothers' fighting, Bucky avoided home as much as possible, spending most of his time at baseball practice or with Joe-Joe, who was dangerously bored now that wrestling season was over. Meanwhile, Melinda, ever the unpleasant daughter, was doing what she could to get under her father's skin, claiming she couldn't wait for him and "the hussy" to resume their "insensate gallivanting" and leave her the hell alone. At this point he had been home for two months, but I sensed another Salt Lake City trip in the making.

The champ of our neighborhood grouchfest, however, was Rebecca Frick. On the outs with her boyfriend, Gordon, she had taken to voicing her displeasure with his "indiscretions" from her porch every morning as he left for his job with the county road department.

"Why don't you have *her* make your goddamn sandwich? And she can buy your shitty Ho Hos, too. Gordon? Do you hear me, Gordon?" or "That's it. Take your goddamn sandwich and get the hell out of my sight. And don't think I'll be here when you get home tonight. I mean it, Gordon. I most definitely mean it." My favorite was when she said, "You can shove your white bread up your sorry white ass. That's the last sandwich you'll get out of me. I'm changing the locks, so don't bother coming back. I mean it, Gordon. Do you understand me, Gordon?"

The neighbors had become accustomed to Rebecca's porch fits, harbingers of yet another breakup. The first one I'd witnessed involved a one-legged bodybuilder named Tim. Bucky, Melinda and I had just gotten off the school bus when a wooden prosthesis flew out from Rebecca's bedroom window and landed in her front yard. Soon after, Tim, wearing nothing but his skivvies and a shoe, hopped out of the house to retrieve his leg with Rebecca following close behind. "My less than perfect derriere has been good enough to pay your goddamn bills!" she had yelled, tossing his clothes one way and a shoe the other. "You can just kiss my sagging ass and my money goodbye!"

Toodle-lo Tim.

For a while a caterwauling cowboy pursued Rebecca, serenading her every weekend with his harmonica and setting every dog in the neighborhood howling, but he, too, was tossed.

At that point Rebecca decided to upgrade the men in her life, no more "suitors who didn't have a pot to piss in." So entered Sir Peter Sebastian, a wealthy, stylish Englishman who wore turtlenecks and tweed jackets and smoked a bent pipe, all of which accentuated his beautiful bald head.

Rebecca met Sir Peter on a Miami excursion and suggested he give the Wild West a try. Once he obliged, Rebecca became his personal tour guide. It was all very respectable. Too respectable for Rebecca, who was eager to show him her wild side yet discovered Sir Peter was a bit of a prude. And light in the loafers, which took Rebecca by surprise because she usually sorted that out. Seems he had developed a thing for men in cowboy boots.

So long, pardner.

To date, Rebecca's most tragic romance was with Dan "Dandy" McDonald, who drove a tanker truck up from Cheyenne twice weekly. Every Monday and Thursday night he'd park his rig in front of Rebecca's house, and every Tuesday and Friday morning she'd send him south with a kiss and a cup of coffee. Dandy had a wife with three kids in diapers living in Cheyenne who did the same thing every Wednesday and Sunday, common knowledge among the truckers who frequented the Bronco Saloon as Rebecca found out.

It wasn't her discovery of Dandy's home life that sent him packing. It was his traveling companion, a meaner-than-snot dump dog named Freeway who Dandy had rescued off Interstate 25. Protective of his master, Freeway didn't take kindly to Francine.

A messy bird, Francine was also noisy and demanding. And prone to depression. Rebecca had to hire a sitter whenever she was away for more than a twenty-four hours, and when Rebecca went on one of her extended trips, she either had to take Francine with her or deliver her personally to a special parrot hotel in San Francisco.

Francine's antics could be quite charming, but she could also bite. Dangling protuberances, particularly earlobes, were the main targets of her aggression. She had been naughty more than once with Dandy, and when she finally drew blood, Freeway took offence. Not long after, he took revenge.

The three of us had been sitting on Bucky's porch swing on a quiet Tuesday summer evening when Rebecca, wearing nothing more than a negligee, ran out of her house and across the street into the Majorses' yard, screaming, "Get me a gun! Get me a gun!" Big Buck intercepted and tried to calm her down, but she remained hysterical. After handing her off to Mrs. Majors, he headed to Rebecca's place, unarmed and uncertain what he would find. What he found was feathers strewn all over the front porch; Freeway, snarling with a foot and a feather in his mouth; and Dandy, buck naked and in a stupor. "Put on some clothes, son," Big Buck had told him. "And if you know what's good for you, you'll take your dog and get the hell out of here."

Exit Dandy.

Poor Rebecca. In a state after Francine's demise, it took three months before she sobered up and swore off booze, and a year after that before she'd have anything to do with a man again. Of course, sobriety and celibacy have their limits.

Enter Gordon.

Rebecca met Gordon during a road-blasting holdup on a one-lane road to Casper while sandwiched between a carload of elderly bridge players on their way to a tournament and a U-Haul filled with the belongings of newlyweds eager to begin their life in Colorado. Gordon was the flagman who swapped stories with the captive travelers while waiting for the all clear. When time came for the motorists to move out, Gordon gave Rebecca a wink. Rebecca decided she could wait a little longer, so she pulled off the road, waved goodbye to her line buddies, and killed time until Gordon got off work so they could drive off into the sunset.

Gordon defined good-looking, tanned and chiseled with perfectly straight, perfectly white teeth and oh, that head of hair, sun-bleached, long and curly. Tall and well-built, he had every female in the neighborhood atwitter. Even Mrs. Mavrakis did a double take every time she saw him outside in his shorts. And Gordon always wore shorts. It could be ten below and Gordon would still venture out while exposing his muscly and befittingly hairy legs to the elements.

Rebecca adored Gordon, and by all appearances he returned her affections. Not comfortable being a freeloader, he took on the role of caretaker, seeing that she, her house, her yard, and her car were well maintained. He was good to her and good for her, but trust did not come easily to Rebecca. She was wary of handing over her heart, and she remained on love's edge. Another bird gave her the push.

Gordon had been running along the dirt road adjacent to the old Beecher property that paralleled the Little Goose River. The cottonwoods were spewing their downy seeds, and the fine white fluff resembled a spring snowfall. Quite a beguiling scene—unless you happened to have allergies. Gordon did, and his run was interrupted by a three-minute sneezing fit. While hunching over, however, he spotted black motion amid the whiteness. A magpie chick had fallen from its nest. Knowing its parents were certainly not nearby or else they would be harassing him, he debated over whether or not to let nature take its course, but decided to intervene. Finding a tossed paper cup, he fashioned a nest, then carried the magpie home and presented it to Rebecca. She fell head over heels, for both Gordon and the bird.

Rebecca named the magpie "Lenore" after Edgar Allen Poe's famous raven. She set up a nursery in Francine's old cage then set about the endless task of hand-feeding Lenore. Grasshoppers, gooseberries, nuts, hamburger—Lenore would eat just about anything. Once the black-billed magpie had imprinted on her non-birdie mom, Rebecca allowed her to fly freely in the house; there would be no clipping this bird's wings, and no dogs allowed anywhere near her. Eventually Rebecca introduced Lenore to the outdoors, giving her permission to come and go. Lenore was happy to explore the neighborhood trees but always returned to Rebecca's porch windowsill, chattering to be let back in.

Lenore was a kleptomaniac. Shiny things were her preferred spoils—keys, earrings, bottle caps—but she also liked to filch hair. No head was safe from her dive-bombing once she had chosen her coif. We had all been her victims and took cover any time we heard the familiar *wock-a-wock* overhead. She was also drawn to smoldering cigarette butts and would stash them along with the rest of her booty between Rebecca's sofa cushions. Gordon had put out more than one fire, the most recent of which had destroyed the couch and filled the entire house with smoke. After that Gordon pleaded with Rebecca to give up cigarettes. She consented, but it did not put her in a good mood. Quite the opposite.

Now one year old, and beckoned by the springtime sunlight, Lenore was coming home less and less. Rebecca surmised her magpie was off cavorting with the opposite sex, and thanks to her nicotine-deprived state, suspected Gordon was doing the same. Little clues cropped up: increased overtime at work, drinks afterwards with "just the guys," unfamiliar perfume lingering on his coat, and all-night weekend poker games followed by "Not now, baby. I gotta get some sleep."

"You've got a corn cob for a brain, you know that Gordon? The only thing worse than a cheating liar is a cheating liar with no imagination. You can just stay at her place tonight. You hear me, you son-of-a-bitch? And you forgot to take your goddamn sandwich!"

Who "she" was, Rebecca didn't know, but in her experience, there was always one eventually. In our experience, whenever Rebecca's outbursts became more frequent, her boyfriend was on the way out. None of us looked forward to that happening. We liked Gordon.

The encumbering funk festered well into April. Our neighborhood was one big pimple, and it needed to be popped. In my case quite literally, which is why I accepted Patricia Simms's invitation for a Sunday afternoon beauty treatment and some serious girl talk.

Patricia Simms had spent the better part of a year trying to get to first base with Joe-Joe's older brother, Ricky, but Ricky wasn't playing ball. Hoping to find a solution to her problem, she had placed her faith in *Cosmopolitan* articles like "How to Get His Attention" and "Try Witchcraft—5 Love Spells" and "What to Do When Your Man is Inhibited." Nothing had worked. "He Loves Me, He Loves Me Not" threw her into depression and "How to Drown the Blues and Get on with It" propelled her into action. She needed a plan and I needed a facial.

Patricia met me at the door wearing one of her father's white doctoring coats. Her long red hair, tightly rolled around empty diet Pepsi cans and held in place with bobby pins and a cellophane wrap, added another five inches to her already tall stature. She immediately handed me a robe, a turban, and a small brown jar.

"Take off your shirt, put these on, then wash your face with this scrub. It's *not* Avon. It's from France and very expensive, so use only a little. After you're through, come into the kitchen and we'll begin."

I trotted off to do as I was told.

The Simms had a bathroom designated for guests, but I never felt comfortable when using it. Too clean and too showy, it always left me with a handwashing problem. Which of the tiny carved soaps to use? And was a fella really supposed to touch the fancy embroidered towels, all precisely folded and draped and color-coordinated? At my house, no two towels were alike, and they seldom hung over anything but the sink's rim or the shower rod. At least ours served their purpose and couldn't be confused with the decorations.

The bathroom's well-lit mirror reaffirmed that a beauty treatment was in my best interests, so after I had slipped into the robe and secured my turban, I opened the jar to inspect its contents. The scrub looked like tile mold and didn't smell much better—which no doubt meant it was good stuff. Taking my chances that "only a little" meant a finger scoop, I tested some on my cheek only to find it wasn't smearable. The scoop fell into the sink, most of it going down the drain. *Adieu.* I picked up what dregs I could and mixed them with water, then gave myself a good rubdown followed by a rinse. Forgoing the intimidating towels, I used the robe to dry my face, then did what I could to restore the bathroom's pristine, pre-Maggie condition.

Patricia was standing beside the dinette table with a pot of steaming water and sundry ingredients. "Am I going to have a facial or a late lunch?" I asked.

Impatient with my sarcasm, Patricia pulled out a chair. "Sit," she commanded, taking my shoulders and pushing me downward.

Patricia positioned my turbaned head over the pot then draped a cloth over it so the steam would target my face. "This will open up your pores. Your skin has a lot of breathing to catch up on, so stay put. I'm setting the timer for five minutes."

She was being downright bossy. Come to think of it, she had been showing signs of a backbone, not starting phone calls with her usual "I hate to bother you" nor ending invitations with "If you're not too busy." Maybe all that magazine reading was doing some good.

I stayed put while Patricia readied her next applications: a rinse of distilled water and lemon juice "to kill any remaining bacteria" and an egg-white mask "for toning and tightening." The first stung like hell, and the second was cold and icky. Once again, Patricia set the timer. "Fifteen minutes. Don't talk or your face will crack."

Next she plopped a stack of *Cosmo* issues on the table. Apparently, I was allowed to read.

"Here, I picked this out for you," she said, opening a magazine to "How to Turn His Head When He Has Eyes for Someone Else."

Her presumption was annoying. Its validity even more so.

"Or maybe you would like to look at this." Patricia reached into her white coat's oversized pocket and pulled out a rolled issue of *Playgirl* magazine.

"Wow. Where did you get that?"

"Don't talk," she ordered, bonking my head with the magazine before handing it over. "I bought it at the drugstore."

I was impressed with Patricia's boldness, but even more impressed with what I saw dog-eared in her pawed-over Playgirl: a full-frontal view of one-hell-of-a-hunk in all his glory. An extremely large glory at that.

"Ish dis da normal shize?" I asked as my face continued to tighten.

Patricia gave my head a gentle slap, then looked over my shoulder. "I'm not exactly sure. And that's kind of what I wanted to talk about. I'm thinking about, you know, sex. Having sex. Going all the way?"

"Hmm," I responded, not so sure this was a topic I wanted to discuss with Patricia.

"I know what people think about me, but I've never done it. Have you?"

I shook my head, glad I wasn't supposed to talk.

"Oh," she said. "I was kind of hoping you had."

"Who'sh da wucky guy?" I asked.

Patricia began to pace. "I'm not sure. I mean, it has to happen with someone, right? Are you going to wait? I really don't see the point. I might as well get it out of the way so it doesn't, you know, get in the way. Make sense?"

"Hmm."

"I don't know, I just wanted to talk to somebody who's been there. I mean, you can only read so much."

"Hmm."

"I asked Melinda to come over today, too, but she couldn't make it. I thought that you two might talk more freely around each other."

"Hmm."

"I know enough about the precautions. And the mechanics. I've been, you know, taking care of my sexual needs since I was ten maybe?"

Holy shmoly! Had Patricia just told me she masturbated? Since she was ten? It took me until fourteen to figure that one out, and it wasn't until I was sixteen when, thanks to a frank discussion with Melinda, I learned there was an actual word to go along with that deed.

No longer in motion, Patricia was holding the chairback beside mine. "Help me out here, Maggie. I'm nineteen years old, with no prospects. What if I peak at twenty? What do you think?"

I thought I didn't want to think—not about *it*, not about me *doing it* and definitely not about her *doing it*. Thank God the doorbell rang. Maybe Melinda had decided to come over after all. Patricia went to answer the door.

"Hello, sweetie. Is your mother home?" The voice was unmistakable. Without waiting for an answer, Rebecca Frick let herself in and came straight into the kitchen.

Patricia, who had always been a little afraid of Rebecca, frantically followed. "No. She's with my father. They took my brother to a—"

"It doesn't matter, honey," Rebecca interrupted as she went about opening the kitchen drawers. "I just came to bum one of her cigarettes. Where does she hide them?"

"Cigarettes? My mother doesn't smoke."

"Yes. Of course. Your mother doesn't smoke. You are absolutely right." Rebecca continued her pursuit, now looking in the cupboards.

"But, I might have one," Patricia confessed. She grabbed the purse hanging from a door handle and searched its innards until finding what was left of a broken Virginia Slim. "But please, you can't smoke in here."

Rebecca eyed the pathetic cigarette with desire but declined. "Thanks, honey, but I wouldn't want to take your last one. How about a drink instead? That bourbon your father is so fond of."

Patricia looked aghast. "There's some in the liquor cabinet, but it's locked up."

Rebecca's shoulders slumped. "Of course it is."

"And I don't have the key."

"Of course you don't."

"How about a root beer?"

Leaning against the wall, Rebecca shook her head. She had come to the end of her rope.

BZZZZZ. My timer went off.

Rebecca turned her attention to me. "What have you got there?"

I had forgotten about the *Playgirl* and tried to hide it behind my back. But seeing this as an opportunity, Patricia snatched the magazine from me and thrust it toward Rebecca.

"Maggie was wondering if this is normal, you know, size wise."

Rebecca took the magazine then sat in the dinette chair next to me. "Normal? Oh my, no. No," she said inspecting the object in question from various angles. "This is definitely extraordinary size wise. And at parade rest, no less. Can you imagine what happens when he stands at attention?" Rebecca ended her assessment with a self-amused snort.

Having only a vague understanding of what she was talking about, Patricia and I laughed with her. My face cracked. Patricia ordered me back to the bathroom for a rinse.

When I returned for the next phase of my facial, Rebecca had made herself comfortable at the table and was sorting through magazines. "I've chosen to stay and watch your transformation," she said.

Patricia patted the chair. "Time to pretty you up."

I had never worn much makeup other than a little eye shadow and mascara, but that was about to change.

"The first thing you need to tackle is those eyebrows," Rebecca suggested.

Patricia agreed and went after me with a pencil in one hand and tweezers in the other, sculpting and plucking and enjoying my winces a little too much. Now that she had a task to draw her focus, Patricia grew more at ease with Rebecca. "I was wondering if you . . . I mean, Miss Rebecca, did you, you know, wait before, you know . . . well . . ."

"Ouch!" I said, twisting my mouth.

"What I mean is . . . what are your feelings about premarital intercourse?"

"Honey, from where I'm sitting now, that's the only kind."

"But you were married, right?"

"I went down the aisle three times."

"Oh. Did you, you know . . . well . . .

"Ouch!"

Did you save yourself for the first one?"

"You mean did I go to the altar a virgin? Well, yes, I did. I was also only fourteen."

"*Fourteen*?" Patricia and I said in unison. All plucking stopped.

"A rather young age, I know, but it was a little more acceptable back then." As we let that sink in, Rebecca continued. "Jay Wayne Rickman. Jay Wayne. That's what he went by. One of those double names so common in the South. Jay Wayne. He was an older man. All of nineteen. A little guy, height wise. But strong, and tender as a newborn's coo."

"Were you madly in love?" Patricia asked, intrigued.

"Oh yes, we were. But my daddy didn't approve. Jay Wayne did not meet his uppity standards. He forbade me to see him. But we pulled a fast one and eloped just the same."

Patricia smiled, happy that love had won out, then came at me again with the tweezers.

"Did your father ever come around?" I asked.

"Hell no. My daddy did not like being disobeyed. My marriage was all of two months old before he succeeded in having Jay Wayne arrested on a trumped-up felony charge."

"Ouch!"

"Soon after, Jay Wayne convinced himself that life without me and my daddy's boot up his butt would be more —,"

"Ouch!"

" — tolerable. Can't say as I blamed him."

Patricia stood back to inspect her handiwork. "That's so sad," she proclaimed.

Rebecca eyed my newly tamed eyebrows. "You got that right."

I wasn't sure if they were appraising the Jay Wayne situation or me.

Patricia put down her brow tools and asked Rebecca to hand her the foundation by her elbow. Then she continued her work while carrying on the conversation. "But you fell in love two more times?"

"Let's just say I moved on."

"Oh. So, you really don't have to be in love to make love."

"Lord, no. You don't have to be in love to have a good time."

"But is sex different when you're in love?"

"Yes. It's different when someone really cares about you, and you feel the same way. It's different."

"So, did you—rouge, please—did you feel different after you'd done it the first time? Did you feel more, you know, womanly inside?"

"Honey, having sex won't give you anything that's not already there. Unless it's a baby. Or a disease."

Patricia stopped to ponder both the moment and my freshly blushed cheeks, which under the circumstances didn't need rouge to turn red.

Rebecca put down her current reading. "What's this all about, anyway? Does this have something to do with Ricky Padilla?"

To my surprise, Patricia took Rebecca's question in stride. "In a roundabout way, it does. Blue shadow, please."

Rebecca did as she asked, then sat back in her chair, strumming her fingers on the tabletop before picking up an eyebrow pencil and positioning it as if it were a cigarette. "Let me tell you something about Latinos. An interesting breed of man, but not the most liberated. They tend to put women in one of three categories: virgins, mothers, and whores. He marries a virgin—and by God she better be one—turns her into a mother again and again, then spends the rest of his life in pursuit of whores."

The wind kicked out of her, Patricia put aside her makeup tools and gave Rebecca a long face.

"Ah, honey. Don't listen to me. I'm just being a bitch." Rebecca placed her hand aside Patricia's cheek. "From what I can tell Ricky's a good guy. And he has a good father. A fine man. That in and of itself lessens the odds of him turning into a total asshole."

More confused than ever, Patricia was losing her confidence. When she picked up the eyeliner and came at me with a terse command not to blink I was a little nervous.

"Have you told him how you feel?" Rebecca asked, softening a bit.

"Well, I've given him enough hints. He ought to know by now."

"Oh, sweetie. Men can be awfully stupid, and women insufferably demure. Take your bull by the horns and tell him — no, show him what you want. What's the worst that can happen?"

"She can look like a complete idiot," I said.

"So what?" Rebecca scolded. "I'd rather be a fool who takes a chance than a smartass who lives life on the sidelines." With that she handed the mascara to Patricia and stood, indicating she should finish the job without her. "I'm tired of dispensing wisdom. I need a drink. You two have fun."

With our sex advisor gone, Patricia wasted no time completing my makeover. As soon as she added the final touch of persimmon gloss and I puckered my lips into a tissue, we parted ways, both wanting to be alone with our thoughts.

Returning home to find I had the house to myself, I immediately went to the bathroom mirror to inspect Patricia's work. The glamour gal looking back wasn't bad, but it wasn't me. My first instinct was to wash everything off. Glamour Gal suggested otherwise. *Did it ever occur to you that maybe you need to change? Be someone different? Maybe take the damn bull by the horns for once in your life?* Straightening my posture, I gave myself the thumbs-up, then marched to the telephone.

"Bucky?"

"Yeah?"

"Let's do something tonight."

"You're not working? What you got in mind?"

"Pick me up at seven and we'll figure something out. Oh, and no Joe-Joe this time."

"Okay?"

This smartass was about to get off the sidelines and into the game. Time for serious seduction.

CHAPTER 16

That night I wore my second best sweater, having shrunk my first in the dryer. Although a tad itchy and prone to shedding angora fluffs, it looked great with a pair of jeans but was overkill for the U-Can Bowl, which was where Bucky and I ended up.

Like my sweater, not my first choice. I had suggested the All-Star Drive-in. After a winter hiatus, its pre-opening-weekend schedule, dubbed "Bring on the Heat," was a selection of bikini beach favorites. Unfortunately, the night was too cold for outdoor movie-viewing without running the heater full blast, and Bucky didn't want to waste his gas on go-go dancing. Disappointed, I went along with his bowling suggestion—it would have to do until I could come up with something that involved the two of us being alone.

It was a typical Saturday night at the U-Can Bowl. The league, whose membership was almost exclusively drawn from my parents' generation, had taken up sixteen lanes. When we arrived, there was a waiting list for the remaining four. Bucky put our name on it.

Bowling aside, the U-Can was known for two things: pinball and french fries. Their pinball machines were well played and well loved— or hated, depending on the temperament of the player. Their fries, long and crispy, were the perfect combination of grease and salt, and came with a dipping sauce that couldn't be found anywhere else in town. Plus, they were cheap. I placed our order while Bucky scouted the pinball situation.

Heavy Hitter, the U-Can's oldest machine and Bucky's favorite, sat on its own next to the men's room. More an object of interest, the game involved batting baseballs and only required a nickel. Unfortunately, Troy Knight was on its flippers. Troy usually monopolized King Kool, a four-flipper favorite. Only out of boredom would he step aside and turn a machine over to another player. Judging by the squint in his eyes and the length of the ash coming from his cigarette, Troy wouldn't be leaving Heavy Hitter anytime soon. He had long surpassed Bucky's run record.

"Hey, Buckaroo. Maggie. Over here."

Steve "The Herc" Kenny had spotted us while tying his shoes. Wearing a tank top and tight jeans, Steve had no qualms about showing off his physique. As he walked towards us I saw Bucky grimace.

"What's up, Buckaroo?" *Bam*. Steve's punch fell on Bucky's upper arm.

Bucky feigned a one-two. "Just waiting for a lane, Herc."

"Why don't you play with us?" Steve waved a hand, indicating where his group was sitting.

"We wouldn't want to butt in," I told him.

"I insist." *Bam*. Another punch to Bucky's arm. "The more the merrier."

Bucky weighed the options given all the pinball machines were occupied. "Sure. Why not?" he said, rubbing his arm.

This was not working out the way I had planned.

The "us" in Steve's group was Freddie Wells and the identical Bigsby twins, Kellie and Connie. On the first day of typing class, Kellie had told me the secret to telling them apart. Kellie had a permanent blue dot on the flesh between her left thumb and pointer, a self-inflicted wound from a number two pencil while playing mumbledy-peg. "It could have been worse," she'd said. "I could have been using a knife."

Kellie and Connie liked to dress in complementing themes. They never wore matching outfits, but often traded back and forth, and when the mood struck they traded boyfriends as well. Their current boyfriends were complete opposites. Muscle-bound Steve was an all-

American jock with short-clipped hair and a letter jacket. Freddie was a tall, lanky hippie whose hair parted in the middle and hung past his shoulders. The only thing they had in common was their preference for Lees over Levis and Colombian over Mexican pot. And the twins.

Surprisingly, Freddie was the better bowler, with a high swing, smooth release and hind foot cross that rivaled any leaguer. Just when Freddie's ball looked like it would go into the gutter, it would spin toward the pins and hit the sweet spot. "The Herc" believed the best way to knock the pins down was brute force. Steve would toss the ball so hard it's a wonder the pins didn't shatter. The loud *whack* drew surprise from the surrounding bowlers, and finger-wagging from the management.

The twins managed to knock pins down every frame with a two-handed toss, and every strike called for smooch time with their respective date. Bucky was also a good bowler, but then he was good at anything with a ball. Not me. I tried to look the part by having model form, but my too-heavy ball carried me past the foul line and into the lane. I led in gutter balls, and seven pins was the best I could do. Needless to say, there was no smooching for me.

Two games down, and with a whopping high score of seventy-eight, I was ready to call it quits. Bucky waited for Steve and Kellie to finish their games, then took his turn and excused himself for the bathroom. Freddie finished with the best score, well ahead of the rest of us. In her final frames Connie bowled three strikes in a row. After jumping into Steve's arms and wrapping her legs around his waist, she planted a juicy kiss that lasted an uncomfortable length of time. Not to be outdone by her sister, Kellie went at it with Freddie. Nobody noticed me changing out my shoes and leaving the party.

I found Bucky by the pinball machines, sharing the flippers on King Kool with Joe-Joe. Not what I had planned.

"Thanks for leaving me," I said cross-armed.

"What's the big deal?" he asked, not so much as glancing my way. "I paid Herc for both of us."

"That's not the point."

Neither Bucky nor Joe-Joe took their eyes off the silver ball. "Nudge it. Nudge it!" Bucky coached.

"Too hard, man," Joe-Joe warned. "You're going to tilt."

Waa waa waa. Bucky tilted. Troy Knight, who was finessing the flippers on Derby Day, gave a smug snort.

Joe-Joe pushed Bucky out of the way, taking over King Kool. "Give me a quarter, man."

I noticed a big red hickey on his neck. Damn, even he was getting some action. "Gross, Joe-Joe. Who's been biting you?"

Joe-Joe grinned. "That's for me to know and you to find out."

"I'm not really that interested."

"What's a matter?" he teased. "You jealous?"

Enough was enough. I shoved King Kool—*waa waa waa*—then grabbed Bucky by the arm. "Can we get out of here?"

Joe-Joe threw up his hands in disgust. "Come off it, man."

Troy added his two cents. "As always, Maggie, you're a barrel of laughs."

"Well who asked either of you?"

Bucky shrugged off my hand. "Yeah, Maggie. What gives? Nothing seems to be hitting your smile button tonight."

He was right. I couldn't stand it anymore. Not the heat from my itchy angora, the *clink-clink* pinball noise competing with the bowling *kapows*, nor my stupid, stupid idea. Thinking I might throw up, I turned and ran out of the U-Can as fast as I could.

The cold slapped me back to reality. After a couple of breaths that left me feeling less lightheaded, I walked to the Blazer and leaned against its grill for support.

It wasn't long before Bucky showed up. He didn't say anything at first, just leaned beside me and looked straight ahead. As I drank in the silence, my head began to clear. When Bucky heard me sigh he asked, "You okay?"

"I'm okay. It's just that . . . well, this isn't what I'd planned."

"Well, what did you plan?"

Without hesitating, I showed him. I leaned into Bucky and kissed him. Right on the mouth. Then I quickly pulled away and traced his lips with my fingers, checking for any inflicted damage.

Bucky was more surprised than shocked. He took my hand, curling his fingers around mine, and then gently pulled my head toward him with his other.

Our breaths passed between us like tasty whispers, an exchange in slow motion. My lips became sensitive feelers, gently scouting his. Our curious yet shy tongues soon joined in the dance. It was scary and exciting, and it felt so right. So ripe. Hunger hit. A gut-wrenching urge to be satisfied. The need to do this very thing and more.

Bucky swung me around, shoving me against the Blazer. When he pressed into me I returned the pressure.

"My God," I gasped, coming up for air. "This is really happening." It didn't matter that we were making out in a well-lit parking lot with people coming and going. Everyone and everything else be damned.

Then the spell was broken.

"Did you hear me, huh? Like, we gotta go." Joe-Joe was standing a few feet from the Blazer, shouting at us.

Bucky spun around, his clenched hands ready to punch. "What's your problem, man?"

"Joel MaCrae just showed up. He got word from Lee Wakefield. You know how his dad's a cop?"

"So?"

"So, it's Melinda. An accident, man. Somewhere along the 87. She's been in a wreck with some guy. We gotta go."

It was close to ten o'clock when we arrived at County Memorial Hospital, Joe-Joe following in his brother's Chevy. First, we went to the emergency room, where the dour nurse on duty told us Melinda had been admitted but wouldn't give out any other details. The equally uncooperative nurse covering the main entrance desk said that it was well past visiting hours and seeing our friend was not going to happen. Bucky was on the verge of banging his fist on her desk when Doc Simms showed up.

"It's okay, Theresa," he assured the nurse, "I'll take it from here."

We hit him with a barrage of questions.

"How is she?"

"When can we see her?"

"Is she going to be alright?"

"What happened?"

"Is she going to die?"

"Slow down," Doc instructed. "First off, she's stable and expected to do well. Right now there's no significant evidence of head trauma, but we'll have to keep an eye on that. She has some lacerations, mild with the exception of one pretty nasty cut on her scalp and forehead. Some fractured ribs and contusions. She's been banged up, but all her vitals are strong. Mrs. Mavrakis plans to stay throughout the night." When we opened our mouth to question this exception, he added, "It's not exactly hospital policy but no one is going to argue with a mother hen who happens to be Greek. The Colonel has also been contacted. He and Mrs. Thomas are in Salt Lake City and will take the first available flight home tomorrow."

"Can you tell us what happened?" Bucky asked.

"Was she drunk?" Joe-Joe wanted to know.

"I'm not going to answer either of those questions."

"Was she driving?" I managed to squeak.

Doc shook his head. "Listen, kids. You can't do anything here tonight, so go home. And for God sake, put on your safety belts."

As we reluctantly walked to the revolving exit doors I looked down the adjacent corridor. With a cigarette hanging from her mouth and another clutched between two trembling fingers, Rebecca Frick sat crying.

Suddenly, I knew who had been behind the wheel.

• • •

Sleep was impossible. I had tried to shove the kiss to the back of my brain, but it desperately wanted to be front and center. Yet how could I go there? My dearest friend was lying in a hospital bed, troubled before she got there and in more trouble now. The "some guy" who had been with her was most certainly Gordon, making Melinda Rebecca's "she".

And Bucky? What was he feeling? How could he possibly be happy about what had happened at the bowling alley considering what came after?

202

Damn, I was being selfish.

When I could stand the tossing and turning no longer, I stacked my stereo, hoping Linda Ronstadt would lure me to sleep.

It was almost noon when I woke up. Still in their pajamas, Mom and Dad sat at the kitchen table sipping their tea and sharing the Sunday paper with Brian. Apparently, they'd had trouble sleeping, too. Mom greeted me with a longer than usual hug. I immediately jumped to the wrong conclusion.

"She's dead, isn't she?"

"What? Oh. No, honey. She's doing good. Mrs. Mavrakis told Doc to make sure you knew, so he called first thing this morning. But Melinda's not up to visitors."

"Well, I'm going to the hospital just the same. I'll stay in the waiting room or something."

"Sure," Dad said. "Whatever helps."

I called Bucky, hoping to catch a ride, but Mrs. Majors told me he was already at the hospital. Brian needed to use Mom's car, so he offered to take me.

On the drive to the hospital, I struggled to keep from crying. Brian didn't pry into my feelings, but he offered a momentary diversion.

"I used to get a kick out of you kids, always thinking up something to do. Whatever happened to that treasure you buried in the back yard?"

"You knew about that?"

"Mom and I saw you digging a hole. Figured it had to do with the cigar box Melinda was holding and the black patch over Bucky's eye."

Bucky's patch had been part of his Halloween costume that year, and he'd continued to wear it long after, commandeering us to be his merry pirate band. Our treasure consisted of Dad's discarded pen knife and Mom's lone fake pearl earring, Mrs. Mavrakises' broken rosary with the plastic beads, and Big Buck's old pocket watch. Bucky thought the watch would never be missed, but he was wrong, which was why we ultimately had to dig up the treasure.

"We plundered our own booty."

"You three have quite the imagination," Brian said as we pulled into the hospital's entrance. "Now's not the time to let it run wild."

I gave him a big hug before opening the door.

"Hey, Mags," he said as I got out. "You're a good friend."

I wondered.

Even though the front-desk nurse was more sympathetic than the one from the night before, she still wouldn't tell me anything. She did say I had just missed Melinda's parents, who would return later in the day.

"I'm sorry, but even if visiting hours weren't over I couldn't let you pass. She's on a restricted visiting schedule. Family only." As the tears welled up in my eyes, she reached for my hand. "It's okay, honey. It's best she get her rest. You'll see her soon enough. So will her boyfriend." She pointed to a figure in the waiting room.

"He's not her boyfriend." I blurted. "Just a very good friend."

"Well, he's been here since early this morning. You might try to cheer him up, or at least convince him to go home."

"Thanks for your help," I replied, trying not to sound too sarcastic.

"Anytime, honey," she assured with a pat. "Just ask for Nurse Angie. Once your friend is cleared for general visitation, our visiting hours for non-family are from two to four, Monday, Wednesday and Friday."

Bucky was fast asleep, slumped in a waiting room chair. I picked up his fallen baseball cap and traced my fingers over the gold Bronco "B" on its crown. It wasn't the first "B" he had worn. The summer after eighth grade Bucky had pitched for the Braves. During the first game of the season he threw a wild fastball that had hit the batter, Ben Jordan, square in the noggin. Ben went out cold. The coaches thought it prudent to call an ambulance. Bucky was beside himself and insisted on riding with Ben to the hospital. Melinda was the one to finally calm him down, getting him to accept that his throw hadn't been intentional and convincing him that Ben wouldn't hold it against him. Bucky was gun-shy his next game, but Melinda and I made sure to cheer him on. He pitched a no-hitter.

I brought the cap to my cheek and wiped away a tear. It smelled so like Bucky. Would he be as determined to see me if I were the one in an accident? Of course he would, and Melinda would be beside him waiting to know if I was okay. That was who we were. As I put the cap back on Bucky's head, he awoke with a start.

"Are there any changes?"

"No changes."

"Is she going to be okay?" he pleaded as if I could make it so.

"Most definitely."

The next day at school the rumors were flying. Melinda and some older guy were on their way to elope when a mysterious driver ran them off the road; now both were fighting for their lives. Some older guy had taken advantage of Melinda's drunken state, forced her into his car, and as she was fighting him off he took a corner too fast and spun out; now both were in a coma. Melinda, drunk off her ass, picked up some older guy at a bar, went on a joyride and while she was giving him a blowjob, he lost control of the car; now he was dead and she was permanently disfigured. When Michelle Fryer told the latter story during lunch, I tossed my chocolate milk in her permanently ugly face.

Joe-Joe got the real story during study hall from Lee via his dad, Officer Wakefield, and relayed it to us after school. Melinda had been at Sherman's Bar in Story, a little town not too far from ours in the foothills of the Big Horns, and Gordon was there as well. Melinda was higher than a kite, even though the bartender claimed he only served her three shots of tequila after seeing a Wyoming driver's license indicating she was of age. When Melinda passed out on a barstool, the bartender was going to call the cops to come and get her for her own safety, but Gordon told him he would see that she got home. Twenty minutes later Officer Wakefield found Gordon's car not three miles from the bar with a splattered deer on its windshield. Apparently, Gordon was going around a bend and hit the doe head-on, causing the car to roll over twice before landing upright. Melinda was still strapped in her seat belt, undoubtedly buckled in by Gordon. Unfortunately, he hadn't done the same for himself. Gordon sustained multiple injuries including a fractured skull with possible brain damage, a fractured larynx, a dislocated vertebrae, a dislocated shoulder, abdominal trauma and a whole lot of broken bones, cuts, and bruises.

Over the next few days Mrs. Mavrakis kept the neighborhood posted on Melinda's progress. She also provided us with mounds of cookies and cream puffs as her way of dealing with misfortune was twofold: bake and pray. So far both were working for Melinda. Not so much for Gordon. He was in a world of hurt.

Rebecca Frick's hurts were of another kind. The night of the accident, after Bucky and I had left County Memorial, she put up a stink about not being allowed to be with her man, enough of one that Doc Simms eventually had to give her a sedative and drive her home. Every night since she had shown up at the hospital drunk and belligerent, demanding to be let in, sometimes declaring her undying love for "the best thing that ever happened to me," sometimes insisting, "I just want to know the son-of-bitch is suffering." Dad and Big Buck had retrieved her three nights in a row. Last night Mr. Padilla was on "Rebecca duty," but the Colonel and Pamela intercepted her meltdown.

It was Friday, almost a week since the accident, and Melinda was finally allowed non-family visitors. As soon as school let out, Bucky and I rushed to the hospital to find Nurse Angie once again manning the front desk.

"I'm sorry, but you can't go in. She's with her father."

"It's supposed to be our turn," Bucky demanded. "This is the time *you* told us we could see her."

"Can one of us visit?" I asked.

"I'm sorry, but the patient's father asked not to be disturbed."

I tried another tactic. "Could you call the room and let him know we're here? I'm sure Mr. Thomas won't mind."

"He only arrived five minutes ago, dear. Perhaps he'll leave before visiting hours are over."

Now Bucky did bang his fist on the desk. Nurse Angie's face turned crimson as she puffed up her checks. "This is a hospital, young man."

"More like a prison."

"We have rules. Our patients and their recovery come first."

I pulled him away. "It's okay, Bucky, it's okay."

"This is stupid," Bucky spewed after we were out of earshot. "The Colonel comes in and out of Melinda's life like a bad radio signal, and now the son-of-a-bitch is always hanging around. It's not fair."

I had no argument there, but I led Bucky outside, hoping he'd calm down. As we were revolving out the door, Joe-Joe was revolving in. I indicated that he should meet us under the hospital's awning, then filled him in on visiting rules.

Joe-Joe gave them a quick dismissal. "So, go in anyway."

"Go in anyway?"

"Yeah. Sneak in when someone comes out."

"How?" Bucky asked. "She watches those double doors like a hawk."

"We don't even know where Melinda is," I added.

"Right. We need a room number." Joe-Joe's wheels were turning. He jumped from one foot to another, cracking his knuckles. "Leave that to me."

I wasn't sure I liked the gleam in his eyes. "What if we get caught?"

"Jesus, Maggie," Bucky scoffed. "It's not like we're robbing a bank or something."

"Just act like you know what you're doing, and act like you know where you're going," Joe-Joe instructed. "You guys go in first. I'll give it a minute then join you."

Trying not to look too suspicious, Bucky and I reentered Nurse Angie's territory, passing her at the front desk then loitering beside the watercooler as we waited for Joe-Joe to finagle Melinda's room number. It wasn't long before he approached the front desk and politely cleared his throat.

"May I help you?" Nurse Angie asked without raising her head from her paperwork.

"I'm here to see Melinda Thomas." Hearing Melinda's name again brought her to attention. "I'm sorry, but Miss Thomas already has a visitor."

"That's okay. I can wait. She's not sharing a room with a bunch of people, is she?"

"No, Miss Thomas has a private room."

"That's good. And she's not on the fourth floor, is she? Man, I hope not. I've got bad memories of the fourth floor. My grandmother was there for almost two months. She's dead, you know."

Recovered from her encounter with Bucky, Nurse Angie was once again her sympathetic self. "Oh, I'm sorry."

"Me too. So please, tell me my friend isn't on the fourth floor."

"No, dear. Miss Thomas is on the second floor."

"Wow, that's good. That's real good. Only she doesn't have a four in her room number, does she? Oh man, she better not. Four is a real unlucky number. That's what my grandmother believed and look what happened to her. I don't know if I can visit her if there's a four in her room number."

"Well, you're in luck. Her room number is 228."

"Wow, that's good to know. Okay. Thanks. I'll just be over there. Waiting, you know. Okay. Thanks."

Joe-Joe joined us at the watercooler, where we turned our backs on Nurse Angie, hoping to remain inconspicuous.

"You heard? Room 228," he whispered.

"But how are we going to get through the doors?" Bucky whispered back.

"Just be ready when I give you the go-ahead."

Joe-Joe took a couple of calculated beats, then sauntered back to the front desk. "Excuse me, ah, it's Nurse Angie, isn't it?"

"Yes?" Nurse Angie put down her pen and folded her arms, awaiting his question. "Could you look at my finger here? I think I got a splinter or something." Joe-Joe extended an open palm.

Nurse Angie pulled it to her face. "I don't see anything."

"Are you sure? I can feel it."

"Well, let me put on my glasses."

After that, it was all in the timing. While Nurse Angie prodded the middle finger of his right hand, Joe-Joe whacked the buzzer with his left, simultaneously letting out a holler that could wake the dead. All eyes were on Joe-Joe, including Nurse Angie's. The double doors opened, and Bucky and I were in.

After taking the elevator to the second floor, we were faced with another nursing station. Fortunately, the two on duty were immersed in a conversation and ignored our presence. We followed the hallway signs directing us through their maze, eventually finding Room 228. Even if we hadn't known Melinda's room number, the agitated voices coming from inside would have given it away. Bucky and I hesitated by the door, listening to Melinda and her father argue.

"I just want to know how he is. Is that too much to ask?"

"He is the reason you are here in the first place."

"Really? If that's what you believe, it's pointless."

"Well that is where the evidence points, and you're not telling us anything different. You're not telling us anything at all."

"I guess that makes us even."

"Melinda, he's more than twice your age."

"Really, Father? You're going to sing that song? Pamela is closer to my age than yours. So, tell me, what's the difference?"

"I can't talk to you when you're being irrational."

"You can't talk to me at all. You haven't a clue who I am or what motivates me."

"I have to make a phone call. I'll be right back."

"But of course. Go. You always do when my inconvenient life gets too uncomfortable for you."

Although taken aback when he saw us loitering by the door, the Colonel made no effort to protest our right to be there. Instead he simply said, "Excuse me, kids," then went on his way. He looked tired. Rumpled.

Melinda was looking out the window and didn't hear us come in. She lay on her hospital bed, propped up by pillows. The right side of her head was shaved, revealing a sewn-up gash that traveled from the top of her ear towards the arch of her eyebrow.

"Anyone home?" I ventured.

Melinda turned towards us. A split extended from her lower lip to her chin, and the rest of her swollen face was speckled with cuts and nicks. Her bloodshot eyes, still masked with bruising, followed us as we came to the foot of her bed. They seemed to ask, *Where have you been?* Instead she said, "Welcome to my world. I bet I'm a sight."

"You are," Bucky squeaked, so unsteady he had to sit.

I knew she'd expect me to make a joke, but all I had was, "Heard you hit a deer."

Melinda nodded. "Have you had any news on Gordon?"

"He's still in a coma," I told her.

"Oh, God." She crumpled into her pillow.

I went to her side, wanting to hug her but not knowing if it would add to her hurt. "Hey. He's alive. That's good news."

Bucky's eyes welled. Having a hard time witnessing Melinda's plight, he moved to the window, placing his forehead on its pane. I kept the conversation going.

"Everyone's been asking about you. Joe-Joe's downstairs waiting to see you and Patricia wanted to come by, but she knew we'd be here first."

"You know we would have been here sooner, don't you?" Bucky finally spoke. "These visiting hours suck."

"I know," Melinda told him. "Thanks for the flowers."

I hadn't thought to send her flowers. Bucky had. Among the many petaled arrangements decorating her room, one was from him.

"I know you don't like red roses," he said, now able to look directly at Melinda, "so I went for yellow."

"They're beautiful," she said with a smile so gracious it put us all at ease. Until the Colonel returned.

"Okay, kids. I need to talk to Melinda in private. I won't be long. Then you can come back in."

"No," Melinda commanded, fixing a red-eyed glare on her father. "They'll stay, and you will go away."

"It's okay, Melinda," I said.

"We'll wait downstairs," Bucky added as we backed our way to the door, but she ignored us.

"Why should they leave? You leave. You're good at that. And when you go, take your wife with you."

Paralyzed by her vitriol, Bucky and I stayed to witness their faceoff.

"Very well, Melinda," the Colonel sighed in defeat. "If you want to do this in front of your friends, so be it. I've arranged for you to be transferred to a facility in Salt Lake City."

"What kind of facility?"

"It comes highly recommended — and it has limited availability, so we're very lucky."

"What kind of facility?"

"You'll be with kids like you, Melinda. Good kids who have trouble . . . coping. Kids who abuse alcohol and drugs."

"What about school?" Melinda asked, suddenly sounding less sure of herself. "I'm about to graduate."

"We have to be realistic. You are in no shape to go back to school."

Terrified, Melinda withdrew into her pillow. "Please don't send me away."

Instinctively wanting to defend her, Bucky took a step forward. I held out my arm and stopped him, saying "no" with my eyes, seeing only panic in his as the Colonel sat on the edge of her bed.

"Melinda, you are in over your head. Our family is in over our head. I should have been paying attention."

"Wow," she chided with a strained laugh. "That's an understatement."

"You need help. More help than I can give you." The Colonel reached for Melinda's hand, but she rebuffed him.

"Have you ever tried?" she said, her voice low and trembling. Melinda's venomous focus on her father shifted inward. "Have I ever been worth the effort?"

"Oh, Melinda," he said, looking as helpless as his daughter.

"Okay, I messed up. I am messed up," she said in a rush. "I'm just one big fucking mess. Thank you for noticing." She started to shake uncontrollably.

The Colonel wrapped his arms around her. At first she resisted, but he kept his hold. "I'm sorry. I am so sorry," he whispered, his voice breaking. "It's going to be alright. Your father's here. Daddy's here. Daddy's here."

Melinda melted as her father rocked her back and forth, years of pent-up sorrow pouring from them both. Bucky lowered his head. I reached for his hand, squeezing it, and my tears. We quietly slipped out the door, leaving Room 228 and the healing going on behind its door.

CHAPTER 17

"Maggie, honey. Please put the cards down and go to bed."

"In a minute, Mom. Just one more hand."

My mother let out an exasperated sigh as she closed my bedroom door, and I shuffled for the umpteenth time, trying to be quiet so as not to disturb her sleep again.

It was well past midnight. Lately I had been playing solitaire into the wee hours. Dad said it was a way to gather my thoughts; Mom said it was my way to avoid thinking. Maybe they were both right. I had a lot on my mind. A lot of things I wasn't ready to deal with, so I dealt the cards instead. *Shuffle, shuffle.*

High School was over, technically. We still had two days to go, but those required nothing more than to show up and goof off. And there was graduation: an evening of boring speeches to sit through with themes of reflection, gratitude, and potential. Hopefully Jeff Perry, our comical and well-liked valedictorian, would spice things up with one last impression of Principal Johnson's notoriously bad impersonation of Elvis Presley. Hopefully Principal Johnson would hand out the 321 diplomas at a tolerable pace so we could throw off our hats and get the hell out of there at a reasonable hour. Hopefully I'd make it through the ceremony without crying. *Shuffle, shuffle.*

As much as I looked forward to receiving my diploma, I couldn't help but ask myself: now what? I certainly wasn't going to follow in my brother's footsteps and become a nurse. The one time I'd tagged along with Melinda during one of her candy-striper shifts it did not go well.

Our first assignment was to bring an elderly gentleman from his room to the x-ray lab. Even though there wasn't much of him, transferring him from his bed into a wheelchair while maintaining a modicum of modesty was no easy task. His hospital gown slipped off more than once, and putting on his shoes was next to impossible. His uncooperative feet provided none of the necessary resistance needed to get the deed done.

"I'll grab his ankle while you try using your thumb as a shoe horn," Melinda suggested. I placed my thumb between his heel and his shoe while Melinda shoved. Bingo. Except my thumb was stuck. Melinda eventually freed me, but not before the exhausted old guy passed gas mere inches from my nose.

Our next assignment was to deliver flowers to a rather chubby young woman who was recovering from surgery. After sipping on the remains of a milkshake, she asked for another — "Chocolate, please" — and Melinda left to do her bidding, leaving me to listen to the ordeal that lead to her hospital stay. During her graphic discourse, her stomach growled and she began to feel uncomfortable. When I reached behind her for a pillow fluff, up came the milkshake — chocolate — and everything else she had eaten that day. I took one whiff and up came the milkshake — strawberry — I'd had for lunch. Shortly after, I went home, deciding I didn't like being sick much less being around sick people. Scratch nursing. *Shuffle, shuffle.*

Even if I had a career in mind, achieving it meant figuring out how to pay for college. My parents could barely contribute to Brian's education. No way could they afford to help me. Plus, it was late in the game. Most kids had sent in their applications months ago and had already been accepted. Our top guy, Jeff Perry, made it into MIT, and Twyla Harper, the second smartest, was heading to Stanford. Carl Roach, who never did forgive me for ditching him on our date, received a scholarship from Colorado School of Mines, where he'd be joined by four other engineering classmates. Michelle Fryer was going to some hoity-toity school back East — good riddance. And Martin

Yazzie was headed back to the Southwest to attend Northern Arizona University. Him I would miss.

Too bad I didn't excel at sports. Steve "the Herc" had received a football scholarship from Washington State. The Cougars also wanted Danny Mazonne, but he held out for the Big Ten, and Michigan State came courting with a full-ride. Wrestling paid off for Joe-Joe—his scholarship was to Boise State University in Idaho. And Bucky, who had been offered baseball scholarships by three different colleges, decided on the University of Wyoming in Laramie so he could be closer to home.

Admittedly, that path worked out better for guys. Liz "Too Tall" Butler was arguably our school's best basketball player—on par with Gary Moss, who had seven schools knocking at his door—but athletic scholarships for girls were almost nonexistent. Fortunately, her brains had landed her a scholarship to Purdue.

More than half my graduating class was college bound, although most planned to remain in-state where tuition was cheaper. Many who weren't seemed content to stick around town, get a job and maybe pick up a few classes at the local junior college. There were a few, like Pete Temple, who were done with formal education altogether and planned to put our town in the rearview mirror and never look back. Others just wanted a break. Susan Weston was taking a year off to bum around Europe, claiming she could do so on five dollars a day. Maybe I could go abroad. Three years of French should account for something. *Shuffle, shuffle.*

There was a rumble in the distance. Thunder. It had been threatening to rain for two weeks now, and we were due. The last time it rained was the day Melinda left for Utah. Melinda. Damn. *Shuffle, shuffle.*

At least I wasn't the only one in the undecided boat. Melinda was trying to figure out her next move as well since she wouldn't be joining my brother at Montana State School of Nursing. After the two-week stint in County Memorial post wreck, followed by most of May at the recovery center in Salt Lake City, she'd had enough of hospitals.

Melinda had made it back to school just in time for final exams, passing them all thanks to Pamela, who had helped her keep up with her studies during recovery by recruiting Bucky's and my help. The three of us ferried teachers' notes and paperwork via phone and special delivery, making one hell of a team.

A flash of light came through my bedroom window. *One Mississippi, two Mississippi, three Mississippi . . .* On twelve Mississippi the thunderclap sounded, immediately followed by a scratch on my door. Putting the cards aside, I opened it for Oscar Doggie, whose squatty legs scurried past me so he could leap into my bed and burrow under the covers. To Oscar, I was an afterthought. The only time he'd come into my room was during a thunderstorm.

Damn dogs, anyway. *Shuffle, shuffle.*

Stew Pot, the Bales mutt, had finally given out at age nine, an old guy in terms of our neighborhood. Rural life was generally hard on any unfenced dog, and most didn't make it past their fourth year.

The Majors went through a slew of dogs before getting Saber, a beautiful German shepherd and by far everybody's favorite. But Saber joined some canine buddies and started chasing sheep. Ranchers didn't take kindly to pack dogs, as once a dog tasted blood odds were they'd kill again. When Saber came home with a red maw the Majors had to get rid of him, one way or another. Big Buck gave him to a family that was moving back East, a heartbreaking decision. Soon after, the Majors broke the cardinal rule of naming a new pet after a departed favorite.

Saber the Second didn't measure up to his namesake. He liked to bark, yet another reason I was having trouble sleeping. I bet I wasn't the only one. My window was closed and I could still hear the damn dog. *Bark, bark. Shuffle, shuffle. Bark, bark.*

Those damn Majors could sleep through anything. Was Bucky awake? Was Melinda? *Shuffle, shuffle.*

Things had returned to normal with Melinda. Better than normal. It felt like the old days when the three of us were inseparable. We spent time together almost every day, talking mostly; Bucky extolled the newest accomplishments of his little sister, who he adored, or railed against the latest exploits of his annoying younger brothers; I reported on the added benefits of having Brian around, or bitched about my boss Pogo and his hissy fits. Melinda listened with great concern — for too long she had chosen to distance herself from us and now she wanted to know everything.

Of course, Bucky and I avoided discussing what had happened between us the night of the accident. Melinda also seemed to want to skirt the particulars of that night, but somewhere in our catching up she decided to come clean, little by little.

Her first confession came during a casual walk along Old Orphanage Road. That was when she told us about her drug use. Primarily black beauties, for when she wanted to be on top of things, and quaaludes, for when she wanted to tune out. An "unbalancing act." She had no preference for one side or the other, she just couldn't cope in the muddled middle.

I was shocked. I knew she smoked pot and sampled the occasional drug but had no idea it had gone so far. Her disclosure pained Bucky, and he was ashamed of himself for not realizing the extent of her use. Melinda assured him his naivety wasn't his fault. She had been a good actress, for a time. But then she screwed up and had to clean up.

Reluctant to go into the details of what went on at the recovery center, Melinda did tell us "doing time" had been a necessary evil and she'd come away with a few nuggets of wisdom. She still had stuff to work out, "issues," but her head was clearer and her relationship with her father was improving. The Colonel had come through, staying in Utah and availing himself to her every step of the way, as did her stepmother.

Melinda also admitted to holding on to an unreasonable amount of anger. Sometimes her dad was its target, sometimes her dead mother. Too often it was Pamela. Mostly the rage was directed towards herself, which didn't make sense to me. Melinda insisted it did, according to her newly discovered world of psychoanalysis.

Crazy stuff. *Shuffle, Shuffle.* But, I was beginning to understand self-loathing. *Shuffle, shuffle.*

Melinda's second confession came three days after the first while we were sitting on Bucky's front porch. That was when she finally told us about the night of her wreck.

After calling it quits with Richard the professor, Melinda had taken up with an oil and gas lawyer from Cheyenne who was in town on business. She fed him some cock-and-bull story about being a research assistant for the Department of Fish and Wildlife. "It seemed like such a fitting title." When the lawyer found out she had been lying—about her job *and* her age—he had left her stranded on the highway outside of Story. She popped a couple of downers and thumbed a ride to Sherman's Bar.

Melinda sat in a back booth and ordered a shot, maybe two before the quaaludes kicked in. Things were fuzzy after that. She did remember sitting at the bar next to Rebecca's boyfriend, Gordon. She remembered feeling safe with him. That was it, until the moment she woke up in the hospital with a hellacious headache and an acute pain in her side.

No one would tell her why she was in the hospital other than she had been in a car accident. It was a nurse who let it slip that Gordon had been the driver. That was when Melinda started putting the pieces together.

"Everyone just assumed I was carrying on with Gordon, but I would never do that to Miss Rebecca. I may be a lot of things, but I'm not a backstabber."

Bucky might have given her the benefit of the doubt, but I was one of those who had made that assumption. She knew and accepted the blame. "My seedy reputation was of my own making, Maggie, and I got a kick out of the notoriety. I only wish Gordon didn't have to suffer the consequences. I'd trade places with him in a heartbeat."

Gordon had certainly borne the brunt of that night's accident. While he had turned a recovery corner, he was still in a head trauma unit in Denver learning to walk and talk again. A slow, difficult process, but Gordon was a fighter and he was determined. So was Rebecca, who had taken an apartment nearby to make sure Gordon was getting the best care possible.

Melinda's third confession had been the hardest for her to make and the hardest for me to hear. It was also the reason why—what time was it, anyway? Shit. Two thirty?—I kept dealing the cards. *Shuffle, shuffle.*

Yesterday had been senior ditch day—a day unofficially sanctioned by the school that allowed us to seemingly snub authority one last time. Most of the kids, including Bucky and Joe-Joe, ended up going to the traditional party at Lake Smitty, but Melinda didn't want to. Too many eyeballs on her, and the temptation to get high would be more than she could handle. I didn't want her to spend the day alone, so we decided to explore Porcupine Falls instead.

Tucked in the Big Horn Mountains, the trailhead to Porcupine Falls was unmarked but easy to find. We could hear the waters' roar from our hike's onset, and by the time we got to the bottom it was deafening. A splendor of nature, the falls sliced through twisted pink and gray mountain rock spotted with rust-red lichen and patches of fuzzy moss before tumbling two hundred feet into an enormous swimming hole.

Melinda brought her camera, a Nikon similar to her mother's old one and a Christmas present from Pamela two years ago. Offended by her stepmother's presumption, Melinda hadn't removed it from the box until last week. Now, fascinated with its possibilities, she clicked away, using me as a model and the falls as a backdrop. When the film ran out we braved a swim.

We ate our sandwiches in that unworried, conversation-less way belonging only to friends, then fell asleep in the sun until the voices of other hikers intruded. It was time to share nature's wealth and go.

Walking up the trail took more huffing and puffing than walking down, and we had to stop frequently. During one rest, Melinda found the perfect log and we sat side by side, taking in the view. That was when the heart-to-heart came.

"I half expected Bucky to show up," she started.

"And miss his chance at showing off in his dad's ski boat? No way. Besides, a lot of people were counting on him to be there."

"I guess you're right. Sorry about that. Taking you away from all the fun."

"Hey, it's been a great day. We'll get our share of skiing this summer."

"Maybe this time you'll be able to keep your top on."

She laughed and I groaned. Last year, after my fourth attempt to get my skis out of water and into the boat's wake, I'd waved to applauding onlookers at the exact moment my bikini snapped, giving everyone a titty show. In my panic, I proceeded to make a less-than-elegant face-plant. Bucky had come to the rescue with his boat and his T-shirt.

Melinda picked up a fistful of dirt and sifted it from hand to hand. "Tell me about you and Bucky," she ventured. "What's going on?"

I shrugged. In truth, nothing was going on. Our kiss remained an unaddressed topic. No talking about it. No joking about it. And nothing had followed. Nothing. Maybe Melinda could make some sense out of it. I decided to confide in her, but before I could speak she pulled her knees to her chest and cried, "Oh, Maggie."

"What's wrong?" I asked, confused by the sudden change of mood.

Melinda lifted her head. "I'm inexcusably jealous. Of you."

Did she know about the kiss? Had Bucky said something to her? "What are you talking about?"

"I've always wanted to be like you."

"Are you kidding?"

"You're funny without trying. You're wise. Fearless. And so sure of yourself even when you're not."

"Melinda, I . . ."

"Don't say anything," she pleaded between shudders. "I've always wanted what you've had. A mom and dad like yours, parents who put you first. Who joke around with you and respect your opinion and think you are the most amazing person on the planet. An older brother. A boyfriend like . . ." Melinda dropped her head again, cradling it with her hands. Suddenly, taking a deep breath, she shot up straight. "It's Bucky. That's why I'm jealous . . . Because, okay, I'm just going to say it. I've always wanted it to be me and Bucky."

I couldn't move.

Scooping another handful of dirt, Melinda kept her eyes on her palms. "The first time I saw him, he was playing in the sand pile with his little brothers. They were screaming, 'My turn, Mr. Horsey. My turn.' He pretended he was annoyed by pawing the ground, but let them jump on his back just the same, whinnying all the while."

Melinda turned her face toward me, smiling at the memory. I wasn't smiling back. She continued.

"From that moment, I knew he was . . . oh god, this is going to sound juvenile. He was my knight in shining armor. Strong and compassionate and . . . well, you know what it's like when you're with him. He's there. I mean really there. Present. He's comfortable with himself. He has courage and curiosity. He's kind, but he's not a pushover. He's got great cars. He's got a great body. And he's so amazingly cute." She rested her head on my shoulder. "And loyal to a fault. You're lucky, Maggie. No, that's wrong. There's a reason why he chose you and not me."

Still dumbfounded, I didn't respond, letting the birds, the breeze, and the falls fill in the silence.

Melinda stood, taking a moment before picking up her camera and handing me my pack. "Please don't tell Bucky what I've told you. He already thinks I'm unhinged. I just wanted you to know so I could make things right between us. I've been ashamed of my feelings for so many years. I'm sorry, Maggie. Can you ever forgive me?"

Rumble, rumble. Whimper, whimper. Bark, bark. Shuffle, shuffle.

Forgive her. She wanted me to forgive her? For what? Being the twin target of Cupid's arrow? Being smitten by the same package of flesh and bones? Being taken in by the same damn dimple? Damn Bucky, anyway. All this time I thought she didn't care about him, at least not in that way. *Shuffle, shuffle.*

Okay, maybe deep down I had known her true feelings. There was no denying how Bucky felt about her. How he had always felt about her. I just thought he'd get over it, eventually. Come to his senses, and I'd be the one.

Crap. Who was I kidding? Bucky had made his choice a long time ago on the steps of my front porch — hell, probably in the club house when I suggested they kiss — and it wasn't me. Too bad he hadn't told Melinda. Maybe he had tried, and maybe she'd refused to listen because it was easier to hurt herself than to hurt me. That was Melinda. Not me, though. Nope. I wasn't that nice. I wanted what I wanted and expected to get it. "All is fair in love and war." That sort of thing.

And Bucky? He had no idea he was being played. Maybe Melinda owed him the apology. Maybe I did, too. *Shuffle, shuffle.*

Another flash of lightning. This one closer. Oscar came out from under the covers, wanting reassurance. I scratched behind his ears then he burrowed back in. Hearing the first drops of rain hitting the roof, I got out of bed and opened my window.

Western rain has its own smell. Like bottled dirt sprinkled by teardrops. *Eau de earth*. A smell that quenches your nostrils. Your skin. Western rain is seldom warm. The dry land screams for relief, and when the water comes it either evaporates like sweat or soaks into the pores of the ground so fast that it creates its own wind. Rain in the West is the reason we have goose bumps.

Shuffle, Shuffle. Bark, bark. Flash!

It hit me. I suddenly knew I had to be the one to make things right. But how? I couldn't just give Melinda my blessing. The go-ahead to go after Bucky. She'd know how I really felt—that Bucky was *my* knight in shining armor first and I didn't want to share him. Since Melinda would never betray me, there was only one way out of this. I was going to have to lie. Lie like a fly with a booger in its eye.

Boom!

CHAPTER 18

"Get that one up front," I directed from the back seat of the Fleetwood.

"No, it's too close," Bucky protested. "Besides, it has a crappy speaker. Remember?"

"That's probably why nobody's there now," Melinda agreed while craning her neck out the window on the lookout for someplace to park.

It was Saturday night and the best spots at the All-Star Drive-In had already been taken. Bucky weaved his mom's Cadillac between the rows until we finally found a speaker pole beside two vacant spots smack-dab behind the projection room and the refreshment stand. Not the best place to watch from—too much ambient light plus disturbance from those en route to the bathroom or the snack bar—but it would have to do until a car ducked out.

We were late because Joe-Joe had ditched us at the last minute. Not that I minded. His absence was essential for putting Part B of "the Plan" into motion. I had been hatching the Plan for two weeks, ever since coming to terms with Melinda's true feelings toward Bucky. Part B included getting them alone together in the appropriate, romantic setting. The All-Star fit the bill.

The All-Star Drive-In had been a summer entertainment staple since my parents were teenagers. Sitting on a rise just a couple miles east of Old Orphanage Road, its screen could be spotted from my front yard, although it appeared no bigger than a postage stamp. When I was a little girl, my parents and I would turn off the porch light, sit on the steps, and try to figure out what was playing. If the movie looked interesting, Dad would eventually spring the buck to go.

Showing up an hour early in hopes of getting our favorite spot, Mom and Dad would join the other moms and dads lining up lawn chairs and wait for the sun to go down while us kids frolicked in the playground beneath the towering screen. There we'd stay until impatient moviegoers sounded their horns demanding showtime. Then we'd watch from atop the hoods until the mosquitoes chased us inside.

The playground wasn't there anymore, and the cost had gone up from a dollar per vehicle to a dollar per person. Management hadn't been happy with patrons overloading their cars. (My brother Brian held the kid-cramming record of twenty-two.) Thus, the change in price. But never underestimate conniving teenagers looking to counteract the price jack-up via deceptive measures, like hiding in trunks or taking cover under well-positioned blankets. Most stowaways showed up after dark when the likelihood of being caught lessened.

By the time Bucky had successfully maneuvered the Fleetwood's front wheels to the peak of the berm and parked, the advertisements were over and the opening cartoon, barely visible in the twilight, was underway. Mrs. Majors's Cadillac was one of the few cars in our neighborhood that hadn't suffered a cracked windshield due to driving dirt roads, and Bucky had to sweet-talk his mom before she agreed to let us use it for the night.

I handed a bottle of Windex to Bucky and he got out to clean the bug splats off the windshield with a towel, leaving the engine on so we could briefly utilize the heater. Even though it was the second week in June and our days had been delightfully warm, nighttime temperatures approached freezing. With the price of gas up to fifty-five cents a gallon, jackets and blankets would have to do.

Melinda rolled down her automatic window to attach our designated speaker, but the pole was out of her reach.

"I'll get it," I announced, opening the back door. The pole's two speakers were on and working. I grabbed them both.

"You know, eventually someone is going to show up and want one of those," she said, her tone meaning *Why do you always do this?*

"And then I will give one back," I answered, my tone meaning *Why do you always question my judgement?*

Having no intention of returning to the back seat, I told her to scoot over, a deliberate move that made certain she and Bucky would have to sit close together. Mindful of the pole, Melinda opened her door and I slid in. I tested both speakers for volume and crackle, hooking the better of the two on the edge of the mostly rolled-down front window. But before I could hang its backup, Roger Dennis pulled up beside us in his van.

Roger's van was known as "the make-out mobile," or as the guys lewdly referred to it, "the cherry buster." Its bucket seats fully reclined when needed, and its vast cargo space, "the moan-zone," carried nothing but an ice chest and mattress, blanket not included. Decked out with a quadraphonic 8-track and loudspeakers that could blast the ditch lights off a freight train, the van had provided the sound system for countless keggers and camping trips. Undoubtedly, Roger had received a warning from the All-Star's ticket-taker because his music wasn't blaring.

Roger rolled down his soon-to-be-steamy window, looked at the pole, then me, then the pole, then me again. He extended his arm to wiggle *gimme, gimme* fingers.

"What's it worth?" I teased.

Roger curled his fingers into a tight fist. "About as much as a knuckle sandwich."

I feigned fear. Roger was actually quite sweet. His van had the bad reputation.

"Hey, man," Roger shouted to Bucky, who was finishing up the Fleetwood's windshield, "while you're at it, give us a shine."

"It'll take more than a rag to clean the crud you've got," Bucky said as he tossed the Windex and towel through Roger's window. Roger got out of the van and inspected his windshield. "I think you're right," he agreed.

Sharon Blakeley, Roger's steady for the past year, appeared in the driver's seat. "Told you we should have brought the squeegee," she said, putting the van's wipers in motion and smearing bugs in their path.

"Okay. That's good," Roger told her, "I'll take it from here."

Sharon turned off the wipers then pulled down the visor to examine her makeup in its mirror. No doubt she was wearing her customary thick black eyeliner and ice-blue lid-to-brow eyeshadow. Sharon considered herself a trendsetter and was the first in our class to get a Farrah Fawcett cut.

Happy with her look, she fluffed her hair and poked her head out the window. "Hi, Bucky," she cooed.

"Hey, Sharon," Bucky said as he peeked in her window. "Who else you got back there?"

"Just us two tonight." Placing her hand on the side of her mouth as if whispering a secret, she asked in a not-so-secretive voice, "Want a brewski?"

"Thanks, but not in my mom's car. She'd have a cow if she smelled spilled beer."

"Well, come knockin' if you change your mind," Roger offered as he handed back the towel and cleaner. Then he put his elbows just below the Fleetwood's window and stuck his head inside. "You too, ladies."

"Thanks but no thanks, Roger," Melinda said, unwilling to jeopardize her sober self with something as mundane as beer. Roger shrugged then gave me the *gimme* fingers again, along with a not-so-subtle hint. "Gary Moss will probably show up sooner or later."

"Okay?" I remarked.

"Think about it, Maggie. Three's a crowd. You wouldn't want to be a third wheel."

I handed him the speaker. "I'll keep that in mind," I said while rolling up the window. "Enjoy the movie, Roger." Roger laughed and got back into his van but not before punching Bucky in the arm as if to say, "Good job."

Bucky returned to the front seat of the Fleetwood and turned off the engine, Melinda's cue to unfold the blanket that had been sitting on her lap. As she draped it over our legs, I adjusted the volume on our remaining speaker. Officially settled in, we waited for *The Graduate* to begin. Although it had been out for several years—the All-Star never showed first-run movies—it seemed a good choice for our current circumstances. Plus, I hadn't seen it before and I loved Simon and Garfunkel.

The movie began with "The Sounds of Silence" underscoring the opening credits as recent college grad, Benjamin Braddock, played by Dustin Hoffman, rides an airport escalator and descends into his uncertain future.

It was time for Part A of the Plan: removing myself from the triangular equation by convincing Bucky and Melinda I had the hots for someone else. Thankfully, I had the perfect someone in mind. Before I could speak, Melinda unknowingly put Part A into action.

"How was the show?" she asked.

"What show?" Bucky wanted to know.

"Maggie went to Casper to see a musical touring group."

"Together We Sing," I reminded him, "Remember, I told you I was going with my mom?"

"Oh yeah, I forgot."

Mom had spotted a poster advertising the performance in the window of the Rexall. The poster also announced that the company, with its cast of young adults between eighteen and twenty-four, was recruiting. Knowing I was down in the dumps about the whole graduation thing and had no immediate plans, she convinced herself it was worth spending the money on show tickets and a hotel in Casper. I agreed to go, after Mom's assurance Together We Sing wasn't affiliated with any church.

So, we went. I dressed in my new "Ain't I Sexy?" top thinking it might help my cause—after all, they were show people. But Together We Sing turned out to be tame. Very Laurence Welk, with ho-hum choreography, innocuous costumes, and peppy people exuberating smiles. The kind of smile I couldn't begin to fake. The show's songs were mediocre and way too sappy for my taste. Still, being part of Together We Sing meant singing and traveling; two things I could see myself doing.

After the show, I hung around the stage with several other hopeful recruits until a cheery twenty-four-year-old interviewer with a perky nose and sparkling teeth called my name. Her name was Ronnie and she was wearing the finale outfit, a white shirt and red vest with the appropriate above-the-knee white skirt. Suddenly my "Ain't I Sexy?" top seemed a little too provocative.

Ronnie handed me a questionnaire then led me to an auditorium. She politely asked questions about my goals, my hobbies, my affiliations. Never once did Ronnie ask to hear me sing. I found out that you really didn't have to be able to sing or dance or play an instrument. You just had to shell out five thousand dollars, and boom, you were in—if your morals and aspirations were in line with the organization's. So much for Together We Sing. However, I did meet Palmer.

Palmer was one of the cast members who really did have talent, and I noticed him right off the bat. Devilishly good-looking, he actually moved his body in time with the music. I saw him in the lobby after my interview, shaking hands with the few lingering fans, and let him know how much I'd enjoyed watching him. He thanked me. He also told me he couldn't help but notice that I had thrown the questionnaire in the trash can. I tried to pretend I didn't know what he was talking about. He teased me with twinkling eyes not unlike Bucky's, then whispered in my ear, "That's where it belongs." Intrigued by Palmer's candid words, I wanted to know more, and he was willing to tell me. Part A of the Plan was falling into place.

"It really wasn't my thing." I summed up the performance to Bucky and Melinda. "But I kinda met someone."

"Someone?" Melinda asked.

"You know. A guy." Hadn't the meaning of "someone" been obvious? Bucky didn't get it either. "A guy?"

"Yeah. A guy," I said, annoyed by my friends' unflattering surprise.

Wanting more details, Melinda reached over me to turn down the speaker. "And?"

"Well, we sorta liked each other." Which was true.

"Who is this guy?" she asked.

"His name is Palmer."

"Palmer?" Bucky popped the *P* as if it were something to be spit out. "Pretty highfalutin name."

I leaned forward and looked at him with disdain. "What's your point, Buckingham?" Bucky folded his arms and jutted out his chin. I knew he didn't like his proper name and I seldom used it, but he had it coming.

"Where's he from?" Melinda continued.

"Connecticut."

"I've never known anyone from Connecticut," Bucky snapped, "much less anyone named Palmer."

"Pamela's from Connecticut," Melinda reminded him.

"Oh." Bucky sank into his seat. If Melinda invoked the name of her stepmother, it meant she was irked with him as well.

"Palmer's in the show. Actually, he's the best thing it has going for it. He plays the guitar and sings. And after the show, he asked me if I wanted to get something to eat. So, we walked Mom back to the motel—she really liked him, but the way—then went for a burger." Which was true.

My mother had been pretty disappointed that the show thing was a bust. She was even willing to try to come up with the money, but I assured her my interest in Together We Sing was next to nothing and something better would come along.

"Anyway, Palmer and I really hit it off and he asked for my phone number." Which was true.

That got Bucky's attention. "You're going to see him again?"

"God, I hope so. He is one handsome hunk. I mean, movie-star good looks. And funny." I let that sink in before adding, "And damn, can he kiss."

Melinda grabbed my hand. "You kissed him?"

"Uh-huh." Which was a lie.

"Wow, I don't think I've ever heard you talk so glowingly about a guy. Tell us more."

Before I could further embellish my encounter with Part-A Palmer, Bucky shushed us.

"Could you both quit gabbing? I'm kind of interested in watching this movie, so turn up the sound."

Melinda gave my hand a little squeeze then pulled the blanket to her chest. I cranked the volume, then snuggled closer, satisfied with my results—Melinda excited with my prospects and Bucky being out of sorts. Although the latter was not something I had expected. Maybe he was jealous. I dismissed the thought and focused on Benjamin Braddock's anxiety instead.

We didn't speak much during the movie's first half other than an occasional comment on the absurd (and familiar) behavior of Ben's parents and their friends and the obvious comparison of Mrs. Robinson to Rebecca Frick. At intermission, Bucky hightailed it to the snack bar while we used the facilities. From stall to sink, Melinda kept at me, wanting information about Palmer.

"How old is he?"

"Twenty-one."

"How long has he been with the show?"

"Three tours."

"Does he plan on continuing?"

"Doubt it."

"Does he have college plans?"

"Not sure."

"What does he want to do?"

"Travel."

"Where were you when he kissed you?"

"No comment."

"When did he say he would call?"

"Soon."

I really didn't have that much to tell. My burger date with Palmer hadn't lasted long because he and the rest of the merry crew had to head back to Denver. Besides, I wanted to play my cards close to my vest. Melinda was no dummy. She'd guess something was off if I swooned too much, too soon. Best to build a believable courtship.

We caught up with Bucky and his tray of Cokes and popcorn outside the snack bar. Gary Moss was standing beside him. Gary and I had been flirting friends since seventh grade, back when he was two inches shorter than me. Now, six and a half feet tall not counting the extra inch added by his thatch of mud-brown hair, he dwarfed Bucky and every other guy in our graduating class. Skinny and spindle-legged, he stumbled through the hallways at school like a foal on stilts, but put him in a basketball game and he was a Lipizzan stallion.

Gary greeted me with shy yet eager eyes. Thinking he might come in handy, I gave him a warm smile in return. Unlike Part A of the Plan (the Moonstruck Maggie phase), the implementation of Part B (the Matchmaker Maggie phase) needed adjusting. Tonight, Gary could be my excuse to part company, leaving Bucky and Melinda to do whatever it was that they might do.

Joe-Joe came out of the snack bar scarfing down a hot dog with one hand and balancing two more in the other. Gary grabbed one.

"You guys come together?" Bucky asked.

"Yeah, man. We caught a ride with Davis," Joe-Joe garbled between bites. "He had five of us stashed between the hay bales in the back of his truck."

"I thought for sure we'd get caught," Gary added. "The blanket was a too small to cover us, and it was all we could do to keep from cracking-up."

I removed a spike of hay that was stuck in Gary's hair.

Joe-Joe laughed. "That ticket-taker. Man, he's missing a few marbles, know what I mean?"

"Anyone seen Roger Dennis?" Gary asked. "He's waiting on me."

Melinda pointed in the direction of the van. "He's parked next to us. We're in the Fleetwood."

"Whoa!" Gary and Joe-Joe exclaimed, simultaneously impressed. Unlike Gary, Joe-Joe hadn't made his seating arrangements known.

"You need someplace to watch?" Bucky asked.

No, no, no, no, no! Now even if I did go to the van with Gary, Joe-Joe would be mucking up Part B. This would not do at all.

Fortunately, Joe-Joe had a plan of his own.

"No, I'm sticking with Davis," he said, chomping down the last bit of his last hot dog. "He's got some smooth shit, man, and he don't mind sharing. You guys want to join us for the time being?"

I glanced at Melinda to see her reaction. Catching my eye, she sighed with resolve, an indication she would not partake in any mood-altering substance no matter how tempting. Joe-Joe picked up on her vibe as well.

"No, I guess you wouldn't want to."

Suddenly, I had idea that didn't involve Gary. I respected him. Even liked him, but not in that kind of way. Rather than lead Gary on only to turn him down, I'd get high with Joe-Joe.

"I'll go," I announced, then turned to Bucky and Melinda for effect. "Do you mind?"

Neither did, however Gary's shoulders drooped in disappointment. Me and him in the van wasn't going to happen. I grabbed my Coke and popcorn, said my goodbyes, and followed Joe-Joe to Dave Davis's truck.

When we got to the truck, Dave was already in a stoned stupor, watching the outdated intermission ads as if they were Oscar-worthy cinematic achievements. Celeste Frost, minus her braces, sat beside him. Notorious for having lunch gunk stuck in her teeth, Celeste had gotten her braces removed just in time for graduation, but after wearing them for four years, hadn't yet adjusted to her wireless look. She was giggling profusely with her lips locked around her teeth.

Neither seemed to notice when we joined. Dave took a hit from an already-lit joint and passed it to Celeste, who took a hit, giggled and handed it to Joe-Joe as if by habit. From Joe-Joe to me then back down the line, the toking relay repeated without so much as a word. I passed along my Coke and popcorn as well. It wasn't until the Two Minutes 'til Showtime announcement that Dave acknowledged our presence.

"Maaaagneeeetoooo," Dave crooned in a controlled inhale, keeping his gaze straight ahead. "Neatooo mosquitooo," came on his exhale.

I had no idea how he knew it was me sitting in his truck. Maybe he smelled me. Dave had an oversized honker that looked particularly big from this side. Could he have picked out my scent amidst the marijuana and Celeste's generous use of patchouli oil? *Fascinating*.

"DeeeeDeeeeDaveDeeee," I answered with a guttural roll.

"Wow, man. How do you do that, man?" Joe-Joe asked, doing a poor job at mimicking our sound. Encouraged by Celeste's giggle, Joe-

Joe launched into a stream of stoned verbal diarrhea, punctuated with the question, "Is anybody hungry?"

Dave grabbed the keys from the ignition and opened the door, releasing a billow of smoke. "I gotta go," he announced before passing the fading roach to Celeste. "See you all later."

"Hey, man, before the snack bar closes why don't you get us some munchies? You fly, I buy?" But before Joe-Joe could reach into his pocket, Dave shut the door and took off. "Bummer, man."

Celeste giggled.

The movie resumed, but I watched without seeing, instead drawn to the occasional burst of a lighter coming from the insides of the surrounding cars. Or the swirling speckles of dust dancing in the beam of the drive-in's projector. Or replaying a snippet of dialogue from the movie until its significance was lost, becoming indistinguishable from the thin, tinny sound emanating from the speaker. A white noise.

My mind ruminated from one thought to another, flowing like cursive letters in a run-on sentence and leaving only a trace of their imprint behind. Some thoughts were random, but most were poignant reminders of the shift in my raison d'être.

Guess I could stay home. Live with Mom and Dad. Watch while everybody else moves on, leaving me behind. Get a better job. Or not. Maybe move away. I wonder who'll make the first move in the Fleetwood? Bucky or Melinda? Probably Melinda.

A car in the front row turned on its lights while it was leaving, casting a spray of white over the screen as Benjamin Braddock's red Alfa Romero sped along the highway, en route to claim the lovely Elaine. Horns throughout the drive-in's parking lot blared at the intrusion.

Joe-Joe joined in the honking. "Turn 'em off, asshole!"

Celeste spoke for the first time since we joined her in the truck. "Human behavior is so predictable." Then, in a manner more curious than accusing, she asked Joe-Joe, "Why do you care?"

"He's messing with the movie, man."

"Most people don't come to a drive-in for the movie," she continued. "They come for privacy."

233

"Hey, I've been watching," Joe-Joe argued. "The guy's screwing around with a hot old lady and now he's got it bad for her daughter, who's also hot. Only she's not too happy finding out about him and Mommy, so she runs away and now he wants to get her back. More power to him, I say."

I was impressed. Joe-Joe had summed up *The Graduate* in a nutshell. Celeste must have been impressed as well because she put her left hand between Joe-Joe's thighs. At the same time, she put her right hand on my knee and said, with the candor of a wise old soul, "Maggie, you know who you are, so how come you don't know what you want?"

Bam. I realized Benjamin Braddock and I were one in the same. Like him, I didn't have a clue what I wanted, just that it was insufferably tied to who I wanted.

Not liking our communal high, I pulled away from Celeste's searing touch and returned to the privacy of my head, no longer trusting my intuition. On one hand, I wanted to do right by Melinda. On the other…*Bucky kissed me! He could love me. He could let Melinda go. I could be the one crossing over the friend-girlfriend line.*

Dammit, why does this whole thing have to be my decision in the first place? Why can't they come out and tell me what they want? Can't Melinda say, 'Listen, Maggie. I'm going to go after Bucky and that's all there is to it.' Period. Can't Bucky just tell me he's in love with Melinda! Exclamation mark. Why do they need my fucking blessing?

I saw my reflection in the condensation collecting on my side window. In it, I wrote the nagging question that had always been there: "Why not me?"

A distinctive moan—one accented by an occasional smack—was coming from my truckmates. By the sound of it, Joe-Joe had his tongue down Celeste's throat, or the other way around. Celeste swung her right leg across Joe-Joe, and he slowly descended into a half-horizontal position as she pressed into him, purring like a kitten. I wanted to look away, but felt compelled to watch. Could Joe-Joe be that good at kissing?

The kiss! What if Bucky tells Melinda about the kiss? That would totally screw up everything. Melinda would back off. She would never, ever, ever believe me if I told her kissing Bucky meant nothing because it meant something. It still means something, and God, I want it to happen again. But it can't. Stupid, stupid, stupid. I should have dealt with the kiss before putting any part of the Plan into action.

The walk back to the Fleetwood wasn't difficult — the movie gave off enough light to allow me to navigate between cars. The night's chill took the edge off my high, allowing me to gather my wits.

Thankfully, Bucky hadn't moved the Fleetwood. I tapped on the window before opening the door, intending to ask Melinda to slide over so I could retake my spot, but she was already sitting close to Bucky. A little too close. Part B of the Plan had worked. They both stiffened as if they'd been caught with their hands in the cookie jar and its sweet goodies were smeared on their faces.

Melinda tried to cover her discomfort. "Damn, Maggie, you gave me a start."

"Sorry," I mumbled. "I'm back."

Bucky acknowledged me with a nod, then reached for the ignition to turn off the motor. "Do you mind keeping it on a little longer?" I asked. "It was a pretty cold walk."

"Sure." There wasn't any hint of annoyance in his response, just good-natured acceptance of my unavoidable return. After making the necessary body adjustments, we watched the rest of the movie in silence. I felt like an intruder. A third wheel.

It was almost midnight when Bucky pulled into Melinda's driveway. They had wanted to grab something to eat at the truck stop after the movie, but I just wanted to go home and Bucky obliged. I thought he would drop me off before Melinda, giving them a little extra time to be alone, but that wasn't the case. The Thomases' porch light came on and Melinda caught a glimpse of the Colonel peeking through the front window.

"In accordance with the powers that be, I'm going to have to call it a night," she said.

I zipped up my jacket, opened the front door and got out. Melinda followed close behind. Before going inside, she grabbed my hand and gave it a squeeze.

"Let's talk tomorrow. I want to know everything there is to know about your potential paramour. I have a feeling you've been holding back."

I don't know what got into me, but I gave her big hug as if we were parting in more ways than one.

Melinda waved goodbye to Bucky then scurried into the warmth of her house. I waved to Bucky as well and began to shut the car door, intending to walk the rest of the way home, but he didn't let me get very far.

"Get back in. I'll drop you off."

The porch lights were on at my house as well. I reached for the door handle of the Fleetwood, then thought twice. Now was as good a time as any.

"Can I talk to you?" I asked, just as Bucky said the same thing.

We laughed and went into an automatic response of "Jinx, you owe me a Coke," a throwback from out childhood, but it was half-hearted.

"Listen, Maggie. That night . . . . at the bowling alley. The night that Melinda had her accident? I've been meaning to talk to you about—"

"The kiss in the parking lot?"

"Yeah. That. I want to explain . . ."

"Bucky, it didn't mean anything. I hate to admit it, but I haven't kissed too many boys and figured I'd try one out on you. Didn't you get that?"

Bucky cocked his head in confusion. I scooted closer to his side.

"I just wanted to see if I had the moves. You know . . . a sexy technique," I said, giving Bucky a nudge with my elbow. "What did you think?"

"Not bad." He nudged me back.

"That's what Palmer said."

Bucky put his hands on the wheel and shook his head. "Palmer."

I took a deep breath before saying what I had to. "Bucky, you and I are friends. The best of friends. That's all."

"I know, I know," he chastised himself, banging the dashboard. "That's what I was thinking. Only I was afraid I had screwed it up."

If he could have felt the punch that landed in the pit of my stomach. In spite of my wound, I put the final part of the Plan in motion.

"I wouldn't say anything to Melinda about that night. She has enough on her mind without dealing with a visual of you and me going at it." As Bucky nodded in agreement, I slid closer to the door, my escape. "She's sweet on you, you know?"

"No."

"Yes."

"Really?"

"Uh-huh."

"How do you know?"

I raised my chin and let out an *argh*. "Sometimes boys are so stupid."

"What would you think if I asked her out? I mean on a real date."

"Where would you go?"

"I don't know, maybe a picnic. Or a ballgame, or maybe—"

"Stop right there. A picnic would be nice. You could drive to Porcupine Falls. She likes it there."

"Yeah, maybe I will."

The conversation was over. I had given an award-winning performance, but my acting ability was fading. Time to bow out. To my surprise, Bucky opened his door as well, wanting to walk me to the door.

"You don't have to do that," I told him.

"Yes I do," he replied. And he did.

Under different circumstances, I would be anticipating a good-night kiss. I would be leaning with my back against the door, hands clasped behind me, head tilted shyly upward. Bucky would be leaning, too, hands braced against the door beside my shoulders in order to maintain a respectful distance between our pounding hearts. My eyes would rise to meet his gaze, then slowly close as our lips met at last. Just as I had always imagined.

Yet there would be no kiss at my door tonight. I turned to Bucky before going inside. "Thanks for the ride. I'll help you clean your mom's car, if we need to."

Bucky reached for my shoulder. "Maggie, are we good? Is everything copasetic?"

I couldn't help but chuckle; Melinda's fancy words had rubbed off on him. "Yeah. A-OK." It was a necessary lie. I knew he knew. He knew I knew he knew.

"Well, see you tomorrow." He hesitated for a moment, then stepped off the porch and headed for the Fleetwood.

"Bucky," I stopped him. "If you do decide to say something to Melinda about . . . just tell her it was an experiment. And a dumb one at that."

He gave me a nod of recognition, waved, then drove away, taking a sizable chunk of my heart with him. Leaving a formidable ache. A hole that would take years to refill.

My mother was waiting up for me, sitting on the couch in her fluffy red robe and reading a book—she always had trouble sleeping unless all her chicks were roosted for the night. Right away, she sensed something was wrong. I could feel her watching me as I took off my shoes and hung my jacket in the closet.

"How was the movie, honey?"

I sat down beside her and shrugged. She gently caressed a strand of my hair that had come loose from its barrette then placed it behind my ear. I curled into a fetal position, making a pillow of her velvety lap.

Looking back, Mom had to have known that my low spirits were due to Bucky, but true to a Westerner's ingrained aversion to meddling, she didn't pry. Instead, she said, "From the time I first held you in my arms, I thought, 'Now, here's a fighter. This child will hold her own.' Mighty Maggie. My inquisitive, determined girl who is now a beautiful young woman, inside and out. I've never had to worry about you, honey. But if and when you need me, I will always be here."

I never needed anyone more. Wrapped in my mother's love, I found the courage to cry.

THE WEDDING

We are outside the Elks Club, lining up on the stairs just to the north of the sidewalk that leads to the getaway car. The Majors boys have been hard at work on Big Buck's brand-new Cutlass Supreme, tying black balloons to its side mirrors and stringing beer cans along its back bumper. A "Just Married" sign hangs off its trunk. Tommy has used shaving cream to add the final touches: tasteless honeymoon tags saying "Legal at Last," "No Sleep Tonight," and "Honk if You're Horny." Billy and Bart get into a spray fight that leaves them and several of the guests, including the three Padilla girls, splattered in foam.

Ignoring her sons' antics, Mrs. Majors assists the flower maiden, her daughter Julie, in passing out little netted bundles of white rice whose tags read, "Mr. and Mrs. Buckingham Majors the Third. June 4, 1978." As she hands one to me, she gives my shoulder a reassuring squeeze. "I wish your fella could have been here."

"Me, too," I answer.

Rebecca Frick staggers beside me. She's holding a cigarette between her teeth, a champagne glass in one hand, and Melinda's tossed bouquet in the other.

"Where is that handsome charmer of yours?"

"He couldn't make it."

"Oh yes, I do understand."

"And Gordon?" I ask.

"A sudden need to see his mother in Omaha. Now how am I going to argue with that?" Rebecca sighs. "What is it that keeps the good men away *from weddings? The ones we have in mind when it comes to catching these damn bouquets?"*

I give her a shrug, not letting on that I had intentionally been occupied during the toss.

Patricia Simms sidles up beside us. She eyes the prized bouquet with envy, then my frilly bridesmaid's dress. *"Where's Mr. Marvelous?"* she asks.

"He couldn't make it," Rebecca answers for me.

"Something came up," I add.

Patricia barely hears us. She's watching Ricky Padilla and his new wife, Roberta. Roberta is six months pregnant and already about to burst. More than likely it's twins. Patricia's eyes tear up. *"Weddings, you know. They make me cry."*

"I know," I sympathize.

"Ah, sweetie, you take this," Rebecca tells her, handing over the bouquet. *"The last thing I need is another last name."*

Patricia's stifled weeping turns into a sob. Rebecca tries to cheer her up with a pep talk.

"You know, honey, the notion of a Mr. Right is pure poppycock. Bull Shit with a capital BS. What's the population of the world now, Maggie? Somewhere in the billions?"

"Four billion," I answer.

"Alright. So, let's take half of that, the male half, throwing away those under, hmm, say sixteen and those over seventy-five — definitely those over seventy-five. That leaves you with a least a billion age-appropriate men."

Patricia's confused brows match mine. Neither of us understand where this is going. Rebecca continues.

"Now toss out the undesirables — depending on your nature, about seven out of ten men are undesirable — then disqualify the idiots who find you undesirable and those who are spoken for. For argument's sake, that leaves us with some one hundred million possibilities spread out from here to Timbuktu."

Rebecca fans herself at the thought. Patricia and I gulp champagne.

"Stay with me, ladies. Say you're in a room with one hundred eligible, desirable men. Chances are at least one is going to float your boat, maybe two. Well? Don't you see? Even if it's just one, one percent of the bigger picture is

one million potential Mr. Rights. Now all you have to do is round 'em up and herd 'em in."

Rebecca raises her glass to Patricia and gives a big yeehaw. "That goes for you, too," she directs at me, "and I'm not talking about Mr. Marvelous."

The Mr. Marvelous they refer to is Palmer. We live together, although I doubt he'll be sticking around for much longer.

• • •

"Don't you think you're rushing things a bit?" Melinda asked after taking a sip from her mug.

"I've known him almost a year. I wouldn't call that a rush," I argued.

We were sitting on my front porch drinking coffee and enjoying the gentle sun after a morning run. It was the last week of March and Melinda was on spring break. I'd enjoyed having her back home, if only for a little while. Plus, letting her know about my decision was better done face-to-face. For some reason, she was seeing red flags.

"What about your mom and dad? What do they think?"

"They like Palmer. What's not to like?"

"Nothing. He's marvelous. Mr. Marvelous. I just don't want to see you get hurt."

What made people assume that extraordinarily handsome guys were constantly on the lookout for someone better? Perhaps that was true of most, but not Palmer.

Less than a year ago, the reality of my strictly platonic relationship with Bucky had left me in shambles. I stayed in my pajamas for six days doing nothing but reading. Mom told everyone I'd caught a bug. On day seven, Palmer called, the first of many conversations in our long-distance phone affair. Sometimes he'd call just to check in. Sometimes we'd chat for over an hour.

Palmer was a lifeline, especially once Bucky left for Laramie and Melinda followed, deciding the University of Wyoming had a lot to offer. Then, in early October, Palmer telephoned from Denver. He had quit Together We Sing and was on his way to Portland for an Elton John concert. Did I want to come with him? I saw no reason not to. Nor did I see any reason not to move to Durango, Colorado, when he called two weeks ago telling me he'd been cast by the Old Opera House to play the hero in their summer melodrama. Convinced I would eventually be hired as well, he rented a two-bedroom apartment. So why wasn't Melinda convinced?

"People get hurt all the time, Melinda. I'm willing to take that chance."

She shrugged then handed me her mug for a refill. "I just want you to be happy."

Happy? I had seen my dearest friends go off to school while I was left out of the college loop. I was working two jobs: one as a receptionist, filling in for Doc Simmses' real one who was pregnant with her first and needed to take it easy, the other at Pogo's Place, slinging burgers and bringing in measly tips — the same old, same old. I was fed up with smelling like a french fry and enduring both bosses' exhausting peculiarities. Moving with Palmer to Durango was my ticket out of Dodge.

"Don't worry, Melinda," I assured my best friend. "I'll be happy." I meant it.

• • •

The Colonel walks down the stairs escorting Pamela, a stunner in her lavender dress and big-brimmed hat. They find a spot at the curb beside Mrs. Mavrakis and her sister, Nerine, who has recently become a resident of our town. With the exception of being a foot shorter, she is a duplicate of her older sister. Both are adorned in their best pearls and flocked-veil pillbox hats, and both are giddy from the day's activities. They unabashedly flirt with Smiley Wooster, a recently widowed grocer and one of Big Buck's and Doc Simms's golfing buddies. Mr. Wooster is all smiles, liking the attention.

I walk down the steps to stand closer to Mom and Dad. They are like lovebirds, holding hands and chatting with Brian, who is fresh from passing his state board exams. Happiness is all around.

Mr. Bales is part of the cheery group. At ninety-five he still stands tall, aided only by an antler-handled cane whittled from a twisty stick of pine, a present from his late wife, Elizabeth. Dressed in his finest leather vest and white felt Stetson hat, Mr. Bales makes it a point to attend as many weddings as he can because he's "sick and tired of damn funerals."

"Where's that fine young feller of yours? That Palmer?" he asks me.

My mother steps in. "He couldn't make it this time, Mr. Bales."

"Well, you better get around to tying the knot soon if you expect me to dance at your wedding."

"Oh, you'll be there, Mr. Bales, kicking up your heels," I tease him.

I am suddenly struck in the face by an elastic projectile. I pick up Melinda's discarded garter. Joe-Joe is nearby, blowing on his finger as if it were the barrel of a gun. He struts over, expecting me to hand back his ammunition.

"So, Mags. You here for long?"

"Just a couple days."

"Then back to Durango . . . and Palmer?"

"Yep."

Joe-Joe takes off his sunglasses and gives me a skeptical look. "What kind of guy goes by the name of Palmer, anyway?"

I want to tell him it's the kind of guy who is willing to go along with a gal's crazy scheme of duping everyone—her family, her best friends—into believing that the two of them are head-over-heels in love. This in exchange for her being his quasi fiancée and reassuring his parents that he is a bona fide red-blooded manly man when in fact he is gay. The kind of guy who, even when he does finally come out of the closet and meets someone he truly wants to be with, puts his life on hold until his pretend girlfriend gets hers sorted out. I want to tell him, but I don't. Yet, Joe-Joe somehow knows. As if reading my mind, he asks, "I don't understand why Bucky and Melinda still haven't figured it out. Your 'relationship' and all."

"They see what they want to see. People do that."

"Hmm," Joe-Joe ponders. "I suppose. You plan on telling them the truth?"

"I might. Someday. Maybe after Melinda hatches her first kid."

Joe-Joe puts his arm around my waist and gives me a squeeze. "You're alright, Margaret Emma Moore." He leans in and kisses my forehead. "And, damn, you smell good."

I give him a sharp elbow to the ribs before laying my head on his shoulder.

The church doors open and the bride and groom emerge. They're back to being casual. She's wearing a tube top and bib overalls. He's in a leather vest and jeans. They pass through the gauntlet of well-wishers pelting them with rice and make their way to the car.

After Bucky opens the door for her, Melinda searches the sea of faces until she finds me. She smiles and blows me a kiss. I grab it in the air, gobble it down, then wave goodbye.

"Alaska." Joe-Joe shakes his head. "Crazy choice for a honeymoon, huh?"

"I think it's perfect."

The wedding is over. Bucky and Melinda drive away. Like the warm tears running down my cheeks, all I can do is let them go.

THE END

Acknowledgements

To my husband, Don Pettit, who has made most of the excitement in my life possible. Without your love, support, and encouragement; without your example of approaching challenges with exuberance and enthusiasm, I could not have completed this book.

To Evan and Garrett, my boys, young men now, who have been around since Chapter Two. Without you I would have never re-awakened my childhood so thoroughly nor realized that whatever age you are, it's the oldest you've ever been.

To my mother, Jeanne Noland, the root of writing, who has always known the importance of generational story telling. You will forever be my rodeo queen.

To my father, James Racheff, Sr. who so successfully combines exasperation with laughter. I will always be your Miss Dolly.

To James Racheff, Jr. and Claudia Allan and their daughters, Natalie Allan and Cait Jones, who cheered me on at every corner. Your brilliance abounds.

To my Racheff siblings all, Jim, Jerry, Joel, Brandon, and their spouses, Adele, Penny, and Patty. You have a huge chunk of my heart.

To Chip Rice of Wordlink, Inc. who took a chance with a newbie, guided her with strength and compassion, then championed her work as though it were his own. You are the best of best.

To Andrea Robinson, whose editing took this book to another level. May we cross paths again.

To John Silbersack, who convinced me a title change was in the book's best interest.

To Black Rose Writing, who has made this book a reality.

To my pre-publishing readers: John McBrine, Jill Cashman, Kelli Glenn, Chris Hadfield, Chris Jones, Ann Meade, Linda Navarro, Regan Orillac (proofer extraordinaire), Mandy Sellers (partner in crime), Melanie Verse, the Bay Forest Book Club, and the workshop ladies (pre- and post-covid).

Thank You!

About the Author

Micki R. Pettit is a former radio personality and voice talent with vocal experience spanning musical theater, opera, big band, rock, and country. She is currently lead female singer with the folk group Bandella and performs with the Bay Area Chorus of Greater Houston. Micki is an experienced copywriter whose personal writing has appeared in various Native American-themed publications. Born in Wyoming and raised in New Mexico, she now lives in Texas with her husband and sons.

Note from the Author

Word-of-mouth is crucial for any author to succeed. If you enjoyed *A Kiss for Maggie Moore*, please leave a review online—anywhere you are able. Even if it's just a sentence or two. It would make all the difference and would be very much appreciated.

Thanks!
Micki R. Pettit

We hope you enjoyed reading this title from:

BLACK ROSE
writing™

www.blackrosewriting.com

Subscribe to our mailing list – *The Rosevine* – and receive **FREE** books, daily deals, and stay current with news about upcoming releases and our hottest authors.
Scan the QR code below to sign up.

Already a subscriber? Please accept a sincere thank you for being a fan of Black Rose Writing authors.

View other Black Rose Writing titles at www.blackrosewriting.com/books and use promo code **PRINT** to receive a **20% discount** when purchasing.

CPSIA information can be obtained
at www.ICGtesting.com
Printed in the USA
BVHW070100041221
623202BV00014B/202